DEATH IN HARLEY STREET

Also available in
Perennial Mystery Library
by John Rhode:

THE CLAVERTON AFFAIR

DEATH IN HARLEY STREET

John Rhode

Harper & Row, Publishers
New York, Cambridge, Philadelphia, San Francisco
London, Mexico City, São Paulo, Singapore, Sydney

To
Robert A. Sturgeon
In deep gratitude

1

A familiar company was assembled in the study of Dr. Priestley's house in Westbourne Terrace. The date was Saturday, January 19th, and the time after dinner. The three guests present had for long had a standing invitation to dine with the Professor on Saturday evenings, should they feel themselves free to do so.

Two of them at least could always manage to accept. Dr. Oldland, a general practitioner, talked a great deal about his practice in Kensington, but this was merely his way of speaking. An elderly and successful man, he had found it possible to relax into a state of comfortable semi-retirement. He now attended only such of his old patients who were personal friends of his, leaving the rest to the ministrations of his younger partners.

Ex-Superintendent Hanslet had, some time earlier, achieved a state of full retirement, after a long career in the Criminal Investigation Department. He was now living—temporarily, as he insisted, until he could find the rose-clad country cottage of his dreams—in rooms in Hampstead. His friends noticed with secret amusement that this temporary arrangement was becoming permanent. The cottage did not materialize, and Hanslet appeared to take no very energetic measures to seek it. In fact, it was more than doubtful that he would ever settle down at any inconvenient distance from his former associates at Scotland Yard, or, for that matter, from his old friend Dr. Priestley's table.

These two, then, rarely missed the Saturday evening meetings. But Superintendent Waghorn, familiarly known as Jimmy, had become one of the chief officers of the Department, and his duties sometimes kept him away. He had gained his promotion less than a year earlier, and was very much on his toes in consequence. On this particular evening, however, he was engaged upon nothing of sufficient importance to prevent his attendance.

And that very fact, though it allowed him to join the party, caused him some slight concern. Dr. Priestley, an eminent if somewhat eccentric scientist in his day, had adopted as his hobby the whole theory of criminal investigation, and, since Hanslet's retirement, had looked to Jimmy for the provision of raw material on which to exercise his art. He was apt, after dinner, to enthrone himself behind his formidable desk, with his secretary, Harold Merefield, not far away. From this commanding position he would listen, apparently in a state of complete torpor, to Jimmy's exposition of his more interesting cases. He would then proceed to construe the facts in a manner peculiarly his own, often enough reaching a conclusion which differed in all its essentials from Jimmy's.

So it was this evening, as the five men settled down in the study after dinner, while Jimmy racked his brains for some topic with which to capture his host's interest. But nothing presented itself. The Professor would not care to hear about cases of pilfering from railway goods yards, or the infringement of the licensing laws by the proprietors of night clubs. Jimmy was still at a loss when, to his intense relief, his rescue came from an unexpected quarter.

"There's something I want to talk about," Oldland remarked, from the depths of his arm-chair. "Usually on these occasions it's you two cops who take the floor and hardly let a chap get a word in edgeways. But this evening I want to hear Priestley's opinion upon one of the most extraordinary things I ever came across. There's no criminal element about it, but I can't help that. You've all heard about that amazing affair of Dr. Mawsley, the Harley Street specialist?"

Hanslet and Jimmy nodded. They had both seen brief notices of Dr. Mawsley's death in the newspapers, but since the incident had not called for the activities of Scotland Yard, they had paid little attention to it. Dr. Priestley was rather more explicit. "I read a very short report of Dr. Mawsley's death, and of the inquest held subsequently," he replied. "The verdict was one of accidental death, I believe. Your interest is purely professional, I suppose?"

"Yes, if you like to put it that way," said Oldland. "I knew Mawsley very well by reputation, for there is no doubt whatever that he was the leading man in his own particular line. Personally, I only knew him slightly, by meeting him now and again at professional functions I've attended. Yes, that was the verdict, accidental death, and nobody who heard the evidence, as I did, could possibly quarrel with it. Mawsley died as the result of making a mistake. And how such a man could make such a mistake is, as I say, one of the most extraordinary things I've come across."

3

"You heard the evidence, you say?" Dr. Priestley remarked. "Does that imply you attended the inquest?"

Oldland nodded. "I did. Not perhaps altogether from motives of idle curiosity. Mawsley died on Tuesday evening last, and that very morning I had posted a letter to him. You've all heard of Sir Matthew Gussage, for you can't glance at the financial columns of any paper without running across his name. He's one of the biggest noises in the City, and incidentally, as mean as they're made. Looks at both sides of a half-penny before he hands it over.

"Well, old Matt Gussage is a patient of mine, and has been for years. We get on all right, though the only way I can get him to pay my bill is to refuse to attend him again till I've got his check. It's his way, and I'm used to it by now. Old Matt hasn't been too perky for some little time, and I'm pretty well satisfied that he's suffering from some obscure glandular complaint. I've been badgering him to let me call in another opinion, but he jibbed at the expense. It was only last Monday that I frightened him into giving his consent.

"I wrote to Mawsley right away, asking him if he would take the job on, and if he would, to fix an appointment. Glands and hormones and all that are what he specializes in, so he was the obvious man to consult. I didn't tell old Matt that his fee wouldn't be less than a hundred guineas, for his reaction to that might have been fatal. Oh, well, he won't have to pay that now, and I shall have to think of someone else."

Oldland paused, and took a sip from the glass of whisky at his side.

"Do you want to hear about that inquest?" he asked.

"If I read the symptoms aright, you have every intention of describing it for our benefit," Dr. Priestley replied dryly.

"I have," said Oldland. "I want to hear what you make of it, all of you. The inquest was held yesterday morning, so the evidence is still fresh in my memory. I'm not going to attempt a verbatim report. I'd rather tell the story in my own way.

"First, something about the fellow himself. Mawsley was fifty-four, and in the course of the proceedings it transpired that he started life under the name of Knapp. I'll tell you later how that came out, though it's of no importance. As Dr. Knapp he had a practice in Bradworth, Yorkshire. Here he met a Miss Wilhelmina Mawsley, married her, and adopted her name, by deed-poll, I suppose. His full name was given at the inquest as Richard Ernest Knapp Mawsley.

"I've told you that my personal acquaintance with him was very slight, but you know how gossip goes round. More than once I've heard it said that Mawsley had married money. Apart from the fact that it's just what one would have expected him to do, the fact that he took his wife's name lends colour to the idea."

"Hold on a minute," Jimmy put in. "Why would you have expected Dr. Mawsley to marry money?"

"Because he never neglected any means of acquiring that useful commodity," Oldland replied. "I may as well say right out that Mawsley was not popular among the members of his profession, for he was an inveterate fee-snatcher. I'm not casting any reflection upon his ability, which I honestly

5

believe to have been exceptional. He was supposed to know more about the mysteries of ductless glands than anybody. But he always took care to put his knowledge to remunerative use. If you asked him to take on the case of some Tom, Dick, or Harry, who had no source of income beyond his weekly pay envelope, you wouldn't get very far. He wouldn't definitely refuse, but he'd tell you that, to his deep regret, he already had so many consultations on hand that for the present he couldn't take on any more. If you cared to communicate with him again in a couple of months' time he would see how he was situated then. I don't know whether he intended to drop the hint that if your patient died in the meanwhile, you wouldn't have to worry him again.

"On the other hand, if your patient was a man of means, no difficulty was raised. I don't doubt that if Mawsley had lived to answer my letter, he'd have written to me making an appointment to see old Matt this very week. And if he had let him off with a hundred guineas I should have been surprised. Naturally, the ordinary G.P. who honestly does his best for all his patients, rich or poor, was a bit shy of applying to Mawsley. But the fact remained that he was the best man at his particular job, and if your patient could afford it, you felt bound to call him in.

"That's the answer to your question, Jimmy. Not to put too fine a point upon it, the fellow was grasping. It would have been quite in character for him to have married a girl with money. I'm bound to say Mrs. Mawsley looks opulent enough. She was at the inquest, a large, imposing lady with a fur coat which would have gone a long way towards liquidating the National Debt. She may be a woman

6

who has perfect command of her feelings. I don't know about that. At all events, she gave me the impression that her grief at her husband's death had not utterly overwhelmed her.

"Perhaps that was because, in recent years, at least, they hadn't exactly lived in one another's pockets. They own a big place, Larch Hall, in Dorsetshire, where the family lives. There are, I believe, one son and one daughter. Mawsley spent the week-ends there, going down on Friday evening and coming back on Monday morning. From Monday to Friday he slept in his suite at Harley Street, looked after by a very decent middle-aged butler, named Phepson. It's a matter of common experience that people who see one another only at the week-ends are apt to acquire divergent interests.

"But I'm not concerned with the degree of affection which may have existed between Mawsley and his wife, for she hardly comes into the picture. I'd better tell you next about his habits while he was in London. I've never been inside the Harley Street suite, but it seems to be fairly extensive. It is on the first floor, and is entirely self-contained. There is a hall, in which a receptionist, who also acts as secretary, sits from ten to four, I suppose with an interval for lunch. In the hall is the telephone, with an extension to Mawsley's consulting-room, in which he spent most of his time. Next to the consulting-room, with a communicating door between them, is another room, known as the dispensary. It is not to be supposed, of course, that Mawsley did any dispensing. But he did carry out experiments, and the dispensary contains a number of drugs and apparatus for that purpose.

"These are the other rooms in the suite: A small dining-room, used occasionally as a waiting-room.

A large bedroom, occupied by Mawsley, and a smaller one occupied by Phepson, the butler. A kitchen and pantry, and a bathroom and lavatory. When he was in London during the week, Mawsley always breakfasted in the suite, usually lunched there, and always dined out, generally at his club. Phepson did the cooking, and most of the housework, assisted only by a woman who came in from eight to ten each morning. Mawsley's orders were that the suite was never to be left empty, that there must always be someone to answer the telephone, even during the week-ends when he was in the country. Phepson was allowed Tuesday evenings out. An arrangement had been made whereby his nephew took his place while he was absent. The nephew's name is Edward Rusper, and he is an assistant in a shop in Oxford Street."

Oldland paused to refresh himself. "I hope I'm not boring you with all these details," he went on. "They're more or less necessary, if you are to understand the rest properly. Now we come to what happened last Tuesday. And it seems important to emphasize that the events of that day were perfectly normal, until the very moment of the tragedy.

"Mawsley had been at Larch Hall for the week-end, and had returned to Harley Street, as was his custom, on Monday morning. Mrs. Mawsley says that during the week-end her husband's manner was perfectly normal, and that he showed no sign of having anything on his mind. He mentioned a plan that had already been discussed, of taking a holiday in the spring and going abroad somewhere with or without the family, saying he thought that early in May would suit him best. Phepson's evidence was very similar. In effect, he says that he noticed no difference in his master when he came back to London, or at any time till his death. His behaviour was just what the butler was used to.

"The coroner took a lot of trouble over this point, going into every detail of what happened on Tuesday. Briefly, this is the picture. Phepson called Mawsley with a cup of tea at eight, and gave him his breakfast in the dining-room at nine. He took in the morning mail with the breakfast, half a dozen letters. Mawsley looked these over, but didn't open any of them. He told Phepson to put them on the secretary's table in the hall. This girl's name is Violet Hilworth. She's a doctor's daughter, and I know her father slightly. Her business was to open the letters when she arrived just before ten, and sort out those of a purely professional nature. She showed them to Mawsley, who told her how to deal with them.

"The charwoman came at eight, swept out the various rooms and so forth, and left about ten. From then till one there was a steady stream of patients for consultation, half a dozen or so in all. The procedure is this: The patient rings the front doorbell, Phepson answers it, and after inquiry turns the caller over to Miss Hilworth. If Mawsley is engaged, the patient is given a chair in the hall. If a second caller arrives while this chair is occupied, he or she is shown into the dining-room. As it happens, there was no duplication of waiting patients on Tuesday. Further, all the patients that day were expected, having called by appointment. Miss Hilworth has no doubt a record of them.

"The last of the morning patients left a few minutes before one. Mawsley called Miss Hilworth into the consulting-room, and dictated some notes to her, again purely professional. At a quarter past one, his usual hour, he had lunch in the dining-room. Simple enough, lamb cutlet, potatoes, bread and cheese. Phepson says that he never had an elaborate lunch. In the course of the afternoon, between two and four, there were a few more callers. Then, when the last had gone, Miss Hilworth took in the letters she had typed for Mawsley's signature, then went home. By a few minutes after four, the only people left in the suite were Mawsley and Phepson.

"Mawsley would never see patients in Harley Street after four. In very exceptional cases he would go out after that and visit them at their houses or in nursing homes. But usually he spent the time from four till when he went out to dinner in the consulting-room or the dispensary. He used the consulting-room as his sitting-room, and would entertain non-professional visitors there. On his table there is a push, which rings a bell in the kitchen. This enabled him to summon Phepson, when he required his presence. It was also Phepson's duty to answer the telephone, which was normally kept switched through to the hall. Phepson's duty outside of what we may call professional hours, that is. If it rang while Miss Hilworth was there, she dealt with it. At other times, Phepson answered the call, and if necessary got Mawsley's instructions. Having done so, he either switched the caller through to the consulting-room, or gave him a message himself.

"On Tuesday afternoon, Mawsley did not go out. While Phepson was boiling the kettle for tea, the telephone rang. He answered it, and was told that the caller was speaking from the offices of Perring & Company, solicitors, Broad Street. Might he be allowed to speak to Dr. Mawsley on a matter of urgent business? Phepson conveyed this message to his master, who said he didn't know who they were or what they wanted, but that he could switch them through. He did so, and a short conversation ensued, which he did not overhear. A few minutes later he took Mawsley's tea-tray into the consulting-room. Simple again, China tea, no milk or sugar, but a slice of lemon, and a plate of bread and butter. On the tray he took three or four letters the post-man had just dropped in the box. As he came out of the room, the doorbell rang, and he admitted the rat-catcher."

"The rat-catcher!" Hanslet exclaimed. "Why, is Dr. Mawsley's suite overrun with rats, then?"

Oldland chuckled. "I thought that would wake you up. I daresay the chap rejoices in some high-falutin' designation, Rodent Extermination Officer, or something like that, but he's the rat-catcher, just the same. You see, it's like this. Mawsley kept rats for purposes of control experiments, having got a special license for the purpose from the Home Office, and this man used to get them for him. He was a frequent, and, I daresay, even a welcome visitor. On this occasion he told Phepson that he'd got a couple of fine young rats, if the doctor would like to have them. Mawsley told Phepson to bring him along, and he remained for the time necessary to transfer the rats from his bag to a cage in the dispensary. When this had been done, and the rat-catcher had received payment, Phepson showed him out, and Mawsley returned to his tea.

"It was a few minutes after five when a second visitor rang the bell. He told Phepson, who let him in, that his name was Forcett, and that he came from Messrs. Perring. It was he who had rung up some little time earlier. He had asked Dr. Mawsley if he might come and see him, and the doctor had consented. Phepson conveyed this to Mawsley, who replied, 'Yes, that's all right. Show him in.'

"Phepson was asked whether Mawsley showed any annoyance at the news of Forcett's arrival. He said none whatever, neither annoyance nor pleasure. No more emotion, we may take it, than he had displayed at the visit of the rat-catcher. You see, he didn't know then what Forcett had come about. But I'll go on with the story as Phepson saw it.

"He showed Forcett into the consulting-room, and went out again, taking the tea-tray with him. He had been in the kitchen twenty minutes or so, when Mawsley's bell rang. He supposed it was a summons for him to show the visitor out, but it wasn't. When he got to the consulting-room, he found Mawsley sitting at his table with some legal documents before him. Forcett was standing beside him, apparently explaining their purport. An attaché case he had brought with him was on a chair. Mawsley looked up as the butler came in. 'Bring the cocktails along, will you, Phepson?' he said.

"Phepson says that he knew at once that his master must be in an exceptionally good humour. He would occasionally have a gin and lime brought to the consulting-room before he went out to dinner, but it was very rarely indeed, even if a friend had called at that time, that he extended this hospitality to his visitor. For that matter, though the order to bring the cocktails along sounded impressive, the only ingredients in the house were a bottle of gin and another of lime juice. These were kept in the dining-room sideboard. Phepson put them on a tray, with a jug of water and a couple of glasses, and took them into the consulting-room. And this was the last time he saw his master, before he made that inexplicable mistake, rather more than an hour later."

2

Dr. Priestley had been sitting with his eyes closed and hands folded, apparently asleep. But his remark, as Oldland paused, showed that he had missed nothing. "May I suggest that the times you mention are regrettably vague?"

"Up to the point of the cocktails being taken in, they are," Oldland agreed. "Phepson thinks that this must have been about half past five, certainly not much later. But after that he began to watch the clock, and his evidence as to the time of subsequent events becomes more accurate."

"One moment, Doctor," Jimmy put in. "What made the butler watch the clock so attentively?"

Oldland laughed. "Observe the darkly suspicious mind of the detective!" he exclaimed. "Actually, his reason was a perfectly simple and natural one. Phepson is a prominent member of the Royal and Antediluvian Order of Buffaloes, a branch of which curiously named but estimable Society meets at the Tabby Cat in Marylebone Road at half past seven on the third Tuesday in every month. Phepson was anxious not to be late for the meeting—I think I told you that he always had Tuesday evenings off. The call for cocktails had suggested to him that Mawsley and his visitor might be in for a long séance. He never left the suite before his master had gone out to dinner, and he was afraid he might be delayed beyond the time of the meeting. Hence his anxiety as to the march of time.

"Well, he sat in the kitchen, with one eye on the clock and the other on a book he was reading. Everything in the suite was quiet. With the consulting-room door shut he could not hear the sound of voices in there, and neither the telephone nor Mawsley's bell rang. Phepson was getting fidgety, when at last the bell rang.

"He left the kitchen to answer it, and as he got to the hall saw Forcett standing in the doorway of the consulting-room, taking farewell of Mawsley. He heard him say, 'Very good, I'll tell him as I go out. Good evening, sir. I'll be round for the papers at ten o'clock tomorrow morning.' Forcett shut the door, and turned to find Phepson coming across the hall towards him. 'The doctor asked me to tell you that on no account is he to be disturbed till he goes out!' he said. Phepson acknowledged this, and opened the front door for Forcett, who left the suite, carrying his attaché case. Phepson looked at the clock in the hall, which is one of those electric ones, run off the mains, and, therefore, presumably accurate, and saw that the time was eight minutes to seven."

"I'd like to put in a word," Hanslet remarked. "What was Phepson's reaction to this message that Dr. Mawsley was not to be disturbed? Did he think it at all queer?"

"Apparently not," Oldland replied. "He took it to mean that if anyone came, or the telephone rang, he was to say that Mawsley was engaged. After Forcett had gone, he pottered about for a few minutes, until sharp at seven the front doorbell rang. He

15

knew who this must be, for, as I've already said, his nephew came to keep watch in the suite while he was out. He opened the door, and, sure enough, it was Edward Rusper. They went into the kitchen together, where they waited for Mawsley to go out. Rusper's presence was extremely opportune, for he was able to confirm his uncle's evidence of the amazing event which took place soon after his arrival.

"But, before I come to that, I'd better switch over to Forcett's story. It will save time if I say at once that Forcett turned up at the suite at ten o'clock next morning, as Phepson had heard him promise Mawsley he would. His evidence, though it throws no light on Mawsley's death, is interesting in other ways. He was the last person to see and speak to Mawsley before the accident, and can give a perfectly impartial opinion as to his demeanour. He and Mawsley were total strangers, having never met before Tuesday evening.

"Godfrey Lionel Forcett is a clerk in the office of Perring & Company, solicitors, of Broad Street. I gather that though their business is mainly commercial, they are at the same time family lawyers. Among their clients was an elderly and very wealthy widow, Mrs. Hilda Somerthwaite, who recently died, Perring & Company acting for her executors. Her will contained a clause, in which a legacy of five thousand pounds was left to 'Dr. Knapp, who attended me when I was staying at Bradworth, and to whom I have always believed I owe my life.'

"Well, that was that. As Forcett told the coroner, the first thing was to hunt up a Bradworth directory. But that didn't help, for no Dr. Knapp was mentioned in it. Mrs. Somerthwaite gave no indication of how long ago she had stayed in the town.

And there was the further complication that she had been married twice. Dr. Knapp might have attended her as Mrs. Somebody Else, or even under her maiden name, before she was married at all.

"In the end, his firm sent Forcett to Bradworth, to make inquiries on the spot. After a good deal of ferreting round, he discovered this. Some twenty-five or thirty years ago a Dr. Richard Knapp had bought a practice in Bradworth, but had not retained it more than three or four years. He had been a young man, not too well off, but had married the only child of a prosperous woollen manufacturer, Jesse Mawsley, who had died not very long after his daughter's marriage. Dr. Knapp had taken his wife's maiden name, sold his practice, and left the town.

"The rest, of course, was easy. A search of the medical directory revealed the existence of a Dr. Richard Ernest Knapp Mawsley, with a string of imposing letters after his name, and an address in Harley Street. There could be very little doubt that he was the fortunate legatee. Forcett was told to get on with the job and verify the fact. Last Tuesday afternoon he rang up Mawsley from the office, and asked for an interview upon a legal matter that had arisen. Mawsley was not very responsive until Forcett told him the matter might possibly turn out to his advantage. Then Mawsley thawed a bit, and told Forcett that if he cared to come along within the next hour or so, he would see him.

"Forcett went, taking with him a copy of the codicil, and a few other papers relating to Mrs. Somerthwaite. His statement as to his arrival at the suite exactly corroborates Phepson's. While he was waiting in the hall for the butler to announce his visit to Mawsley, he had glanced at the clock, and had seen that the time was between five and ten minutes past five. He was thus within Mawsley's limit of an hour or so.

"Admitted to the consulting-room, Mawsley told him to sit down and asked him pretty curtly what his business was. Forcett, who, of course, had never set eyes on Mawsley before, realized that some diplomacy would be needed. His job was to establish the fact that Dr. Mawsley, the Harley Street specialist, and Dr. Richard Knapp, late of Bradworth, Yorkshire, were one and the same. His first approach was not very successful. When he first asked Mawsley whether, many years ago, he had practised in Yorkshire, Mawsley countered by telling him that before he answered questions of that kind, he demanded to be told for what purpose they were put.

"I knew enough of Mawsley to understand that he would not care to recall his early struggles as an impecunious G.P. And Forcett, who strikes me as a pretty shrewd young fellow, no doubt tumbled to this. He gave Mawsley a hint of the good things in store by telling him that his firm was administering the estate of a lady who at one time might have been a patient of his. I should explain that Forcett, tracing Mrs. Somerthwaite's history, had found out that during the period twenty-five or thirty years ago her name had been Gunton, her first husband having been Captain Gunton, who was killed in action in 1918. So he asked Mawsley if he remembered attending, many years ago, in Bradworth, a Mrs. Gunton.

"This broke the ice a little, but Mawsley still retained a certain reserve. He said that he remembered the name well enough, but that obviously he could not be expected to divulge professional secrets. Forcett, pretty well satisfied by now, assured

18

him there was no question of that. The lady was dead, and had mentioned her benefactor in her will under the name of Dr. Knapp. Inquiry had shown the probability that Mawsley was the individual in question.

"Mawsley immediately became more genial. He admitted that, as a young man, he had for a short time held a practice in Bradworth, purely, as he was careful to emphasize, for the sake of acquiring general experience. During that time he had attended Mrs. Gunton, who, while her husband was in France, was staying with her people in Bradworth. He had diagnosed her trouble as an unusual glandular complaint, which, if left to run its course, might well have ended fatally. He remembered the name and the case very well indeed, for the success of his diagnosis and of his subsequent treatment had been one of the factors deciding him on the subject on which to specialize.

"From that moment the two seem to have got on famously. And when he was told that he had been left five thousand pounds, Forcett says Mawsley was delighted. I'll bet, knowing his avidity for money, that he was as pleased as Punch. Anyhow, he rang the bell and told the butler to bring in cocktails. They came, and each of them had a couple of glasses of gin and lime. Meanwhile, Mawsley expanded. He told Forcett that he had documents which would show that, as Dr. Knapp, he had practised in Bradworth, his case-book for that period, in which a record of his treatment of Mrs. Gunton appeared, and a copy of the deed-poll by which he had changed his name. All these were in his safe at Larch Hall. He would bring them up to London with him on the following Monday. Meanwhile, he would like Forcett to leave the papers he had brought, so that he could study them at his leisure. Forcett agreed to do so, and to call for them next morning.

"Stimulated by the news of his good fortune, and possibly also by the gin, Mawsley became most affable, and indulged in reminiscence, insisting that his visitor should not hurry away. At last Forcett managed to disengage himself, he says about seven. We know from Phepson that it was actually eight minutes to. As he got up to leave the consulting-room, Mawsley rang the bell. He told Forcett that he would meet the butler in the hall, and that he would let him out of the suite. Mawsley went on to say that he wanted to go through the papers very carefully, there and then, and asked Forcett to tell Phepson that he was on no account to be disturbed till he went out.

"You may wonder why all this, which had no direct bearing on Mawsley's death, was brought out in such detail at the inquest. The reason was that the coroner, as I think, quite properly, wanted as much light as possible thrown on Mawsley's demeanour immediately before the event. Forcett's visit was purely fortuitous. But he was the last person to whom Mawsley spoke, and for that reason his evidence was of considerable value.

"But, of course, since this was the first time Forcett had met him, he couldn't tell whether his demeanour was normal or not. All he could say was that at first he had seemed slightly suspicious of the visit of a strange lawyer. Quite naturally, in my opinion. Medical men are a sitting target for vexatious proceedings on the part of disgruntled patients. But as soon as Mawsley understood what his visitor had come about, his manner changed completely. He became friendly and hospitable. His conversation proved him to be in full possession of all his faculties.

"Forcett described the last sight he had of him, as he said good evening to him from the doorway of the consulting-room. He was sitting at his table, with an extremely satisfied air, smoking a cigar which he had lighted a minute or two earlier. He had offered his visitor one, but Forcett, being a non-smoker, had declined. The papers which Forcett had brought were on the table in front of him, as was his glass of gin and lime, not quite empty. His last words were the message he asked Forcett to give the butler as he went out."

Oldland paused, emptied his glass, and refilled it. "Forcett went out, and Phepson shut the front door behind him. You understand that I'm trying to tell you the story, not repeating the evidence in the sequence it was given. After Forcett's departure, which we know to have been at eight minutes to seven, there were first two, then three people in the suite, Mawsley, Phepson, and his nephew Rusper. Mawsley in the consulting-room with the door shut, gloating over the codicil to Mrs. Somerthwaite's will, and, as it transpired, calculating how far the money would go. Phepson pottering about, acutely aware of the passing minutes, and watching for the first sign of Mawsley preparing to go out. Rusper sitting in the kitchen, reading an evening paper he had brought in with him.

"Time went on, with Phepson growing more restive every moment, and wandering up and down the hall listening. Remember, he was very anxious to be able to get away in time for his meeting. But it seemed an age before he heard anything. Then, at ten minutes past seven, he heard a dull thud from the consulting-room, as though Mawsley had dropped a book or something on the floor. A hopeful sign, that he was preparing to make a move, Phepson thought. Listening still, he heard the handle of a door rattle. It could only be the door between the consulting-room and the dispensary. Phepson supposed that before he went out Mawsley wanted to see how the rats that had been brought him were getting on.

"He thinks a minute, or maybe a couple of minutes passed, during which he could hear sounds of movement in the dispensary. Only faintly, of course, for the door between the dispensary and the hall was shut. He couldn't form any idea of what Mawsley was about. Then, suddenly, Phepson, whom I suspect of being a reader of sensational fiction, heard what he describes as a blood-curdling cry and a sickening crash.

"Rusper heard this, too, and came dashing out of the kitchen. For a second or two they stood, but all they could hear was a rapid hammering noise. Phepson called out, 'Are you all right, sir?' or something like that. Then he opened the door, the door between the hall and the dispensary. There's a minor point there, by the way, which isn't of any importance, but you'd better have it. It didn't occur to Phepson until later, but that door, which was usually kept locked, was not so at that moment. Phepson's explanation of this is that Mawsley had let the rat-catcher out that way, and had omitted to lock the door behind him. The key is on the inside, naturally.

"Well, Phepson and Rusper burst into the dispensary together. Mawsley was on the floor, speechless and writhing in agony, his heels kicking, which accounted for the hammering they had heard.

Phepson seems to have kept his head admirably in this emergency. Obviously, the first thing to do was to summon medical aid. He hadn't far to go for that for, although Mawsley was the only occupant of the house who actually lived in it, half a dozen other specialists have consulting-rooms there. Phepson, telling Rusper to stay where he was and not to stir till he came back, rushed to the front door. As he did so he was aware that the telephone bell was ringing, but obviously he couldn't stop to answer it. He ran downstairs first, but found that all the ground floor people had gone home. Then he started upstairs again, and was lucky enough to meet Dr. Chilvers, who has a consulting-room on the second floor, coming down.

"Now for Chilvers' story. He's a urologist, and though certainly not such a star as Mawsley, is an extremely capable man in his own line. He had finished for the day, and was about to go home. As he came downstairs, he was intercepted by Mawsley's butler, whom he knew well enough by sight. This man told him that his master had been taken very queer, and would he come and see him. Phepson led him into the suite, and to the dispensary, at the door of which Rusper was standing. Phepson says that he can't have been away more than three or four minutes. When he came back, the telephone had stopped ringing. Rusper says that during Phepson's absence he did not move from the spot where he was standing, and that no one had entered or left the suite.

"I won't bore you with the technicalities of Chilvers' evidence. By the time he arrived on the scene, Mawsley was lying still, obviously past all human aid. Satisfied on this point, Chilvers began to look about him. He found that Mawsley's coat sleeve and

23

cuff were rolled up on his left forearm, in which was a recent puncture. On the floor lay a hypodermic syringe, with the glass barrel broken. And on the bench stood a phial, the rubber cap torn off and lying beside it, bearing a label, written in ink, 'Inj Strych Hyp.' Or, translating that for the benefit of our policemen, hypodermic injection of strychnine. The phial still contained a quantity of liquid.

"What had happened was perfectly obvious. Mawsley had given himself a fatal injection of strychnine. For the sake of continuity, I'll anticipate the evidence a little. The body was removed to the mortuary that evening, and a post-mortem was performed. The public analyst was called in, and found strychnine in the tissues in sufficient quantity to cause death. The liquid in the phial was found on analysis to be a solution of strychnine hydrochloride, of a strength of eight grains to the liquid ounce. The fragments of the broken barrel were collected, and on being tested revealed the presence of strychnine. There is no room for the slightest doubt of the cause of Mawsley's death.

"But to get back to Chilvers. He was not in any way intimate with Mawsley, who was apt to keep himself aloof from his colleagues of the same profession. He had never before been inside the suite, and his intercourse with Mawsley seems to have been restricted to occasional exchanges of greetings if they happened to meet on the stairs. From what he could see for himself, and from what Phepson told him, he came to the conclusion of suicide. At his suggestion Phepson rang up the police, and in due course an Inspector, Lambourn by name, arrived on the scene.

"Lambourn considered it his duty to call in the police surgeon, so there was quite a party. Between

24

them they had a good look round, beginning with the dispensary. There they found, besides the rats in their cages, and a lot of medical equipment and apparatus, a cupboard containing an assortment of drugs. Among these were a number of phials, precisely similar to the one found on the bench, with labels indicating that they contained hypodermic injections of various kinds, some extremely powerful, others comparatively innocuous. The assumption being that Mawsley induced glandular disorders in rats, and then experimented in the control of them by the administration of different drugs.

"The coroner tumbled at once to the significance of these phials, and asked if it would be possible to mistake one for another. The answer was that though the phials themselves were exactly similar, each bore a distinctive label in Mawsley's handwriting. The wording of the labels, though abbreviated, was perfectly intelligible to anyone with a knowledge of pharmacy. The cupboard was open, and fitted with a lock, in which was the key.

"The party then entered the consulting-room, the door between which and the dispensary being wide open. Here the light was on, a powerful reading lamp on Mawsley's table. The first thing they noticed was that the chair in which Mawsley always sat, and in which he had been sitting when Phepson last saw him, was lying on its back on the floor. This probably accounted for the first dull thud Phepson had heard while he was listening. There was no other sign of disorder. The tray, with the bottles of gin and lime juice, the jug of water, and one empty glass, was on a side table. On the main table, at which Mawsley had been sitting, were the papers Forcett had left. Beside these was a half-burnt cigar resting on an ashtray, in which was the stub of another cigar. Also on the table was an empty cocktail glass, a silver pencil, identified as Mawsley's, and a sheet of his notepaper, with pencilled figures in his handwriting. At the head of the sheet was written £5000, and the rest of the figures appeared to be calculations based on that amount.

"Everything in the consulting-room was left undisturbed until the following morning when, at ten o'clock, Forcett turned up to keep the appointment he had made. Lambourn was there to meet him, and after hearing his account of his previous visit, took him to the consulting-room, and asked him to point out any difference in its appearance since he was there last. He pointed out the overturned chair at once, and said that Mawsley had been sitting in it when he left. Then he looked round carefully, and noticed one or two other things. He remembered that the tray had been on the central, not the side, table, for he had put his empty glass on it. Mawsley had not then finished the other glass, now empty, which was standing at his elbow. He had finished his first cigar, and put the stub in the ashtray. He had lighted a second cigar not more than three or four minutes before Forcett's departure.

"Then Forcett, seeing the pencil and the sheet of paper, said they were not there when he left. He thought he could explain the calculations. Mawsley had asked him what legacy duty would be payable. Forcett had replied that he was not quite sure, offhand. He thought about twelve per cent, but would look the matter up and tell him when he next saw him. The calculations on the paper showed a deduction of twelve per cent from the sum, and the income to be derived from the remainder if invested to yield four per cent. All this is not so irrelevant as it seems, for it reveals Mawsley's train of thought after Forcett left him.

"Well, that's about all, for Mrs. Mawsley's evidence didn't carry matters much further. She was perfectly calm and collected, and might have been giving evidence in the case of a casual friend. She had last seen her husband during the previous weekend, which he had spent at Larch Hall. He had then seemed perfectly normal, and had certainly given no indication that anything was worrying him. She knew for a fact that he had no financial troubles, and she had no reason to suppose that he had any professional ones either. She could not believe that he had intentionally taken his own life.

"The coroner took the only reasonable view. He said that the evidence showed conclusively that deceased had died from strychnine poisoning, self-administered. How he came to poison himself must remain a matter of conjecture. Mr. Forcett was the last person to see him before the event, and his evidence showed that he had had the pleasant duty of informing the doctor that he was the recipient of a substantial and unexpected legacy from an old patient, whom he had benefited in the early days of his career. Mr. Forcett had told us that he showed no sign of depression. On the contrary, he seemed cheerful, and indulged in reminiscences as they drank cocktails together. The material evidence showed that after Mr. Forcett had left him, the doctor's thoughts were engaged upon the legacy, and the use to which it could be put.

"The post-mortem showed that deceased was in good health, suffered from no organic complaint, and that his general condition was normal for his age. The only thing abnormal was the presence of a lethal amount of strychnine in his system, thus clearly indicating the cause of death. Dr. Mawsley's financial position was sound, and his medical reputation of the highest. He had carried on his work with skill and efficiency right to the end. This evidence nullified any suggestion of deliberate suicide.

"The only alternative was that of a ghastly mistake having been made. Dr. Mawsley deliberately took out a poison from his poison cupboard and administered to himself an injection of fatal proportions. For a medical man of his experience to make such a mistake was extraordinary, but no purpose would be served by conjecture as to how the deceased made it. The evidence was sufficient proof of the fact, and his duty was to give a verdict of accidental death. The Court would, he had no doubt, wish him to express their sympathy to his widow and family for the loss of a distinguished husband and father."

Oldland emptied his glass with an air of finality. "Your move, Priestley," he concluded.

3

Dr. Priestley opened his eyes and surveyed his guests gravely. "A most remarkable narrative," he observed. "I gather, from what you have told us of the evidence, that there can be no question of the correctness of the verdict. Your difficulty is to imagine how such a man as Mawsley could, under any circumstances, make such a mistake. I agree that it is surprising. But, before I express any opinion, I should like to hear the views of one more experienced than myself in the occurrence of violent death. What remarks have you to make, Hanslet?"

Hanslet took a long, slow pull at the glass of beer beside him. As he put it down he chuckled. "Experience!" he exclaimed. "You know very well, Professor, that when I've managed to muddle through a difficult case, more often than not it's been thanks to you. But if you want to hear what I've got to say, I'll tell you. Whenever I've found a chap dead in circumstances difficult to explain, I've asked myself: Murder? Suicide? Accident? in that order."

"I don't doubt you have," Oldland remarked acidly. "But in this case your rather elementary question is already answered."

"Never mind," Hanslet replied. "I'm an old-fashioned old stager, and I can't get away from the routine I've been used to all my life. As I say, my first question has always been, murder? And from that follow two other questions, motive and opportunity. And I've always taken motive first, and had a look round for anyone who might have had a reason for getting rid of the chap. And that sort of reason usually turns out to be a financial one."

Oldland shrugged his shoulders. "All right, if you like to be obstinate. But I can't help you, for the subject of Mawsley's will wasn't mentioned. I imagine that the only people who benefit financially by his death are his wife and family. He may have left a small legacy to Phepson, who's been with him some time."

"What about the five thousand pounds the old woman left him?" Hanslet asked. "Who gets that now?"

"Not being a lawyer, I couldn't say," Oldland replied. "It'll be shared out with the rest of his estate, I suppose."

"His wife and family again," said Hanslet. "You gave us to understand that Mrs. Mawsley didn't seem overmuch upset by her husband's death. Well, never mind. Had he any enemies? Jealousy? Revenge?"

"How the dickens do you expect me to know that?" Oldland demanded. "I thought I had made it sufficiently clear tha' acquaintance with him was of the slightest. I've .old you that he wasn't generally popular among the fellow members of his profession, and I suppose a man in his position is bound to arouse a certain amount of enmity. Beyond that I can't go."

"All right," said Hanslet tranquilly. "Motive at present not clear. Next, opportunity. At the time when Mawsley jabbed himself with the needle, there

30

were only three people in the suite—himself, the butler, and the butler's nephew. There's no doubt about that, I suppose? There can't have been anyone else lying doggo about the place?"

"I've given you the evidence," Oldland replied patiently. "It's for you to explain how a fourth person could have got in and out."

Hanslet knocked out his pipe and began to refill it. "I don't want to seem captious, Doctor," he said. "But there's one little point in which I can't quite agree with you. When Phepson heard Mawsley cry out, and tried the door between the hall and the dispensary, he found it unlocked. You say that isn't of any importance, but I'm not so sure of that."

"It would be interesting to learn what importance you attach to the fact," Dr. Priestley murmured.

"Why, this," Hanslet replied. "We're told that door was normally kept locked, with the key on the inside. Quite right, too, if the dispensary is full of rats and deadly poisons. When the door was locked, the only way into the dispensary was through the consulting-room. Phepson says it must have been left unlocked when the rat-catcher left, and he may be right. That was at half past four or thereabouts. From that time onwards, anyone could have got into the dispensary without going through the consulting-room, and, therefore, without Mawsley's knowledge."

"Quite a good point," said Dr. Priestley approvingly. "This person having previously hidden in some other part of the suite?"

"That's right, Professor," Hanslet replied, encouraged by this approval. "This chap slipped into the dispensary while Phepson wasn't about. While he was taking the cocktails into the consulting-room, if you like. He waited there for Mawsley, then when

31

he came in took hold of him and jabbed him with the syringe, which he had already filled. He ran into the consulting-room, and slipped out of the suite, and out of the house, while Phepson was hunting for a doctor and his nephew was watching Mawsley. What do you say to that, Doctor?"

"I say it's fantastic," Oldland replied testily. "There's no evidence of such a person. That's the worst of you policemen. Once you get an idea into your heads, you start imagining evidence to bolster it up."

Hanslet grinned. "Sorry, Doctor, but if we didn't use our imagination sometimes we shouldn't get very far. But you don't care about the idea of murder, I can see that. Very well, suicide comes next."

"Equally out of the question," Oldland replied. "I won't labour the point that there was no possible reason for Mawsley to take his own life. It is just possible that he had some secret motive for doing so which hasn't come to light. I won't even ask you to explain why a man should entertain a stranger most cheerfully one moment and kill himself the next. But I will say, and that most definitely, that no man with any knowledge of poisons and their effects would have deliberately chosen the method Mawsley chose.

"Look here. I may lay claim to at least an elementary knowledge of the subject. Chilvers saw, in that poison cupboard, quite a formidable collection of drugs, prepared as injections, most of which possessed lethal properties. It is notorious that of all forms of poisoning, that by strychnine is the most painful. I refuse to believe that Mawsley, with a dozen injections to choose from, all certain and comparatively painless in their effects, deliberately gave himself a fatal shot of strychnine."

"Well, you know best about that," said Hanslet. "So, like the coroner, we're driven back to the theory of accident. And, so far as I can see, the only way Mawsley can have made such a mistake was through sheer damn carelessness. What was he playing about with a hypodermic syringe for, just then?"

"That's just the question," Oldland replied. "No doubt he was in the habit of playing about with hypodermic syringes, as you put it. Not giving injections to himself, but to his rats, for experimental purposes. But why just then, before he was going out to dinner? I've an idea, which I'll give you for what it's worth."

Fortified with a sip of whisky, Oldland went on. "We must try to imagine Mawsley's state of mind after Forcett left him. He was a chap with a passion for money, and here was a fat and entirely unexpected legacy fallen from the blue into his lap. He wanted a chance to gloat over that, to consider all the rosy prospects it offered. Hence, his message to Phepson, that his golden dreams were not to be disturbed. We know that he spent the next quarter of an hour or so smoking his cigar, finishing his cocktail, and indulging in satisfactory calculation. Then his insides reminded him that it was time to go out and get something to eat. By Jove, he would! He'd give himself a slap-up dinner, with a bottle of fizz to go with it. And what about a shot of something first, something that would key his sense of enjoyment up to the very highest pitch?

"I suppose that all of us have experienced, at least once in our lives, something so pleasurable that it produced a sense of intense excitement, more or less suppressed. For a while, at least, our behaviour is slightly abnormal. I imagine Mawsley to have been in such a state at that moment. He jumped up so abruptly that he upset his chair. What did a little thing like a chair matter? He would pick it up in a minute. Then he went into the dispensary, determined to give himself an injection of some pleasure-stimulating drug. Cannabis, which you know as hashish, perhaps.

"It is a commonplace that familiarity breeds not only contempt, but carelessness as well. It isn't the man using a circular saw for the first time who cuts off his fingers, but the chap who's been using the thing every day for years. Anyone else would have read very carefully the label on the phial he took out. But not Mawsley. Why should he? He knew exactly the position of each drug in the cupboard. The cannabis was the third from the left. He reached for that phial, filled the syringe from it, and gave himself the injection. We know the result."

"Excellent!" Dr. Priestley exclaimed. "All our doubts are set at rest. What is your opinion, Superintendent?"

Jimmy, to whom the Professor's question was addressed, smiled. "I'm very much impressed by the doctor's vivid reconstruction, sir," he replied. "But there are a few technical details I should like to ask him about. Isn't it just possible that Mawsley mistook, not the nature of the drug, but the quantity of it that he introduced into his system?"

Oldland looked doubtful. "You mean that his intention was to give himself a shot of strychnine, but that he miscalculated the dose? Well, I suppose that is just possible. Strychnine certainly has tonic properties. For that matter, it is often prescribed in cases of dyspepsia. Mawsley may have been having trouble with his digestion, and thought that he'd better take precautions before that marvellous dinner he'd promised himself. It strikes me as being highly unlikely. And still more so that with his experience he should have given himself a fatal dose."

"I'm working my way towards that," said Jimmy. "You told us about the liquid remaining in the phial. On analysis it was found to contain eight grains to the liquid ounce, I think you said. Is that the usual strength?"

"My pharmacy is a bit rusty," Oldland replied. "I couldn't say offhand. You've got a *Codex* here, haven't you, Priestley?"

Harold Merefield got up and from one of the glass-fronted bookcases that lined the walls of the study produced a bulky volume. This he handed to Oldland, who turned over the pages. "Here's your answer, Jimmy," he said. " '*Injectio Strychninae*, B.P.C. 3 5/32 grains to one fluid ounce.' That seems to be the usual proportion. But Mawsley probably made up his solutions himself, in the proportion that best suited his purposes."

"Well, yes," Jimmy agreed. "But I'm thinking of Hanslet's point about the unlocked dispensary door, and this is what's in my mind. Suppose that Mawsley was in the habit, now and then, of giving himself an injection of a minute quantity of strychnine, using for the purpose a solution of normal strength, three and a bit grains to the ounce. Someone who was aware of this hotted up the solution to double strength. Injecting the same quantity of this as usual, Mawsley would have given himself a double dose of the drug. Will that do?"

Oldland shook his head. "I'm afraid not, Jimmy, and I'll try to explain why," he replied. "If Mawsley was in the habit of taking strychnine injections, it must have been in minute quantities, since they produced no ill effects. So minute that doubling the quantity would not have produced fatal results. Or, at all events, not results so immediately fatal as was the case. Do you see what I mean? I'll put it another way. Mawsley certainly cannot have been in the habit of injecting himself with half a lethal dose of strychnine. The results would have been far too unpleasant."

"There's something in Jimmy's idea, just the same," Hanslet remarked. "About the poisons having been monkeyed with, I mean. You pictured Mawsley reaching for the bottle without troubling to look at the label. Perhaps he did. But what if someone had shifted the bottles round without his knowledge?"

"Oh, come now!" Oldland protested. "That's a bit farfetched, even for a policeman determined to find foul play where it doesn't exist. If I were setting out to murder anybody, I should take care to adopt a surer means than that. If Mawsley's mind had not been occupied with his windfall to the exclusion of everything else, he would at least have glanced at the label. How on earth could anyone have known in advance that he would be wealth-intoxicated that evening? You'll have to think again, my friend."

"A word you've just used makes me think," Hanslet replied. "Intoxicated. Not only by the news of his legacy, but by the cocktails he'd been drinking. Perhaps he was just a wee bit fuddled, and didn't quite realize what he was doing."

"That's rather more reasonable," Oldland agreed. "But it wants some modification. A seasoned cocktail drinker would hardly get fuddled on a couple of glasses of gin and lime. On the other hand, the alcohol may have contributed to the negligent frame of mind I suggested. Well, Priestley, it's your move now, surely."

"I have listened with close attention to the various conjectures which have been made," the Professor replied. "I am in agreement with some of them, but not with others. Let me say at once, however, that I find the problem raised by Mawsley's death of the greatest interest. The problem, stated in its simplest terms, is this. Under what circumstances did a lethal quantity of strychnine find its way into Mawsley's system?

"This problem is by no means solved by the statement that he administered the fatal injection himself. We are left with the even more puzzling query which Oldland has so ably expounded. But, first of all, we must establish that basic fact. Was the injection self-administered? What is the alternative? That it was forcibly administered by some other person. It is worthwhile examining that alternative, if only to reach the conclusion that it may safely be discarded.

"I find it very difficult to envisage any unauthorized person lurking in the suite, on the watch for an opportunity of murdering Mawsley. Apart from the negative evidence on this point, such conduct would appear incredible, if only by reason of the risk of discovery such a person would have run. It seems more reasonable to assume that the facts are as stated, that at the time of the injection the only people in the suite besides Mawsley were Phepson and Rusper.

"Following Hanslet's line of approach, a very sound one, we ask ourselves first whether Mawsley can have been murdered. I do not look with any great favour upon suggestions that the poison cupboard, or the poisons it contained, had previously been tampered with. It seems to me that the chances of Mawsley's death resulting from any such tampering with criminal intent would have been too remote. Murder then can only have been committed by those actually in the suite at the time. I leave to your consideration the possibility that the butler and his nephew between them overpowered Mawsley and administered the injection. If you reject this, you must accept the fact that the injection was self-administered, as established."

"I don't think anybody in Court ever had the slightest doubt about that," Oldland remarked.

"Even Coroners' Courts have been known to reach incorrect conclusions," Dr. Priestley replied dryly. "But in this case I am inclined to agree with the verdict, in so far as I believe the injection was self-administered. But I am by no means so easily satisfied that, this being so, Mawsley's death was necessarily accidental. Hanslet's second alternative, that of suicide, to my mind has not been disposed of."

"Oh, dash it all, Priestley!" Oldland protested. "People, especially prosperous, go-ahead people like Mawsley, don't take their own lives on a sudden whim. You've heard the evidence as to his demeanour, perfectly bright and cheerful. And the probability that he was suddenly seized with suicidal dementia is so remote that it can be dismissed."

"In attempting the solution of a problem, every possibility, however remote, must be considered," Dr. Priestley replied. "I cannot help thinking that, however prominent Mawsley may have been in his profession, little or nothing has been revealed of his private life, at least in the course of the inquest.

You speak of the evidence adduced as to his demeanour, which all goes to show that his conscience was clear and untroubled. Who gave that evidence? His wife, who saw him last during the week-end. Phepson, who judged apparently by the incident of his sending for the cocktails. Forcett, who, as a stranger, and, therefore, lacking a basis of comparison, was hardly in a position to testify whether his manner was normal or not.

"The judgment of these three people may have been correct, within the time limit of their observations. I will go so far as to suggest that, up to the moment of Forcett's departure, and for some minutes after that, Mawsley cherished no thought of suicide. Let me recall a very minor point in the evidence you repeated for our benefit, Oldland. When Phepson took the tea-tray into the consulting-room, there were on it three or four letters which had just arrived. When, if at all, did Mawsley open and read those letters?"

"I don't know," Oldland replied. "That was the only mention of them. One of them was the one I posted to him about old Matt Gussage, I expect. He can't have had much chance of reading them. The rat-catcher came almost immediately, and Forcett soon after he had gone. And Forcett's news probably put the letters out of his head."

"Probably, for the moment," Dr. Priestley agreed. "But let us consider again that critical period following Forcett's departure. The evidence shows that Mawsley devoted some part of this at least to calculations regarding the legacy. At this point I may be allowed to follow the example of my guests and indulge in conjecture. It is at least possible that, the calculations finished, the neglected letters caught Mawsley's eye, and he opened them.

"We do not know what has become of those letters, and any theory based on them must be purely tentative. It is, therefore, with extreme caution that I suggest the following possibility. The contents of one of those letters were such as to utterly wreck Mawsley's peace of mind, so much so that he found himself abruptly faced with the alternatives of ruin or suicide. We can all of us, I daresay, imagine how this could have arisen. Mawsley may have practised euthanasia, and been threatened with exposure by some relative of his patient. Again, I remind you that perusal of the letters he received that afternoon may show my suggestion to be entirely without foundation.

"But, if it can be shown to have any basis in fact, it might explain what followed. Mawsley, having received a shock which drove him into unreasoning panic, leapt violently from his chair, upsetting it as he did so. He rushed into the dispensary, and seized the hypodermic syringe and the phial of strychnine injection. The fact that the cap was torn off, not punctured in the normal manner, suggested disturbance of mind. I have this to say regarding your objection, Oldland. It is true that the effects of the administration of strychnine are agonizing. But, on the other hand, as the event showed, the agony is rapidly terminated by death."

"Well, that's an idea, Professor," said Hanslet thoughtfully. "But if there was such a letter, what became of it? Lambourn, who seems to have explored the consulting-room, wouldn't have overlooked such a vital clue as all that."

"The existence of the letter is a pure hypothesis on my part," Dr. Priestley replied. "We are told that Mawsley received three or four letters by the afternoon post. We are ignorant of their contents, except that we have reason to believe that one of them may have been Oldland's. Since those that may have been found were not mentioned in the course of the inquest, we can assume that they were irrelevant to the issue. But they may not all of them have been found. One of them may have been destroyed, by Mawsley himself, or some other person."

Dr. Priestley glanced meaningfully at the clock, the hands of which pointed to an hour considerably later than that at which his guests were accustomed to take their departure. "It is late," he said. "But before we seek harbour from the ocean of conjecture upon which we have embarked, just one brief point. What was the source of the strychnine with which Mawsley was fatally poisoned?"

"Why, I told you that!" Oldland exclaimed. "The phial containing what remained of the injection was found uncapped on the bench in the dispensary, beside which Mawsley had fallen."

Dr. Priestley smiled. "The obvious, again," he replied. "But it has passed through my mind that rat-catchers are among the few people who are able to obtain strychnine in the ordinary course of their business."

4

Jimmy was not altogether surprised when, on the following Monday, he was rung up by Harold Merefield. "Is that you, Jimmy?" Harold said. "Listen. All the week-end the Professor has been worrying his head over that yarn Oldland told us on Saturday evening. He told me to ring you up and ask you if you could manage to come round this evening after dinner. I'm pretty sure he wants to talk it over with you quietly. Come if you can, it may set his mind at rest."

Jimmy promised to do so, and was faithful to his word. He found nobody in Dr. Priestley's study but the Professor and Harold, and the former lost no time in getting down to the subject. "It is good of you to humour the whims of an old man, Superintendent," he said warmly. "Especially as the affair which has captured my attention is at present no concern of the police. But I will ask you a question which I hope you will answer, not as a member of the Criminal Investigation Department, but as an intelligent member of society. After what you heard on Saturday evening, and I do not suppose you have derived information from any other source, are you entirely satisfied that the verdict in Mawsley's case is the correct one?"

Jimmy hesitated. It was not always easy to answer the Professor's questions in such a way as to meet with his approval. "Well, sir, on the evidence the coroner heard, I don't see what other verdict he could have given," he replied in some trepidation.

"On the evidence he heard, certainly," said Dr. Priestley, and Jimmy congratulated himself on having put in the saving clause. "But was all the evidence available to him? I cannot help wondering."

Dr. Priestley paused, and then went on rather more briskly. "You know my attitude towards these matters, Superintendent. I am not concerned with the individual, but with the interpretation of facts. It is of no concern to me how Mawsley met his death. But I maintain that if the truth is as the coroner expressed it in his summing up, I find it as inexplicable as Oldland appears to. And when the truth appears inexplicable, my critical sense is immediately stimulated. Do you follow me?"

"Perfectly, sir," Jimmy replied, perhaps not altogether truthfully.

"Very well," said Dr. Priestley. "My first step in criticism is to ask whether there may not be some alternative explanation of the tragedy. And, in that connection it occurs to me that the proceedings were to some extent perfunctory. Had a skilled investigator, such as yourself, been summoned immediately he might—I say only that he might—have observed indications that passed unnoticed. Mind you, I am not blaming any of those concerned. I imagine that each of them told the truth as he saw it. I do not for a moment suppose that any of them made a false statement or withheld a particle of evidence. But perhaps they failed to look beneath the surface of the obvious.

"You will reply perhaps that a skilled investigator

was in fact summoned, in the person of Inspector Lambourn. I know nothing of the Inspector's ability, but I fully appreciate the position in which he found himself. Having heard what Dr. Chilvers, Phepson, and Rusper could tell him, he can have had no suspicion of foul play. Mawsley had quite clearly died as the result of suicide or accident. He found none of the conventional indications of suicide, such, for instance, as a note of farewell left behind by the victim. Apparently he didn't find any other suggestive evidence, such as a letter upon which I allowed myself to conjecture. In any case, the probability of suicide could only be determined by those who knew Mawsley best. It could not be determined by any minute examination of the premises, for instance. He satisfied himself, no doubt, with a close interrogation of those present, and a careful, though superficial, inspection of the dispensary and consulting-room. I maintain, therefore, that the investigation was not as thorough as it might have been."

As Dr. Priestley paused, Jimmy ventured a question. "Have you formed any suspicion that Mawsley died as the result of some action on somebody else's part, sir?" he asked rather awkwardly.

The Professor's reply was prompt. "If anything is certain in this most puzzling case, it is that Mawsley died by his own hand. That being so, you may say that whether he killed himself intentionally or unintentionally is a matter of purely academic interest. This may be so, from the police point of view. But to the student of criminology it is a question of enthralling interest. If Mawsley committed suicide, what compelling terror drove him to the deed? If his death was due to a mistake, how did that mistake arise?"

"I don't know that the interest is entirely academic, sir," said Jimmy. "If the police had any reason for doubt, they would not let the matter rest. But, in the light of the coroner's verdict, I hardly see what action they could take. Unless—"

The Professor looked intently at Jimmy as his sentence remained unfinished. "Unless?" he asked sharply.

"Well, sir, I'll put it this way," Jimmy replied hesitantly. "The Chief has never forgotten how you came to the rescue over that Lake House affair. Whenever a puzzle crops up now, he always says, 'We shall have to send for Dr. Priestley to unravel this for us.' I'm quite sure that if I were to tell him you were not quite happy about the verdict on Mawsley, he'd let me make investigations on any lines you cared to suggest. Very quietly, and without any fuss or publicity, of course."

Dr. Priestley frowned slightly. "I do not wish the Assistant Commissioner to acquire the impression that I am a meddlesome busybody," he said. "And I should prefer you not to use the expression unhappy, for the issue is not of a nature to disturb my equanimity. You may say, if you think fit, that the version of the evidence I have heard does not entirely explain to my satisfaction how Mawsley came to administer to himself a lethal injection."

Jimmy smiled. "I think I can promise you in advance that will be good enough, sir," he replied. "The Chief is sure to tell me to get on with it. But I should very much like your advice as to where I ought to start."

"At the suite in Harley Street," Dr. Priestley replied unhesitatingly. "It is most unlikely that, after the interval that has elapsed, you will find any material evidence there. But you will have the opportunity of talking to Phepson, and forming your own opinion as to his veracity. In the course of conversation with him you may elicit further details of the events immediately preceding Mawsley's death.

"There is another person whom I think you should see. Oldland mentioned a girl, with whose father he was acquainted, a Miss Hilworth, who acted as Mawsley's secretary and receptionist. Although apparently it was not thought necessary to summon her to give evidence at the inquest, her duties must have given her some insight into her employer's professional affairs. It is possible that the letters received by Mawsley by the afternoon post on Tuesday have been handed over to her.

"Too much emphasis has, I think, been laid upon Forcett's visit, or rather upon the news which he brought Mawsley. It seems to have been assumed that a man who has just learnt that he was the recipient of an unexpected legacy would not commit suicide shortly afterwards, an assumption with which I cannot entirely agree. Five thousand pounds is a very pleasant sum of which to become possessed, but it could hardly have made any vital difference to a man in Mawsley's position. Unless, of course, his prosperity was merely superficial, and he had financial worries unknown to anyone but himself. You should, for your own satisfaction, interview Forcett and hear at first hand his account of what took place during the interview. But the true facts of Mawsley's financial position must obviously be sought elsewhere.

"That brings us to his wife and family, and so to Larch Hall. And here I may issue a warning, probably unnecessary to one of your experience. The only real issue at the inquest was to decide whether

Mawsley's death was due to suicide or accident. In such cases the evidence of friends and relatives may be assumed to have a certain natural bias. A verdict of accidental death is obviously more acceptable to them than one of suicide, and they will abstain as far as possible from saying anything which might tend to sway the balance towards the latter. I am not, of course, imputing perjury to anyone in this case.

"It would be of considerable interest to ascertain the provisions of Mawsley's will, and more particularly, the amount of his estate. I do not consider it very likely that he committed suicide owing to financial embarrassment, but the possibility should not be overlooked. Equally important are his relations with his family and with other people, his friends. Oldland rather gave us the impression that he was not a man to make friends readily. But he may at least have had acquaintances, to whom he confided matters withheld, for instance, from Mrs. Mawsley.

"A hint of this is afforded us in the course of Phepson's evidence. You will remember that Old-land told us the butler was much impressed by Mawsley offering his visitor the hospitality of a cocktail. But such a gesture on his part, though rare, was not entirely unprecedented. Phepson said that, even if a friend called before his master went out to dinner, it was very rarely that he offered him a cocktail. That remark suggests that people did occasionally call after consulting hours. Were these visits professional, or purely social? Did Mawsley ever invite any of them to spend the week-end at Larch Hall?

"I think you will appreciate the reasoning which

prompts these suggestions. Whether Mawsley's death was due to suicide or accident can only be determined by a process of elimination. Not until every possible motive for suicide has been eliminated can we safely conclude that the occurrence was purely accidental. And even then we should ascertain whether the accident could have been precipitated by events. Hanslet has suggested some disarrangement of the contents of the poison cupboard, with the implication that it was done with criminal intent. The disarrangement appears possible, but, for the reasons which Oldland touched upon, criminal intent appears unlikely.

"We do not know who, besides Mawsley himself, was in the habit of entering the dispensary. It may transpire that some person, or persons, had permitted access to the room. If so, the contents of the poison cupboard may have been disarranged inadvertently. Even so, I find it difficult to believe that Mawsley would have charged a syringe without so much as glancing at the label on the phial from which he did so.

"Your own suggestion, that the mistake lay in the strength of the injection, appears to me more reasonable. Mawsley may have believed that he had measured into the syringe a quantity of liquid containing merely a tonic and stimulating dose of strychnine. He supposed, in fact, that the phial contained a solution of strychnine hydrochloride in proportion of, say, one-fifteenth of a grain to the fluid ounce. Let me impress upon you as emphatically as I can, that this is no more than unsupported conjecture.

"But, following up this line of thought, how could the error have arisen? In the cupboard there may have been two or more phials of strychnine solution, of different strengths. But, had this been the case, one would have expected the labels on these phials to be clearly marked with the strength of the solution each contained. Alternatively, there may have been a single phial, containing a weak solution, into which an additional quantity of the drug had been introduced. There may be a supply of some strychnine compound, in crystalline form, on the premises, particularly if Mawsley was in the habit of making up his own injections.

"I am not suggesting that the solution was deliberately strengthened with a view to causing Mawsley's death. That would involve the existence of someone who was aware that he was in the habit of giving himself strychnine injections—a habit of which we have no evidence—and that he would do so once more within a reasonable time, at least before he had discovered, by the effects of his experiments on the rats, that the strengthening had taken place.

"But there is one curious point, which should not, I think, be ignored. The visit of the rat-catcher that evening. It would appear from the evidence that Mawsley took this man into the dispensary, for the transfer of the rats he had brought to the cages there. It may be, and probably is, a coincidence, to use that word for want of a better. But strychnine in any form is not an easy drug for the ordinary person to obtain, while, as I pointed out, rat-catchers use it in the course of their destructive activities.

"Beyond that, Superintendent, I have no advice to give you. If an investigation is to be undertaken, it should be conducted with an impartial mind. I have done my best not to prejudice you in either direction. And I may be allowed to add this. If at any stage of the inquiry, with which I hope you will be entrusted, you care to consult me, my time is unreservedly at your disposal. I shall be most happy to see you, whenever you care to call."

Next morning Jimmy sought an interview with the Assistant Commissioner, to whom he expounded Dr. Priestley's doubts as tactfully as possible. "I know the Professor pretty well by now, sir," he concluded. "And I'm quite sure that he wouldn't have sent for me as he did unless he was honestly convinced that there was something behind the affair."

The Chief nodded. "I don't doubt that," he replied. "But it doesn't follow that what lies behind it is any affair of ours. Still, I'd like to set his mind at rest, if only to repay the debt of gratitude we owe him. He saved us from what might have been a very awkward blunder, not so long ago. All right, fit the job in with your other duties, and see what you can make of it. I give you a free hand, unless and until something more important crops up."

Dr. Priestley had recommended Jimmy make a start at Mawsley's suite in Harley Street. But before he did this, he felt that he should see Inspector Lambourn who might otherwise feel aggrieved. So he called at the police station, and had a word with the Inspector. "You remember that affair of Dr. Mawsley, a week ago?" he said. "You went to Harley Street and had a look round, I believe. Have you done any more about it, since the inquest?"

"Why, no, I haven't," Lambourn replied. "After the verdict there didn't seem any more to be done by us, anyhow."

Jimmy nodded. "Quite right. But one or two minor points have been raised, and the Yard has been asked to take them up. You won't think I'm butting in if I go and look over the place myself?"

"Not in the least," Lambourn replied. "You'll find the butler in charge there, I believe. He seems quite a good chap."

"All right, I'll ask him to show me round," said Jimmy. "And while I'm here, you might tell me what you know."

But Lambourn could tell him little more than Oldland had already reported. He had, on exploring the consulting-room, seen some letters lying on a desk. He had glanced at these, and found that they were all of a business nature, asking for appointments, and so forth. He had had no reason to doubt that the various statements made to him were anything but accurate. "In fact, sir," he concluded, "when I heard the evidence given at the inquest, I could see that the doctor hadn't committed suicide, but had killed himself by accident."

Just so, Jimmy thought, as he made his way towards Harley Street. The evidence given at the inquest. Nobody, basing his opinion upon that alone, could disagree with the coroner, however puzzling Dr. Mawsley's mistake might seem. But evidently the Professor suspected the existence of additional evidence, which had not been given at the inquest. Well, if he was right, it was Jimmy's task to unearth it. Not a very hopeful prospect, a week after the event.

It was a few minutes after three o'clock in the afternoon of Tuesday, January 22nd, when Jimmy reached the suite. He rang the bell, and the door was opened by a middle-aged man in a black suit, who he knew must be Phepson. The man's face, he thought, indicated honesty of purpose, if not perhaps exceptional intelligence. "You are Phepson, Dr. Mawsley's butler?" he said, presenting his card. "I should like a few minutes' talk with you. Who else is here?"

Phepson's eyebrows lifted as he read the wording of the official card. "There's nobody here but me," he replied, in a tone which betrayed his surprise. "You want to talk to me? I hope there's nothing amiss, Superintendent?"

"Nothing whatever," Jimmy reassured him. "It's just this. When an important man like Dr. Mawsley dies, we folk at Scotland Yard like to have full particulars for our records. You're alone here, you say? All the better. Can we sit down comfortably somewhere and have a chat?"

"Certainly, sir," Phepson replied, apparently satisfied with this explanation. He led the way into the dining-room, a rather sombre place, in which the only objects of interest were the central table, with chairs set round it, a heavy Victorian sideboard, and a few pictures, which Jimmy judged to be valuable. He took a chair at the table, and nodded to Phepson to seat himself at the opposite side. "Now then," he said encouragingly, "tell me the story of what happened here last Tuesday afternoon. In your own words, just as you'd tell a friend who had asked you about it."

Phepson complied, readily and at length, for he was obviously still bubbling over with the experience. His account deviated in no way from Oldland's report of his evidence. To Jimmy it was an indication of his reliability that more mature consideration had not led him to modify any of his statements. He felt quite satisfied that if evidence had been suppressed or distorted, Phepson at least was not responsible.

"Thank you," he said, when the butler had finished. "That's all perfectly clear. Now, you won't mind if I ask you a few questions, just to get the details clear in my mind. You say that when you ran out to find a doctor, the telephone bell was ringing. Was it answered?"

Phepson shook his head. "I had other things to think about, sir. And my nephew Ted didn't answer it, for he never left the dispensary door till I came back with Dr. Chilvers. It had stopped ringing then, or at least I think it had. I wasn't taking much notice of things like that."

"I'm sure you weren't," Jimmy agreed. "The caller, whoever he was, getting no reply, must have given up trying. Did he ring up again later?"

"No, sir," Phepson replied. "No calls came in for the rest of the evening. The only time I used the telephone again was when I rang up Mrs. Mawsley at Larch Hall, a good while later."

"Then the call can't have been of any great importance," said Jimmy lightly. "Now, I want to get this telephone business quite clear. The extension was not switched through to the consulting-room. If a call came, you answered in the first place, then asked Dr. Mawsley if he wished to speak. If he did, you switched him through. Is that right?"

"Perfectly, sir," Phepson replied. "That's just what happened when Mr. Forcett rang up soon after four. And that was the last call that came through that day."

"And what if Dr. Mawsley wanted to ring someone up himself?" Jimmy asked.

"It didn't often happen that he did, sir. The master never used the telephone more than he could help. But if he wanted to speak to anyone, he'd ring for me and tell me to put the extension through. After consulting hours that is, of course. But I don't remember the master himself putting a call through in the evening for a long time."

"After consulting hours, naturally," said Jimmy. "You weren't concerned with the telephone between ten and four. It was Miss Hilworth's job to answer it then. By the way, what time did she leave here last Tuesday?"

5

It seemed to Jimmy that Phepson's eyelids flickered, almost imperceptibly, at the mention of Miss Hilworth's name. But the quiet, respectful tone of his voice did not alter in the least as he replied. "I did not actually see Miss Hilworth go, sir. She always let herself out. But the last patient left a few minutes before four, and I think she went very soon afterwards. The last I saw of her, she was coming out of the consulting-room with the letters for the post."

"The last you saw of her that day," Jimmy remarked. "Miss Hilworth came here next morning at her usual time?"

Phepson shook his head. "No, sir, she didn't," he replied with peculiar emphasis. "When I say that was the last I saw of her, that's what I mean. I haven't set eyes on her since a minute or two before four last Tuesday afternoon."

"Perhaps, having heard what had happened, she didn't think it worthwhile coming any more," said Jimmy casually. He didn't want to discuss Miss Hilworth with the butler until he knew more about her. "She always let herself out of here, you say. Did she let herself in? Has she a key to the front door?"

"Not to my knowledge, sir," Phepson replied. "When she came in the morning she always rang the bell, and I let her in. So far as I know, there are only two keys to the front door. The master had one, and I had the other."

"I see," said Jimmy. "Now, what about the house door, the entrance from the street. When I came just now, a porter let me in and asked me who I wanted to see. Is there always a porter on duty in the lower hall?"

"Only in the daytime, sir," Phepson replied. "He comes at eight and goes at seven. My nephew Ted told me that he was just packing up when he came last Tuesday evening. And he'd gone by the time I ran down to see if any of the other doctors were still here."

"The door is shut when he goes, I take it," said Jimmy. "How does one get in after that?"

"Well, it's this way, sir," the butler explained. "Everyone who has rooms in the house has a key. The master had one, and I've got one. And you must understand that the other doctors are here only in the daytime. They wouldn't be likely to want to come in after the porter had gone, and, of course, no patients would call on them here then. They've all got night addresses, where they live, I daresay. As for us, there's a bell-push down there with a brass plate, 'Dr. Mawsley, Night only.' The bell is in the kitchen here and if it should ring I go down to the outer door. But it's not very often that's ever happened."

Jimmy nodded. "So that if you or Dr. Mawsley were out in the evening, you could get in without any trouble. Now, I want to ask you about something else. You told me that you took cocktails into the consulting-room that evening. How many do you suppose Dr. Mawsley and Mr. Forcett had between them?"

Phepson got up and went to the sideboard. "You can judge for yourself, sir," he said, as he put a couple of bottles on the table. "They're just as I put them away last Wednesday. When I took them in, the lime juice was full, for I'd opened a fresh bottle only the day before, and the master hadn't had any out of it. And the gin was just about level with the top of the label."

Jimmy contemplated the two bottles, one of Rose's Lime Juice Cordial, the other of Gordon's gin. The level of the liquid in the first was about a couple of inches down the neck, and in the second perhaps an inch below the top of the label. This hardly suggested a debauch. Jimmy estimated that Mawsley and his visitor could not have had more than a couple of cocktails each, and not very potent ones at that.

The butler evidently guessed his thoughts. "The master was never one to take very much to drink, sir," he said. "Sometimes he'd have a glass of white wine with his lunch, but as often as not he'd only have iced water. Every evening before he went out to dinner he had a glass of plain gin and water, but I think he took that as medicine as much as anything else. He'd usually come in here and get it himself, and I've seen him put a little tablet in it, which fizzed. Then before he went to bed he'd come in here and pour himself out a glass of whisky, and that's all."

"He wasn't what you'd call a heavy drinker," Jimmy remarked. "Well, you've told me quite a lot of interesting details, Phepson. Now, I wonder if you'd mind showing me the consulting-room?"

This, it turned out, was the largest room in the

suite. As the butler showed him in, Jimmy stood just inside the doorway and looked about him. He saw a table, at which were set two chairs. This stood, not in the centre of the room, but rather to one side. A Venetian screen stood a short distance within the doorway, in such a way that, when the door was open, very little of the interior was visible to anyone in the hall. In the wall facing the door was an open fireplace, now empty, on either side of which were large bookcases, filled with medical works. The wall to the right of this was occupied by a big desk, and a chair, and an extensive filing cabinet. On the further side of the room was a second door, leading into the dispensary. At one side of this door was an adjustable couch, and beside it a large and formidable cabinet, on which were a number of switches. A flexible metal arm extended from this over the couch. On the other side of the door was a smaller table. Beside the fireplace stood a couple of upholstered arm-chairs.

Jimmy looked round, making a mental note of this furniture. "Now, Phepson," he said, "tell me exactly what you saw when you brought in the tea last Tuesday evening. Where Dr. Mawsley was sitting, and what he was doing."

"The master was sitting at his desk, sir," Phepson replied. "He was writing something in a book. When I put the tray on the middle table he got up. He picked up the letters I'd brought on the tray and looked them over. He didn't open them, but put them on the desk. Then he sat down at the table, in the chair with its back to the desk, the one he always sat in."

Jimmy nodded. "This suite is centrally heated, I notice. But there's a fireplace here. Was it ever used?"

"Always, sir, in winter, during the week," the butler replied. "The master always liked to see a fire burning. I don't think it was the warmth so much as that it looked cheerful. There was a fire in here last Tuesday afternoon."

"Very well," said Jimmy. "The next time you saw and spoke to Dr. Mawsley was a few minutes later, when the rat-catcher came?"

"That's right, sir," Phepson replied. "I came in here and told the master that the man had come and brought a couple of rats with him. He was sitting at the table having his tea, and he told me to show the man in. I did, and left him there. It wasn't much later, ten minutes or so, I daresay, when the dispensary door opened. The master and the rat-catcher were in there, and then the man came out, and I let him out by the front door."

"You knew the rat-catcher, of course?" Jimmy asked. "He'd been here before?"

"Oh, yes, sir, I knew him well enough," Phepson replied. "He used to come here pretty often, once a fortnight or three weeks, as a rule. He didn't make an appointment, so to speak. The master used to tell him when he'd next be wanting any rats, and that he could bring them along then. He's got a sort of haversack he brings them in."

Jimmy smiled. "Well, he was the first visitor. Mr. Forcett was the second. What was Dr. Mawsley doing when you showed him in?"

"He'd finished his tea, and was smoking a cigar and looking at a book. Just as I'd seen him scores of times when I'd come in to take away the tray. He asked Mr. Forcett to sit down in the other chair at the table. I put a bit of coal on the fire, then went out, taking the tray with me."

"Just one point," said Jimmy. "Did you notice

whether Dr. Mawsley had opened his letters by then?"

Phepson frowned in an effort of recollection. "I can't say that I did particularly, sir. But I fancy I caught sight of the envelopes lying on the desk just where he'd put them. I think he must have opened them after Mr. Forcett had gone, for they were there lying open on the desk later on."

"What became of them?" Jimmy asked.

"The Inspector looked them over, sir and then told me I'd better put them aside somewhere. So I clipped them together and slipped them into the top left-hand drawer of the desk. I was going to tell Miss Hilworth what I'd done when she came, but she hasn't, so far. There have been several other letters come by the post since then, and I've put them in the same place."

"Nothing in here was touched till the Inspector came?" Jimmy suggested.

"Nothing, sir. And when he left that evening he locked the door and took the key away with him. He came here next morning to meet Mr. Forcett, and they came in here together. It was after Mr. Forcett had gone that the Inspector told me about the letters, and that I might tidy the room up. Mrs. Mawsley had gone back to the hotel where she was staying, by then."

"Ah, yes, Mrs. Mawsley," said Jimmy. "She was here on Wednesday morning? Who told her of her husband's death?"

"I did, sir. You see, it was this way. When the Inspector came, one of the first things he asked was whether the master had any relations. I told him he had a wife and family in the country, and he said they'd have to be told. So I put a call through to Larch Hall and spoke to Mrs. Mawsley. I told her as best I could what had happened, and that the master's body was being taken off to the mortuary. Naturally, she seemed very much upset, and said she'd come up as soon as she could. It was about nine o'clock next morning when she got here, and she told me she'd driven up in the car and was staying at the Langham. I told her what I could, and then she saw Dr. Chilvers and then, when they came, the Inspector and Mr. Forcett. I think the Inspector took her to the mortuary to see the body."

"Was Mrs. Mawsley still very much upset when she came here?" Jimmy asked.

Phepson rubbed his nose thoughtfully. "Well, sir, that's hard to say. She talked to me quite quietly and without making any fuss. But then she's the sort of lady that doesn't let you know what she's feeling. It seemed to me she was more surprised than upset, if you understand me, sir. Just as if she could not make out how it could have happened."

Jimmy nodded. "I know what you mean. Is Mrs. Mawsley still staying at the Langham?"

"Oh, no, sir. She left for home after the inquest on Friday. You see, the master was taken to Larch Hall that afternoon, and buried there on Saturday. Mrs. Mawsley saw me before she left, and asked me to stay on here till she'd made arrangements about what was to be done with the suite. The master had it on a long lease, I believe."

"Did Mrs. Mawsley often come here when her husband was alive?" Jimmy asked.

"No, sir, hardly ever. She'd come up to London now and again for a few days at a time, but she'd always stop at the Langham, not here. I don't think she's been inside the suite half a dozen times all the years I've been here."

"She saw her husband every week-end," Jimmy

remarked. "Did Dr. Mawsley have many visitors here, apart from his patients?"

"After consulting hours, you mean, sir? Not very many, as a rule. It wasn't more than once or twice a week that anybody came to see him then. A doctor might come to talk about a case, but hardly anyone else, except Mr. Weedon."

"And who is Mr. Weedon?" Jimmy asked.

"The manager of the branch of the United Bank in Wimpole Street, sir. The master had known him for a long time. I think when Mr. Weedon came here it was usually on business, but he and the master were very friendly, all the same. He was the only gentleman except Mr. Forcett that I've ever known him to give cocktails to."

"I daresay Dr. Mawsley had other friends whom he met in the evening when he went out," said Jimmy. "Now, do you think I might glance at those letters that came last Tuesday afternoon?"

"Certainly, sir," Phepson replied. He opened the drawer and took from it a pile of letters which he laid on the table. On the top were a dozen or so envelopes, unopened and with postmarks showing that they had been delivered since Mawsley's death. Under these were three letters, held together by a paper clip. "Those are the ones, sir," Phepson remarked, as Jimmy came to them.

"What about the envelopes they came out of?" Jimmy asked.

"I don't know, sir. I didn't find them on the desk. I expect the master threw them into the waste paper basket after he opened them. I remember there were some envelopes in it when I emptied it."

Jimmy turned his attention to the three letters. At the foot of the first he recognized Oldland's angular signature. It dealt with the obscure complaint of Sir Matthew Gussage, and asked for an appointment. The other two, both from medical practitioners, were of very similar nature. "These were all that came by the afternoon post?" Jimmy asked.

"They were the only ones lying on the desk, sir," Phepson replied. "I can't be certain, but I think I brought four in on the tray. If I did, the fourth may have been a circular, or something like that, and the master threw it away as soon as he opened it."

"What did you empty the waste paper basket into?" Jimmy asked.

"Into a sack the porter keeps, sir. And that's collected every Monday morning."

But, Jimmy thought, if the fourth letter had been of a compromising nature, Mawsley wouldn't have dropped it into the waste paper basket. He would have thrown it onto the fire that was burning at the time. "Never mind," he said cheerfully. "Now, can I have a look into the dispensary?"

Phepson opened the inter-communicating door, in the lock of which Jimmy noticed there was no key, and they went in. This room was slightly smaller than the consulting-room, and was equipped for severely utilitarian purposes. Wide benches, occupying two sides of the room, took up most of the floor space. Besides these there were a sink with water laid on, and several steel cupboards, one of them with a key in the lock. On one of the benches stood a number of empty cages. Jimmy glanced at these with interest. "Hullo, where are the rats?" he asked.

"There were only the two the rat-catcher brought that afternoon, sir," Phepson replied. "And I drowned them in a bucket, I didn't know what else to do with them. I didn't think anyone else would want to be pestered with the things."

Jimmy smiled. "I don't suppose Dr. Mawsley's executors will want to include them in his estate. They were much better got rid of. How did you dispose of the bodies?"

"I gave them to the porter to burn in the central heating furnace, sir. That's what I've always done when the master gave me dead rats to get rid of, as he often did. Sometimes they were just dead, and sometimes they were all cut about, where the master had been looking at their insides, I suppose. He didn't keep them as pets, you understand, sir."

"Yes, I understand that," said Jimmy. "By the way, talking of Dr. Mawsley's executors, do you know who they are?"

Phepson shook his head. "I couldn't say, sir. The master never spoke to me about things like that. But Mr. Weedon could tell you if you were to ask him, I daresay."

"Perhaps I will," said Jimmy. He went round the room, examining the objects it contained and opening the cupboards in turn. He found a large quantity of surgical instruments, dispensing apparatus, hypodermic syringes, X-ray apparatus, with racks of numbered negatives, a couple of microscopes with a cabinet of slides. All the paraphernalia that might have been expected, in fact. The cupboard in which was the key was full of drugs, in bottles and jars. Each shelf bore a label in Mawsley's handwriting, one of which read "Injections."

On the shelf thus labelled were scores of phials, each inscribed with the nature of its contents, and each sealed with a rubber cap. Among these Jimmy recognized some that were known to him—aconite, curare, hyoscine, morphine, and so forth—but the majority were unfamiliar. He found that none of the phials bore the word strychnine. But on one of the other shelves, labelled "Alkaloids," was a small jar bearing the inscription "Strych. Hydrochlor," containing a quantity of crystalline powder.

"There's one of those little bottles gone, sir," Phepson remarked. "The one we found standing on the bench with the cap off. The Inspector took it away with him, and he's never brought it back."

"He wanted it for analysis," said Jimmy. "Now, who came in here besides Dr. Mawsley? Who kept it swept and dusted, for instance? The charwoman, I suppose?"

"Not she, sir," Phepson replied. "I asked her once when she first came to wash the floor over, but she wouldn't come inside, not when she'd seen the rats. So I've had to do it myself. I come in every morning and sweep round and wash out the sink and that. And in the week-ends when the master was away, I used to give the rats the food he'd left measured out for them."

"That door leading into the hall was always kept locked, wasn't it?" Jimmy asked.

"Yes, sir, that's right. I never used it, but always went through the consulting-room. The only time I've ever known it left unlocked was the other evening, when the master forgot to lock it again after the rat-catcher had gone. It was kept locked because once, a long time ago now, a lady patient waiting in the hall opened it by mistake and nearly had hysterics when she saw the rats."

"I don't wonder," said Jimmy. "Now, who else besides you and Dr. Mawsley came in here? Did Miss Hilworth?"

"I really couldn't say, sir," Phepson replied firmly. "I've never known her to use the door into the hall.

But she was in the consulting-room a good bit, and she may have come in and out of here that way. Of course, I wouldn't know."

Jimmy was inclined to wonder what the butler didn't know, or at all events suspect. But he was not yet prepared to encourage tittle-tattle. He asked Phepson to show him exactly how he had found Mawsley when he burst open the door, and the positions of the phial and the broken syringe. Then he pointed to the cupboard in which the drugs were kept. "The key is in the lock now," he said. "Do you know where Dr. Mawsley kept it?"

"I don't know that I've ever seen it anywhere else," Phepson replied. "It's always been in the lock like you see it now, whenever I've come in here. Whether it was turned or not I couldn't say, for I've never tried it. There wasn't much need to put the key away, for nobody could come in here prying about. There was always somebody in the suite when the master was out. He was very particular about that, because of the telephone."

At Jimmy's request, Phepson showed him all over the suite, taking him into every room. By the time he left, he was satisfied that there was only one means of entry, the front door which, the butler assured him, was always latched.

6

Jimmy's next call was at the United Bank in Wimpole Street. Although it was by now after banking hours, his official card gained him access to the manager's room. Mr. Weedon was a man in the middle fifties, tall, spare and genial. He welcomed Jimmy readily enough, asked him to sit down and offered him a cigarette.

The pretext which had sufficed for Phepson would not have sounded very convincing here. "I've come to you in search of information, Mr. Weedon," Jimmy said. "Scotland Yard have been asked to find out what they can about the affairs of Dr. Mawsley, who died at his suite in Harley Street a week ago."

Mr. Weedon nodded. "And anything I say may be used in evidence against me. What do you want to know, Superintendent?"

"Anything you care to tell me," Jimmy replied. "Not only about Dr. Mawsley's affairs, but about the man himself."

Mr. Weedon exhaled a cloud of smoke. "That's rather a large order. I'd better begin by saying this. When I read of Mawsley's death, and the manner of it, I was so astounded that I had the curiosity to attend the inquest. I, therefore, heard the evidence and the verdict which, incredible though it seems, was the only possible one."

"Did you, before you heard the evidence, entertain any suspicion that Dr. Mawsley might have committed suicide?" Jimmy asked.

"Never, for a moment," Mr. Weedon replied emphatically. "Look here, Superintendent. I think I can claim to have known Mawsley better than anyone, except his wife and family. I was not only his banker, but our business association had led to a personal friendship. I often used to go to Harley Street for a chat and a cocktail, and Mawsley as often dropped in to see me. I should explain that I live in a flat above the bank here. Knowing him as I did, I can imagine no reason whatever which could for a moment have caused Mawsley to contemplate taking his own life."

"Had he any interest apart from his profession?" Jimmy asked.

"He had one absorbing interest, to which his profession was the means," Mr. Weedon replied. "He had an absolute passion for money. I don't know if you'll understand me when I say he collected it for its own sake, as people collect postage stamps or Chinese jade. The point I'm trying to make is that I don't believe he had any idea of what use he meant to put it to eventually. He never, for instance, spoke of retiring one day and enjoying himself."

"His expenses must have been pretty considerable?" Jimmy suggested.

Mr. Weedon shook his head. "Not so much as you might imagine. There was the upkeep of the Harley Street suite, but for many years past the income from his investments had been more than sufficient to cover that. You're thinking of Larch

Hall, I daresay. Well, I may tell you in confidence that was not Mawsley's show. His wife is a rich woman, who inherited a pot of money from her father, who was a Yorkshire manufacturer. It was her money that bought Larch Hall, and kept it up. For that matter, she not only brought up the two children, but she subsidized Mawsley pretty generously during his early years in London, before he had found his feet.

"Apart from his professional expenses, Mawsley spent very little money, relatively speaking. He smoked very good cigars, and he was a connoisseur of wine, though he drank very moderately. You could hardly call him a miser, but he would rather see money accumulating than spent on things that didn't interest him particularly. I shouldn't like to say that he was unsociable, for he could be a very good companion when the mood was on him. But he never sought companionship. He told me that although he had been a member of his club for goodness knows how many years, he had no more than a nodding acquaintance with any of his fellow members. He only belonged to it because he found it convenient to dine there, and it had a very good cellar."

"He was hardly what you would describe as a popular figure?" Jimmy asked.

"Respected for his professional abilities, but popular, no," Mr. Weedon replied. "He was perfectly well aware that people didn't take to him very readily, but that didn't worry him in the least. I'm inclined to think that he was deliberately distant in his manner, because he didn't want to be bothered by unprofitable people. It may sound uncharitable, but I have thought that he wouldn't have been so pleasant as he was to me if I hadn't been of some use to him. Of course, with his patients, profitable people, it was quite a different matter. He made himself perfectly agreeable to them, and usually managed to do them a lot of good, if not to cure them."

"I understand that he was considered the leading specialist in his own line," said Jimmy. "Could you give me, in the strictest confidence, of course, some idea of Dr. Mawsley's financial position at the time of his death?"

"Well, seeing who you are, I don't see why I shouldn't," Mr. Weedon replied. "In general terms, he has deposited in our strong-room here securities to the value of about a hundred thousand pounds. His current account is no doubt in credit, but I cannot say offhand to what extent."

"Thank you," said Jimmy. "That's quite near enough for me. You have the advantage of me, in that you heard the evidence given at the inquest. I gather, however, that Mr. Forcett got the impression that Dr. Mawsley was delighted to such an extent that one might say excited, at the news of his legacy. Isn't that rather surprising in the case of a man who already possessed so much capital?"

Mr. Weedon shook his head. "I don't seem to have made Mawsley's devotion to money clear to you. I haven't the slightest doubt that he was excited, wildly excited. Forcett's evidence was probably an understatement. The excitement not so much of a man given extra money to spend, but of a collector who unexpectedly acquires a valuable piece for nothing. I don't mind betting that, but for that extraordinary accident, he'd have come round here as soon as he'd had dinner, to tell me all about it. And he'd have spent hours discussing the best use to which the money could be put."

"Have you formed any idea of how he came to make the mistake he did?" Jimmy asked.

"Only a very vague one," Mr. Weedon replied. "To begin with, Mawsley was always very careful about his own health. Not that he believed he had anything the matter with him, but, as he told me more than once, he believed in taking precautionary measures. For instance, he always carried a box of tablets, and used to drop one in almost everything he drank. I've had a gin and lime with him at his place, and I always gave him a whisky and soda when he came to see me in the evening, and he always put one of the tablets in his glass. I believe the idea was to stimulate the digestive juices.

"That's only by the way. Now, I'll tell you what's in my mind. Mawsley mentioned to me, not so long ago, that he found it beneficial to give himself an injection of some drug or other, now and then. When he'd had a hard day with a lot of difficult cases, for instance. It bucked him up, I suppose. He told me the name of the drug, but I didn't take any particular notice. It may have been strychnine. You see what I'm thinking?"

"That he inadvertently gave himself an overdose," said Jimmy. "It does seem the only possible explanation. But to return for a moment to the financial question. Can you tell me who inherits Dr. Mawsley's money?"

Mr. Weedon shrugged his shoulders. "I was his banker, not his solicitor. I did once, very tentatively, ask him if he had made a will, but he sheered off the subject. I don't think he cared to contemplate a universe from which the famous Dr. Mawsley had departed. Which is one of the reasons for my conviction that he would never have committed suicide. What will become of his money I have no idea. I can't imagine anyone apart from his wife and family to whom he could have left it. And somehow I don't fancy that charities will benefit."

"Dr. Mawsley was on affectionate terms with his wife and children?" Jimmy suggested.

"I am hardly in a position to know," Mr. Weedon replied. "I said a moment ago that I knew Mawsley as well as any of his acquaintances. That being so, it may astonish you to know that the first time I saw Mrs. Mawsley was at the inquest. The children I have never seen. Mawsley never produced his family for my inspection, and only rarely mentioned them in conversation."

"Did you get the impression that there was any estrangement?" Jimmy asked.

"Well, I don't know," Mr. Weedon replied. "Mawsley spent practically every week-end with his family, at Larch Hall. How they all got on together there I haven't the remotest idea. I don't think it ever entered his head to invite me down there. It always seemed to me that he kept his two lives in entirely separate compartments. In one, his Harley Street existence, with his professional activities, his financial interests, and his club. In the other, his family associations at Larch Hall, whatever they may have amounted to."

Jimmy nodded. "And when did you last see Dr. Mawsley?" he asked.

"One day the week before last," Mr. Weedon replied. "Let me see; Thursday it must have been. I should explain that the first things he looked at in his paper every morning were the current market prices of the various securities he held. He came round to see me that evening after dinner, his usual time. Peebles Corporation three and a half per cents had fallen half a point, and he was rather fretting about it. He gave me instructions that if they fell any further I was to sell his holding, but as it turned out they began to rise again next day, so all was well.

"Because I say he was fretting, don't run away with the idea that the incident had thrown him into a state of depression that might have led to suicide. Far from it. He sat with me for an hour or two, and had a whisky. Apart from the regrettable weakness of the Peebles stock, he had nothing whatever on his mind, and was perfectly cheerful. More so than usual, in fact. He told me, as a great secret, that he had had a tip from official quarters that his name would appear in the next Birthday Honours list. He was looking forward to that eagerly, because he believed that it would bring him more patients. No, Superintendent, I can only repeat what I said before. Nothing will ever convince me that Mawsley committed suicide."

Jimmy left the bank, and knowing this was a suitable time to find Oldland at home, made his way to his luxurious establishment in Kensington. As Jimmy was shown into the lounge, Oldland put aside the evening paper he was reading. "Hullo, Jimmy!" he exclaimed. "Come in and make yourself comfortable. It isn't often that you find time to pay me a visit, and I'm delighted to see you."

"I only looked in for a minute," Jimmy replied. "Didn't you say the other evening that you knew the father of Miss Hilworth, who used to be Dr. Mawsley's receptionist?"

Oldland looked at him speculatively. "Eh, what's this? Do I gather that the Yard has taken up that business?"

"Well, yes and no," Jimmy replied. "We haven't started an official investigation. But the Professor has suggested that it might be worth our while to look into things quietly."

Oldland laughed heartily. "I thought I'd given Priestley something to sharpen his teeth on, but I didn't know he'd take it as seriously as all that. Well, I'm very glad you're taking a hand, for you may be able to get to the bottom of the mystery. I can't help feeling that there's rather more to it than came out at the inquest. But why this reference to me? I don't know the girl at all, and her father only slightly."

"Miss Hilworth left Dr. Mawsley's suite about four o'clock last Tuesday," Jimmy replied simply. "She hasn't shown up since."

"Hasn't she?" said Oldland. "Well, you can't expect me to tell you why she hasn't, for I know nothing whatever about her. I meet Hilworth from time to time, not professionally, but because we happen to have mutual friends. He has a small, and I should imagine not very lucrative, practice in Hammersmith. He told me, a couple of years ago or so, that his eldest daughter had got a job in Harley Street with Mawsley, and that's all I know."

"Miss Hilworth lives at home, one may suppose," said Jimmy. "Can you tell me Dr. Hilworth's address?"

"Not offhand," Oldland replied. "You'll find the telephone directory over there, and you can look it up."

Jimmy consulted the directory and found the entry "Hilworth, V. N., Physn. & Srgn., 7 Briston Road," with a Hammersmith number. "That's the chap," Oldland remarked, as Jimmy read this out. "Going to call?"

"Yes, I think so," Jimmy replied. "I'm collecting information about Dr. Mawsley and his habits, and

Miss Hilworth may be able to contribute a few items. Tell me more about her father."

"I can't tell you much," said Oldland. "He's somewhere about fifty, I should think, pleasant enough, but with a rather care-worn expression. He's a widower with children, and I don't suppose his practice brings in a lot. I daresay he finds it none too easy to make ends meet, and that's why his daughter had to go out to work. I like him personally, but of his professional ability I can offer no opinion. And that's all."

Jimmy declined Oldland's invitation to stay for dinner, and went on to Hammersmith. Briston Road was a turning off King Street, and on the door of Number 7 was a brass plate, bearing Dr. Hilworth's name. He rang the bell, and the door was opened by a tall dark girl in a black frock. She was obviously not a parlour-maid, and Jimmy thought she might well be the Miss Hilworth who had been employed by Dr. Mawsley. He introduced himself, and asked if he might speak to Dr. Hilworth.

The girl showed no surprise at the visitor's designation. She led him along a narrow passage, lit only by a feeble lamp, to a poky little surgery. Left there, with the promise that Dr. Hilworth would join him shortly, Jimmy looked about him. The room was clean and tidy, but everything in it showed evidence of extreme economy. And when, after a short interval, Dr. Hilworth came in, Jimmy appreciated the accuracy of Oldland's description. He had a pronounced stoop, and his face, though friendly enough, was lined and drawn. The suit he was wearing was well cut but shiny with wear. "Good evening, Superintendent," he said. "What brings you here?"

"A thirst for knowledge, Doctor," Jimmy replied.

"I am making inquiries about Dr. Mawsley of Harley Street, who died very suddenly last week. Your daughter worked for him, didn't she?"

At the mention of Mawsley's name Hilworth frowned. "I can't tell you anything about Mawsley's death," he said curtly. "Though you are quite right about my daughter Violet working for him, she left her job, a week ago today."

"Dr. Mawsley died that evening," Jimmy remarked. "I didn't expect you to be able to tell me anything about his death, Doctor. I daresay you read a report of the inquest, which resulted in a verdict of accidental death. I'm trying to find out how such a strange accident could have happened. Perhaps, if I were to talk to Miss Hilworth, she might give me some ideas on the subject?"

But Hilworth hardly rose to this suggestion. "I don't see how Violet can tell you any more than I can," he replied. "She had left the suite for the last time some hours before Mawsley died."

That was just it, Jimmy thought. Why had she left her job on that particular day? It was unlikely that he would get a satisfactory reply to a direct question. The matter would have to be approached by a roundabout route. "Yes, of course," he said smoothly. "But Miss Hilworth must be familiar with Dr. Mawsley's habits. She had been with him for some considerable time, hadn't she?"

"Familiar with his habits!" Hilworth growled. "That's true enough. It was because she was getting too familiar with Mawsley's habits that she left him. He was an unpleasant sort of beast, let me tell you."

"You knew him well?" Jimmy asked swiftly.

"I never set eyes on him," Hilworth replied. "Harley Street specialists and panel doctors in unfashionable districts move in very different circles,

I assure you. Their orbits do not intersect. If I had known the sort of chap Mawsley was, I should never have let Violet go to him. But I didn't, then."

He paused, frowning at the table in front of him, then continued abruptly. "I'll tell you how it happened, if it's of any interest to you. Violet always had an ambition to become a qualified dispenser, and for that reason took the pharmacy course and passed her examinations. A couple of years or more ago, Mawsley advertised for a receptionist secretary, who must be a qualified dispenser and a capable typist. Violet, who was both, answered the advertisement. Mawsley sent for her, interviewed her, and took her on then and there.

"She liked the job at first, and she liked her employer. She used to come home and tell me of his kindness to her, and what a great man he was. Between ourselves, Superintendent, I fancy Mawsley must have been one of those strong silent men who exert an uncanny fascination over women. The snake and the rabbit, you know. Until the women find them out, that is. I've always heard that Mawsley was a tremendous success with his lady patients.

"Well, I was very glad that Violet had found a congenial job. When she had been with Mawsley about a year, a fellow came to see me in this consulting-room. I knew him well enough, though I had never attended him before. He had a small tobacco and sweet business in one of the back streets round here, and had done an immense amount of unselfish work among his poorer neighbours. A thoroughly fine character, in fact.

"He complained of certain rather puzzling symptoms, and after watching him for a bit I came to the conclusion that something very unusual must be wrong with one of his ductless glands. It struck me at once that was where Violet's great kind man came in. Glandular trouble was what he specialized in, and surely he would be only too eager to do his best for such an eminently deserving case. I wrote to Mawsley at considerable length, outlining the case, and going on to say something of my patient's circumstances and activities, explaining that he couldn't possibly afford to pay any whacking great fee.

"Mawsley didn't trouble to answer my letter. He gave Violet a verbal message, to repeat to me when she got home. He regretted that he was far too busy to be able to spare any of his time on relatively unimportant patients. I was thoroughly snubbed for my temerity in suggesting that the great Dr. Mawsley should demean himself by any consideration of the case of an impecunious shopkeeper. I got the poor fellow admitted to a hospital, where he died soon afterwards. I gather, by the way, that Mawsley didn't waste much of his valuable time in the wards of voluntary hospitals. Mind you, I don't say that he could have cured my man. But the incident gave me my first inkling of the real Mawsley behind the gracious and dignified façade.

"I didn't say much to Violet, for I didn't want to disturb her faith in her idol, and she didn't say much to me, whatever she may have thought. I noticed that from then on I didn't hear so much about how wonderful Mawsley was. And gradually it began to seem that she wasn't so happy in her job as she had been at first. I asked her if anything was the matter, and she told me it was nothing. Quite obviously, she didn't want to talk to me about it."

Again Hilworth paused, and fidgeted uneasily. "There's bound to be a certain restraint between father and daughter on some subjects," he went on. "If her mother had been alive, it would all have come out long ago, I don't doubt. As it was, it wasn't till last Monday that I knew. She came home that evening quite hysterical, and she poured it all out incoherently, hardly knowing what she was saying.

"As a man of the world, Superintendent, you can guess what the trouble was, and I needn't go into details. To use a favourite expression of my young women patients, Mawsley had been getting fresh. Asking Violet to stay after consulting hours, and go out to dinner with him. She's a sensible girl, and could see very well what all this was leading up to. On the other hand, she didn't want to lose her job. Mawsley paid her well and that's a consideration in this family. She managed to stave him off, as long as she could.

"But it seems that on Monday, when he came back from the country, his patience was at an end. He told Violet that he was tired of being treated by his wife and family as an unwanted stranger. He suggested that the following week-end they should go away together and have a good time, giving her to understand that a substantial fee would be forthcoming for services rendered. It was typical of the man to assume that money could buy him anything he wanted. She was to fix things up at home, and let him know about it in a day or two's time.

"Well, you can imagine my feelings when Violet told me all this. My first instinct was to go straight to Harley Street and tell Mawsley a few pointed truths, but I thought better of it. It was no use making any sort of fuss. Mawsley might blandly deny the whole thing, and say that Violet had invented the story as a means of blackmail. I told Violet she had better go to work the next day and behave as though nothing had happened. Then I sat down and wrote Mawsley a real stinker, telling him just what I thought of him. I pointed out that if I cared to report his conduct to the General Medical Council, that would be the end of his professional career. And I didn't forget to express in the plainest possible terms my opinion of the message he had sent me about my patient. I finished up by saying that he wouldn't see Violet again. And now you know why she left her job."

7

Jimmy felt that he was on very treacherous ground indeed. Hilworth's outburst of confidence had seemed quite spontaneous. But, after all, he and his daughter had had a whole week in which to concoct a plausible story. Jimmy nodded sympathetically. "It was the only course Miss Hilworth could have taken, under the circumstances," he said. "Did you post your letter to Dr. Mawsley?"

"At Violet's suggestion, I gave it to her to post as she went to work next morning," Hilworth replied. "Mawsley would then get it in the evening, after she had left. She didn't want to risk a scene, naturally, and she had no intention of ever entering the suite again. I hope Mawsley read the letter before he died, that's all."

"May I see Miss Hilworth?" Jimmy asked. "I shall, of course, make no reference whatever to what you have been good enough to tell me. I merely want to ask her one or two quite impersonal questions."

"I don't see why you shouldn't talk to her," Hilworth replied. He opened the door and called out, "Violet! Come here a minute, will you?"

A voice answered him, and the girl who had admitted Jimmy appeared. His closer scrutiny revealed her as decidedly good-looking, with a capable

81

and rather calculating expression. The sort of girl, Jimmy thought, who was quite able to take care of herself. "The Superintendent wants to talk to you about your late employer," said Hilworth.

"Dr. Mawsley?" she replied, perfectly equably. "What do you want to know about him, Mr. Waghorn?"

"How he came to make the fatal mistake that cost him his life, Miss Hilworth," Jimmy said. "You can't tell me that, of course, for you weren't there at the time. You know what happened, I suppose?"

"Father and I read the report of the inquest in the paper," Violet replied. "We didn't know of Dr. Mawsley's death till then."

"You saw him last about four o'clock that afternoon, I believe," said Jimmy. "Did you notice anything unusual in his manner? Or did he, on Tuesday, seem to you very much as you had always known him?"

Violet shook her head. "I can't say I noticed any difference. But then I didn't see very much of Dr. Mawsley that day, not to speak to him alone, I mean. He was very busy with a full list of appointments, and patients were coming and going all the time I was there. After the last one had gone I took in the letters to sign, and he was quite normal then."

"You tell me that you read a report of the inquest, Miss Hilworth," said Jimmy. "You know what the verdict was. In your opinion, was Dr. Mawsley the sort of man who was likely to make such a disastrous mistake?"

Violet looked towards her father, and the pair exchanged a rapid glance. "It does seem most extraordinary," she replied. "I never knew him to make a mistake while I was with him. Not that sort of mistake, anyhow."

"Has it occurred to you that it mightn't have been a mistake, after all?" Jimmy said, very quietly.

There was a tense pause, before Violet burst out passionately, "Yes, it has! He couldn't have given himself a fatal injection by accident. And why should he have wanted to take strychnine, of all things, unless he meant to kill himself?"

"You say strychnine, of all things, Miss Hilworth," said Jimmy. "Was Dr. Mawsley in the habit of taking injections of other drugs?"

"I don't know that you could call it a habit," she replied, more calmly. "He wasn't a drug addict, if that's what you mean. He used regularly to take tablets, which he dissolved in anything he drank, as a preventative of indigestion. They were perfectly harmless, and consisted mainly of papain. And he told me that sometimes, when he felt tired after a particularly strenuous day, he gave himself an injection which he called M and C, for short."

"Do you know what this M and C was made up of?" Jimmy asked.

"Why, yes, of course," she replied. "It was a mixture of mescaline and corynanthine. Dr. Mawsley told me that he found it a wonderful pick-me-up, far better than alcohol in any form."

"You said that last Tuesday had been a busy day," said Jimmy. "The sort of day perhaps after which Dr. Mawsley might have felt in need of his favourite stimulant. Let me ask you this question, Miss Hilworth. Do you think it possible that he took out the wrong bottle by mistake? That he gave himself an injection of strychnine, believing it to be M and C?"

Violet shook her head firmly. "Doctors with his experience don't take out the wrong bottle. They were all clearly marked with labels which he wrote himself. And he was using them every day. He used to keep rats, in which he induced certain disorders, and then gave them different injections, to observe the effects. I simply can't imagine him picking out the strychnine injection when he meant to use the M and C."

"You were familiar with the contents of the drug cupboard?" Jimmy asked. "Your duties took you into the dispensary?"

"Why, yes," she replied. "I didn't care much for the rats at first, but I soon got used to them. I used to measure out the diet that Dr. Mawsley ordered for each of them. And I made up the various injections as required."

"Then you probably made up the strychnine that Dr. Mawsley took?" Jimmy suggested.

"I did," she replied. "And I remember doing it. I found the phial of strychnine injection very nearly empty, not long ago, and made up a fresh supply from the jar of strychnine hydrochloride."

"Do you remember what strength you made the solution?" Jimmy asked.

"Of course," she replied. "Dr. Mawsley had given me a list of the proportions I was to use in dispensing the various injections. In the case of strychnine the proportion he ordered was eight grains to the fluid ounce."

"Did you make up the injection which Dr. Mawsley called M and C?"

"No, that was the only one I didn't dispense," she replied. "He said that was his own secret, more as a joke than anything, I think. He made it up himself, and I don't know what proportions he used."

"I have been told that the door between the dispensary and the hall was always kept locked," said Jimmy. "Was that the case?"

She nodded. "That's perfectly right. Whenever I had to go into the dispensary, I always went through the consulting-room."

"Did anyone besides you and Dr. Mawsley ever go into the dispensary?"

"Not when I was about," Violet replied. "I believe that Phepson used to sweep it out before I got there. I don't suppose anyone else ever went in. There was no reason why they should."

"Dr. Mawsley was perfectly satisfied with Phepson?" Jimmy suggested. "He found no fault with him?"

"Not that I know of," she replied. "He'd have sacked him soon enough if he had. Phepson always struck me as the typical butler. Respectful enough, but inclined to pry into things that weren't his business."

This seemed to confirm Jimmy's idea that there had been no love lost between Phepson and Miss Hilworth. "Old retainers are apt to be inquisitive," he said. "Can you give me an instance of his prying?"

"No, I can't," she replied shortly. "It was only my impression, nothing more."

Jimmy thanked Violet and her father for the information they had given him, and left the house. While he remembered the names of the unfamiliar drugs Violet Hilworth had mentioned, he went back to see Oldland once more. Oldland had finished his dinner, and was sitting beside the fire in the lounge with a glass of whisky beside him. "Hullo, Jimmy!" he exclaimed in some surprise as his visitor was shown in. "Back again? Had anything to eat?"

"Well, no, I haven't," Jimmy agreed. "But it doesn't matter. I only dropped in to ask you a few medical questions."

"It does matter," said Oldland firmly. "The brain

won't function properly unless sustained by regular meals. There's an excellent York ham in the house, and I'll have some sandwiches cut off it for you. You can eat them with a bottle of beer while you talk." He rang the bell and gave the necessary order. "Well," he continued, "you've seen Hilworth?"

"Yes, and his daughter," Jimmy replied. "And I'm blest if I know what to make of them. But I'll tell you this. The more I hear of your friend Dr. Mawsley, the less I'm inclined to regard his death as a disaster to the community."

"He was no friend of mine," said Oldland. "And however much of a rotter he may have been, his death will be a disaster for some people. My close-fisted patient, old Matt Gussage, for example. I doubt there's anyone else who'd be able to fathom his trouble. In which case Matt isn't very long for this world, I'm afraid. Oh, well, his heirs won't pine away with grief, I daresay."

The parlour-maid came in with a tray, which she set beside Jimmy. "There you are," said Oldland. "Now that you're supplied with the essential nourishment, fire away with your inquisition."

"I want to hear what you can tell me about certain drugs I've never heard of till this evening," Jimmy replied. "To begin with, what is papain, and what do you use it for?"

"Papain is an extract obtained from a tropical plant," Oldland replied. "It is used to promote digestion. So far as I know it is perfectly harmless. I've prescribed it myself, and have never known ill-effects to result."

"Good," Jimmy said. "That confirms what I've been told. Next, what is mescaline?"

"This sounds like a new Child's Guide," Oldland replied. "Or are you putting me through an oral examination in materia medica? You won't have heard of mescaline. It is very little known, and has not yet come under the Dangerous Drugs Act. It has properties not unlike hashish, or Indian hemp."

"I've heard of hashish," said Jimmy. "We run across cases of smuggling the stuff now and then. What effect would an injection of this stuff mescaline have?"

"In small doses, quite a pleasant one," Oldland replied. "Mild excitement and a sensation of happiness. When these symptoms passed, they would be followed by a carefree drowsiness. Large doses would produce a nasty hangover of depression. But I believe mescaline is rarely or never fatal."

"Good again," said Jimmy. "The last on my list is corynanthine."

"Eh!" Oldland exclaimed. "I wasn't expecting that one. Corynanthine is a stimulant, possessing peculiar and rather unusual properties."

"Is a mixture of mescaline and corynanthine normally used as an injection?" Jimmy asked.

"I have never prescribed such a mixture," Oldland replied. "An injection of it would almost certainly have curiously stimulating effects. Any more questions? My curiosity is thoroughly aroused."

"Mawsley occasionally used an injection of those two drugs," said Jimmy. "I'm told that he called it M and C, and described the composition as his secret. I saw a bottle labelled 'Inj. M and C' among the injections in his dispensary. Well, if I have aroused your curiosity, listen, and I'll tell you rather a queer story."

He proceeded to repeat what Hilworth and Violet had told him. "Whether or not their statements were the exact truth, I can't say," he went on. "I think that in the main they may be trusted. Now,

I'll tell you something else. I went to Mawsley's suite this afternoon and interviewed Phepson, who is in charge there. He told me, among other things, that to the best of his recollection four letters came for Mawsley by the afternoon post. Only three were found after his death. There was a fire burning in the consulting-room grate that afternoon.

"Now, if Phepson's memory can be trusted, the missing fourth letter can only have been Hilworth's. And I'm inclined to wonder whether this is what can have happened. After Forcett had left him, Mawsley opened his letters, one of which, by the way, was yours. Three of them were quite innocuous, but the fourth, if it was Hilworth's, was what he himself described as a real stinker.

"We don't know what Hilworth actually wrote, or how far he carried his threats. I think it quite possible that he told Mawsley he meant to show him up, and you know better than I do what an effect such an exposure would have on a specialist's practice. You remember the Professor's suggestion, that Mawsley might suddenly have found himself faced with professional ruin, and I'm inclined to believe that his guess was right. What was Mawsley's reaction? He jumped up and threw the letter into the fire, for that must not be found after his death. Then he went into the dispensary, and gave himself a thumping injection of strychnine. He knew that it would be painful. But he also knew that it would soon be over."

"Well, I don't know," Oldland replied doubtfully. "It's a possibility, certainly. But somehow it hardly seems to fit in with Mawsley's character for him to throw up the sponge like that, without making a fight for it. After all, as you say Hilworth himself remarked, it was only the girl's word against his.

He might have turned the tables by accusing Hilworth and his daughter of conspiring to blackmail him."

"That's true," Jimmy agreed. "You don't think it can have been a put-up job on the part of the Hilworths?"

"That the girl invented the story of attempted seduction?" Oldland replied. "I don't know. But I will say this. From the comparatively little I know of Hilworth, I should hesitate to accuse him of deliberate blackmail. No doubt he believed what his daughter told him, and was naturally furious. And there's another thing which tends to support his story. Mawsley's use of corynanthine suggests very strongly that he was of amorous tendencies. I should imagine that the evenings after he had given himself an injection of his secret M and C were not devoted to entirely innocent diversions.

"But there you are. Mawsley is dead, and this Hilworth girl is the only one who knows the truth of any intimacy there may have been between them."

"I have an idea, from Phepson's manner, that he had his suspicions," Jimmy remarked.

"What the butler thought is not evidence," Oldland replied. "Who did Mawsley leave his money to?"

"I haven't found out yet," said Jimmy. "His banker professes to know nothing of his will. In the course of his evidence Forcett mentioned that Mawsley had told him that he had certain documents in a safe at Larch Hall. It strikes me that safe is the most likely place to look for the will, if it hasn't been found already."

Oldland nodded. "You're probably right. You'll make it your business to see the will, I don't doubt. What if you find it in a clause running something like this? 'To my faithful and conscientious secretary, Miss Violet Hilworth, I bequeath the sum of five thousand pounds.' Eh?"

"My belief in Miss Hilworth's veracity would suffer a shock," Jimmy replied. "What exactly are you driving at?"

Oldland sipped his whisky thoughtfully. "I like Hilworth, and for that reason I don't care to cast aspersions on his daughter's character. But you've got to face the fact that she may have been a trifle more complacent than she led her father to believe. She may have persuaded Mawsley to leave her something, though until you've seen the will, that's a matter of pure conjecture.

"Now, as to what happened last Tuesday evening. There I'm with you, up to a point. Mawsley read Hilworth's letter, and chucked it in the fire. But with a gesture of contempt rather than of despair. Let the fellow do his worst, he was quite capable of bluffing his way out of the situation. Nuisance losing that girl, though. Oh, well, let's go out and have a good time and forget about it. So Mawsley went into the dispensary and gave himself an injection of strychnine."

"As a preliminary to having a good time?" Jimmy suggested. "Not on this earth, surely?"

"Ah, wait a minute!" Oldland replied. "Strychnine, administered in small quantities, produces effects not dissimilar to those caused by corynanthine. Mawsley may have intended to take just enough for his purpose, as a variant from his favourite M and C."

"Which merely brings us back to the original problem," said Jimmy. "How did he come to make such a glaring mistake?"

"Who dispensed the injection he took from the

phial?" Oldland demanded. "The Hilworth girl, you tell me. How can you be sure that Mawsley ordered her to make it up eight grains to the ounce? What if his instructions really were that the proportion was to be one-fiftieth of a grain to the ounce? What then, I say?"

Jimmy looked a trifle incredulous. "You won't mind if I say it doesn't sound altogether convincing?"

Oldland laughed heartily. "Of course it doesn't!" he exclaimed. "But let me tell you this, Jimmy. If you can find some explanation of Mawsley's death which does sound altogether convincing, I shall be the first to congratulate you."

8

Next morning, Jimmy called on Messrs. Perring and Company in Broad Street. The offices were extensive, and it was evident from the number of people about that the firm was in a pretty big way of business. Jimmy presented his card, and asked if he might see Mr. Forcett.

With only a moment's delay, he was shown into Forcett's room. He was a young man of thirty or thereabouts, with a keen, intelligent face, and a businesslike manner. "Come in, Superintendent," he said, rising from his chair as Jimmy entered. "Sit down and tell me what I can do for you."

"I'm going to ask you to spare me a few minutes of your time, Mr. Forcett," Jimmy replied. "I am engaged in making certain inquiries regarding the late Dr. Mawsley."

Forcett nodded comprehendingly. "I thought that matter wouldn't be allowed to rest," he said. "It's the most extraordinary affair I ever came across. I'll willingly tell you anything I can, but I'm afraid I shan't be able to add very much to what I said at the inquest. What is it exactly that you want to know?"

"I should like, first of all, to hear your personal impressions," Jimmy replied. "Rather less formally than you felt yourself able to convey them in evidence. You only met Dr. Mawsley on that one occasion, of course. What did you make of him?"

"I'm bound to say he puzzled me rather," Forcett replied. "I'd better tell you how my impressions developed. You know the facts, of course, so I needn't repeat them. And you'll understand that I had to go rather cautiously. I wanted to ascertain that Dr. Mawsley was in fact the Dr. Knapp mentioned in Mrs. Somerthwaite's will before I said anything to him about the legacy.

"My first approach to him was on the telephone, asking for an appointment. He was rather sticky at first, perhaps imagining that I wanted to serve him with a writ, or something like that. I made it as clear to him as I could that my business was not of an unpleasant nature, and might possibly turn out to his advantage. He agreed to see me, not very enthusiastically, and said I might come along in an hour's time.

"I kept the appointment, as you know, and was welcomed rather coldly. Dr. Mawsley told me to sit down and tell him what I wanted in as few words as possible. His manner was very much that of the important personage who has no time to waste on trifles. And the atmosphere didn't get any more genial when I began to talk about Bradworth and a Dr. Knapp who had once been in practice there. That subject didn't seem to appeal to him.

"However, he began to brighten up when I mentioned Mrs. Somerthwaite, or rather Mrs. Gunton, as she was then. He remembered her case as having been one of his earliest successes, but had entirely lost sight of her. This seemed good enough, so I told him of the legacy, and showed him a copy of the codicil I had brought with me.

"I never in my life saw such a rapid change in anyone's manner. You might have thought he was a criminal lying under sentence of death, and that I had brought him news of a free pardon. From that moment, nothing could be too good for me. He offered me a cigar, which I didn't accept as I very rarely smoke, and sent for cocktails. His delight at the legacy was so childlike that I was amazed. His attitude when I first came in had given me the impression that five thousand pounds would be a mere flea-bite to him. But not so. He became so voluble about it that I had quite a job to tear myself away."

"I have been told that Dr. Mawsley had a collector's passion for money," said Jimmy. "May I ask what he talked to you about while you were enjoying his hospitality?"

"The legacy mainly, and what the duties would amount to," Forcett replied. "I promised to tell him that exactly when I saw him next morning. For the rest, he talked entirely of himself, and of how since those early days he had climbed to the very top rung of the profession's ladder. He seemed immensely pleased with his own achievements."

"Did he make any mention of his private life?" Jimmy asked. "Was there any reference to his wife and family?"

"Only by implication, when he told me that his home was in the country. A place called Larch Hall in Dorsetshire, where he had documents proving his identity with the former Dr. Knapp of Bradworth."

"I suppose there can be no doubt about that identity?" Jimmy asked.

Forcett shook his head. "Not the slightest. I had made inquiries personally in Bradworth, as a result of which I had practically no doubt when I asked Dr. Mawsley for an appointment. His recollection of Mrs. Somerthwaite as his patient seemed to settle the matter. Since then I have received positive proof.

"I'll tell you how that came about. After the inquest Mrs. Mawsley approached me and asked me what would happen about the legacy now that her husband was dead. I explained that first of all it would be necessary to establish the late Dr. Mawsley's identity with the person mentioned in the codicil. To that end I said that Dr. Mawsley had told me that in his safe at Larch Hall he had a copy of the deed-poll by which he had changed his name. If Mrs. Somerthwaite's executors might be allowed to see this they would no doubt be satisfied, and would hand over the money to Dr. Mawsley's executors for allocation in accordance with the terms of his will.

"Mrs. Mawsley said that there could be no question of identity. When she became engaged to her husband he was in practice in Bradworth under the name of Dr. Knapp. However, she promised to look in the safe for the document and send it to me. She did so, and I received it yesterday morning. In her covering letter she omitted to give the names of the executors of her husband's will. I have written to her, asking for that information."

"You think that the news of this legacy came as a complete surprise to Dr. Mawsley?" Jimmy asked.

"I'm quite sure it did," Forcett replied. "He and his former patient had entirely lost touch with one another. As the wording of her codicil shows, she did not know he had changed his name, and he was equally unaware that she had changed hers. And I assure you, Superintendent, that the change in his manner showed clearly enough that my news

95

was not only a surprise to him, but a very welcome one."

"Dr. Mawsley's manner is a matter of considerable importance," said Jimmy. "The evidence shows that you were the last person to hold any conversation with him before his death. For that reason anything you can tell me, however trifling, which might throw any light upon his state of mind, would be welcomed."

"I quite understand that," Forcett replied. "You are, quite rightly, trying to eliminate any possibility that Dr. Mawsley committed suicide. During the initial steps of our interview, before he had any inkling of the purpose of my visit, Dr. Mawsley's manner was not that of a man who had anything on his mind, except perhaps a rather exaggerated idea of his own importance. At the end of our interview, his manner was that of a child who has just found his Christmas stocking full of new toys.

"At the time I left him, his demeanour was as much unlike that of a man who contemplated taking his own life within the next half hour as could possibly be imagined. His last words to me were that he would be delighted to see me next morning as near ten o'clock as possible. And would I be so good as to tell his butler as he let me out that on no account was he to be disturbed until he went out himself. I know, from what I saw next morning, that after I'd gone his thoughts were occupied with the legacy."

"Thank you, Mr. Forcett," said Jimmy. "Nothing could be clearer than that. Now, I want you to try to remember a detail. While you were with Dr. Mawsley on Tuesday evening, did you see any letters in the consulting-room, opened or unopened?"

"Let me think," Forcett replied. "There was certainly no correspondence of any kind on the table at which we sat. But I believe that on the desk behind the chair in which Dr. Mawsley sat there were some envelopes. I'm not sure enough about that to make a statement on oath. Whether they had been opened or not I cannot say. I don't remember seeing them there when I went back next day."

"You spoke of cocktails," Jimmy said. "Can you tell me how many Dr. Mawsley had?"

Forcett smiled. "I do not think you need entertain the idea that his mistake was due to the influence of alcohol. He had one cocktail, a not very strong gin and lime, into which he dropped a tablet taken from a box he carried in his pocket. He remarked that it was a preventative against dyspepsia, to which he was occasionally liable. When he had drunk the first, he poured himself a second, which he had not finished by the time I left. It did not seem to me that this very small amount of spirit had any effect upon him."

Jimmy nodded. "Now, next morning," he said. "You called at Dr. Mawsley's suite at ten o'clock, as you had promised you would. Will you tell me what you found when you got there?"

"The first thing I found was an Inspector of Police, who greeted me with the amazing news that Dr. Mawsley was dead," Forcett replied. "He took me into the consulting-room, where he assured me nothing had been touched, and asked me to point out any changes in it since I was last there.

"The most obvious thing was that the chair in which Dr. Mawsley had been sitting during our interview was lying on its back on the floor. Apart from that, the differences in the appearance of the room were only minor. The tray with the bottles and the glass I had used had been moved from the table at which we had sat to one at the side of the room. Dr. Mawsley had finished his second cocktail after I left, for his glass was empty. A few minutes before I went out, he had lighted a second cigar, having finished the one he was smoking when I came in. He must have gone on smoking this, for the half-burnt cigar lying on the ashtray on Wednesday morning was very much shorter than when I last saw it in his mouth.

"Lying on the table were two documents which I had left, a copy of the codicil of Mrs. Somerthwaite's will, and a document I had had typed for Dr. Mawsley's signature. This declaration had not been signed when I left on Tuesday evening, but on Wednesday morning I found it signed, R. E. K. Mawsley, and dated January 15th, which was Tuesday, of course. In addition to these documents was a sheet of paper, which had not been on the table at the conclusion of our interview. On it were certain pencilled words and figures which, I was told, were in Dr. Mawsley's handwriting. These showed that he had been calculating the sum that would remain after the payment of duty, and the income it might be expected to yield on investment. Beside this sheet was a silver pencil, identified as the one that Dr. Mawsley always carried in his pocket."

"You were able to form a pretty good idea of how Dr. Mawsley had spent at least part of his time after your departure on Tuesday evening?" Jimmy suggested.

"A very good idea," Forcett replied. "He must have sat, finishing his cocktail and smoking his cigar, while he worked out the additional income the legacy would bring him. I've explained to you, as carefully as I can, Superintendent, the mood he was in when I parted from him. I have, of course, no knowledge of him beyond that I derived at our interview, but I cannot believe that this mood was assumed for my benefit, or to conceal any sort of despondency. If I may say so, common sense revolts at any suggestion that he deliberately committed suicide within a few minutes after I left him."

"We don't know what may have happened during those few minutes," said Jimmy. "You told me that, during your interview, Dr. Mawsley only barely mentioned his wife and family. Did he speak of his secretary, Miss Hilworth?"

Forcett shook his head. "Not a word. The first I heard of a secretary was when the butler mentioned her at the inquest."

"Did you notice what sort of a fire was burning in the consulting-room on Tuesday evening?" Jimmy asked.

"Why, yes," Forcett replied. "It was a pretty good one when I left. The butler made it up and put some more coal on when he showed me in. On Wednesday morning it had gone out and had not been relaid."

"Neither you nor Dr. Mawsley went into the dispensary during your visit on Tuesday?" Jimmy asked.

"We neither of us left the consulting-room the whole time," Forcett replied. "I saw there was a second door there, but I had no idea where it led to. It was not until next morning that the Inspector took me into the dispensary."

"Well, I won't occupy your time any longer, Mr. Forcett," said Jimmy. "I'm very grateful for the opportunity to talk things over with you. You have formed no private ideas of your own upon the subject?"

"One can't help guessing about how Dr. Mawsley made such a tragic mistake," Forcett replied. "But it is no affair of mine. My business, as representing the executors of Mrs. Somerthwaite, is to insure that the legacy shall reach the Dr. Knapp mentioned by her, or, as things have turned out, his legal heirs." He paused and held out his hand. "It will be interesting to learn who those heirs may prove to be. Good morning, Superintendent."

Jimmy's next visit was to a small house in Marylebone. He had ascertained the name of the official rat-catcher of that borough, Jack Thrisk, and his address. Having been told that he was usually to be found at home for his midday meal, Jimmy timed his visit accordingly, and was admitted to the kitchen.

Thrisk, a burly, red-faced man, was ready enough to talk. "Dr. Mawsley?" he replied to Jimmy's opening question. "Why, yes, I've known him these many years. And mighty sorry I was when I read in the papers what had happened to him."

"You saw him a few hours before he died, I believe," said Jimmy. "Tell me about that."

"I don't know that there's very much to tell," the rat-catcher replied. "I just went along to see him, like I often used to. When I'd been there just before the New Year, the doctor told me that he'd like me to bring him a couple of strong young males in about a fortnight's time. So I went along that Tuesday afternoon with a nice couple I'd got that very day. The doctor had told me long ago that when I came to see him it must be after four, when he'd finished his work."

"You'd seen Dr. Mawsley often enough before," said Jimmy. "Did you notice anything different about him that Tuesday?"

"I can't say that I did," Thrisk replied. "Everything was just as usual. I rang the bell and the butler let me in and went to tell the doctor I'd come. Then he took me into the room where the doctor was, and I said I'd got two lovely young rats that I thought would just suit him. So he took me through into the room where the rats were kept, and—"

"Hold on a minute," Jimmy interrupted. "Dr. Mawsley took you through. You mean through the doorway that leads from the consulting-room to the dispensary?"

Thrisk nodded. "That's right. I didn't recollect the proper names of those two rooms till you spoke them. As I was saying, he took me through, and I opened my bag and put the two beauties into their cages, one in each. The doctor said they'd do very well, and gave me my five bob. That's what we'd agreed long ago, half a crown for each one that suited."

"You and Dr. Mawsley didn't talk about anything else, besides the rats you'd brought?" Jimmy asked.

"Why, no," Thrisk replied. "What else should we talk about? I don't suppose I was in the place longer than five or ten minutes. And when the rats were in their cages and the doctor had paid me for them, he let me out through the other door, the one leading into the hall."

"Do you remember if that door was locked before he opened it?" Jimmy asked.

"Yes, it was locked, with the key inside," Thrisk replied. "The doctor had to turn the key before he opened it. And as I left him the butler came up and let me out by the front door."

"It didn't strike you that Dr. Mawsley looked or spoke as though he was worried or upset in any way?" Jimmy asked.

Thrisk shook his head. "I didn't notice anything strange about him. He seemed to me just the same as I'd always found him. He didn't say very much, but then he never did. Besides, his tea was waiting for him, and I daresay he was in a hurry to get back to it."

"I daresay he was," Jimmy agreed. "By the way, your job is more to kill rats than to catch them alive, isn't it? You lay down poison for them, I expect. What do you use?"

Thrisk put his hand in his pocket and produced a small bottle with a screwed cap, containing a blue powder. "That's what I always use," he said. "I mix it myself as I want it. It's strychnine, that's what it is. I've got a permit to buy that, and I mix it up with flour and a little prussian blue to colour it. So that it won't be taken for anything else, you follow. And that's what I always use to put in my bait."

"Dangerous stuff to leave lying about," Jimmy suggested casually.

"You don't suppose I leave it lying about, do you?" the rat-catcher demanded indignantly. "Not likely! That bottle never leaves my pocket. Why, even the baits when I've got them ready are kept well out of harm's way. Look over there yonder, you'll see for yourself how it's done."

He pointed to the wall, against which rested a long bamboo rod, with a spoon tied to one end. "That's what I use," he went on. "I put the bait on that, and then shove it into the run as far as I can get it to go. Where dogs and cats can't get at it. I know my job better than to leave stuff like that lying about. And you can ask who you please, and you'll never hear that there's been an accident where I've been."

9

Jimmy had plenty of things to occupy his time besides this semi-official investigation into the circumstances of Dr. Mawsley's death, and these engaged him that afternoon. But in the evening he sought out Hanslet, knowing that he would be interested in a report of his progress, and that he might let drop a helpful word.

Over a glass of beer in Hanslet's favourite house of call, Jimmy unfolded his story. "Well, there you are," he concluded. "I'm bound to admit that I haven't picked up anything very startling to tell the Professor. There is, I suppose, just a chance that Mawsley was driven to suicide by Hilworth's letter, but it seems to me a very slender one. I'm of the opinion that the coroner was right, and that it was just an accident, though a very surprising one."

"Well, you've seen and talked to these people, and I haven't," Hanslet replied. "But I've been thinking a lot about it, since Oldland told us the yarn the other evening. And I've wondered if things really happened exactly as we're told they did. Whether Mawsley was alone in the dispensary when he let out that yell."

Jimmy nodded. "Yes, I know. We have only the evidence of Phepson and his nephew. All I can say is this. Wherever I have been able to check Phepson's statements, they have been confirmed exactly."

"Wherever you have been able to check them," Hanslet replied. "That's just the point. The people you have seen bear out Phepson's version of affairs up to a certain point. Up to the time when Forcett left the suite, in fact. It seems pretty certain that we know the truth about what happened up to that moment. But after that, until Dr. Chilvers appeared on the scene, it seems to me there's some room for doubt."

"Yes," said Jimmy. "I've thought of that, and this is the way I look at it. If the statements of Phepson and his nephew covering that period are not correct, it can only be because they have some object in lying. In other words, because they somehow contrived, or at all events connived at, Mawsley's death. Why?"

Hanslet shrugged his shoulders. "Conjecture is apt to prove unprofitable, as the Professor would say. All the same, one might risk a guess at their motive. There may have been some object of value in the suite, the existence of which was known only to Mawsley and his butler. Phepson decided to secure it for himself, and by this time has done so. That will do for motive, and he had every possible opportunity."

"Would he have seized his opportunity on the very evening of the week that his nephew came to the flat?" Jimmy asked.

"Of course he would, if the nephew was in the plot!" Hanslet exclaimed. "He would have come in very useful as a witness to corroborate his uncle's story. Besides, it may have taken two of them to do the job. Perhaps they had fixed it up between them for that evening. And, after what you've been telling me, I can see how they could have managed it."

Jimmy called for more beer. "Tell me about it," he said encouragingly.

"Phepson had been Mawsley's butler for a long time," Hanslet replied. "He was obviously perfectly familiar with Mawsley's habits. He said that he always went out to dinner, a fact you've been able to verify. But he didn't say that before he went out he always went into the dispensary. We know, from another source, that he went in there now and again at that time. To give himself an injection of M and C. It seems to me quite likely that he always went in, to see how his rats were getting on, perhaps. Or to fill up his box of tablets.

"Phepson knew this, and when his nephew turned up, the two of them slipped into the dispensary. No difficulty about that, for the door had been left unlocked after the rat-catcher had gone. They waited there in the dark, until Mawsley opened the other door and walked in. They overpowered him— that's why the help of the nephew was wanted— and while one of them held him, the other pumped in the strychnine. They had got the syringe already charged while they were waiting, I daresay. And before Phepson went to look for help, they arranged things as they wanted them found."

"Well, yes, that's all right," Jimmy agreed rather doubtfully. "But what would they have done if the dispensary door hadn't been left unlocked? They couldn't have counted on that."

"Of course they couldn't," Hanslet replied. "That was just a stroke of luck. But we're told that when the door was locked, the key was left in position on the inside. And, as any burglar will tell you, that situation is easily dealt with. All you want is a pair

105

of pliers with which you can grasp the end of the key. You can turn it from outside then, easily enough. No doubt Phepson had provided the necessary tool.

"It's rather interesting that Phepson should, entirely of his own accord, have made that remark about the door being unlocked, and that it was normally kept locked. The explanation is, I fancy, that when a man embarks upon a sea of lies, he's always keen to make every possible use of any islands of truth there may be in it. Phepson must have guessed there would be some sort of investigation. It would be obvious that the door had not been broken open. Miss Hilworth, if asked, would say that it should have been locked. Phepson's unsolicited remarks would be taken as evidence of his veracity."

"He admits that he knew his way about the dispensary," said Jimmy thoughtfully. "But would he have known which injection, and how much of it, to use so that it would be almost immediately fatal? He had to be quite sure that Mawsley, if not dead, would at least be incapable of speech before help came."

"He wouldn't have gone to find a doctor until he was satisfied about that," Hanslet replied. "And he had plenty of opportunity of learning all he wanted to about poisons and their effects. You say the consulting-room is full of medical books. He may have studied them at his leisure during the weekends, when he had the suite to himself."

Hanslet took a drink of beer, and, thus inspired, went on. "There's another thing I've been wondering about. It's a detail which doesn't appear to be of the slightest importance, and that's just why

I'm going to mention it. I've often found that it's the things which don't appear to be of any importance that in the end turn out to be the clues. That business of the telephone bell ringing as Phepson left the suite to hunt for a doctor.

"He says that he couldn't be bothered to answer it, and that it had stopped ringing by the time he got back with Dr. Chilvers. Nothing remarkable about that, you may say. The caller, failing to get an answer, gave up trying. But isn't it rather odd that he didn't try again? Phepson says he didn't.

"Now, if the caller was only slightly familiar with Mawsley's arrangements, he wouldn't have given up so easily. He wouldn't have believed it possible that there should be no reply from that number. Mawsley, we are told, insisted that there should always be someone on the spot to take messages. That was the very reason for Phepson's nephew being in the suite. To answer the telephone when both master and butler had gone out.

"So I'm inquisitive enough to ask a question or two. Did the telephone really ring when Phepson says it did, and remain unanswered? If it didn't, why should Phepson have invented the incident? If it did, was it answered by either Phepson or his nephew, with the intimation that Mawsley was out or too busy to be disturbed? If so, to whom was that message given? Finally, is it really the case that Phepson's nephew came regularly to the suite on Tuesday evenings, or did his uncle arrange for him to come on that particular Tuesday only?"

Jimmy laughed. "Your mind's set on murder," he said. "But, quite frankly, I don't see Phepson in the role of first murderer. He gave me the impression of being far too stolid and unimaginative. And Mrs.

Mawsley, at least, seems to consider him entirely worthy of trust, since she's left him in charge of the place."

"Well, it's your show, not mine," Hanslet replied. "But this is how it seems to me. Take suicide first. You have in that young lawyer chap Forcett an entirely independent witness who had nothing whatever to gain whether Mawsley lived or died. He says that when he left, shortly before the event, Mawsley was most certainly not in a suicidal mood. And I can't feel very enthusiastic over your theory that he lost his head on reading Hilworth's letter, after Forcett had gone.

"The alternative, you say, is accident, genuine or contrived. Everyone seems to be agreed that a genuine accident appears amazing. It is almost incredible that Mawsley should have injected himself with a fatal dose of strychnine by mistake. It's possible, I suppose, that Miss Hilworth may have monkeyed with the poisons in some way. And if she did, I fail to see how she could have known that Mawsley would help himself from the strychnine bottle that evening. No, Jimmy, my lad, I don't care much for either of your alternatives. And the only thing that remains is deliberate murder."

Jimmy shook his head. "That's even more improbable than either of the other two. It means that Phepson was in the plot, which I simply won't believe. Nobody could have got in or out of the suite without his knowledge."

"I wouldn't be too sure about that," Hanslet replied. "I've known of people getting in and out of places when such a thing has seemed quite impossible. And in this case, it doesn't seem to me all that difficult. We'll suppose, if you like, that Phepson's story is the truth down to the last detail, and that neither he nor his nephew had any hand in the business. Where was he during the few minutes between his letting Forcett out and his nephew in? In the kitchen, I gather. You've seen the layout of the place. Would it be possible for anyone to get from the front door across the hall to the dispensary without being seen from the kitchen?"

"Well, yes, I daresay it would," Jimmy replied doubtfully. "But—"

"Wait a minute," said Hanslet. "This person presented himself at the house door, and was let in by the porter. He asked for someone in the house, Dr. Chilvers, for instance. The porter, knowing that Dr. Chilvers had not gone yet, sent the inquirer upstairs. Or perhaps the person didn't have to enter the house as he was already there. One of the people who have rooms in the building. You hadn't thought of that."

Jimmy smiled. "No, I hadn't. You see, doctors don't murder one another as a rule."

"How do you know that?" Hanslet demanded. "They would never be found out, if they did it neatly enough. For all you can tell there may be another specialist on the premises in the same line as Mawsley. He murdered his rival in the hope of getting his practice. There's a jolly good motive for you.

"But we're getting away from the point. This person had a key to the front door of the suite. Phepson says there were only two, his and Mawsley's. But that doesn't cut any ice, for it's easy enough to get a duplicate cut. The fellow lets himself in and slips across to the dispensary, where he fills up the syringe and waits. As Mawsley comes in, he jabs the syringe into his arm, then bolts into the consulting-room.

"His get-away was perfectly simple. Phepson dashes out of the suite, leaving the front door open, while his nephew stands in the dispensary doorway, goggling at Mawsley. The fellow merely slips out of the consulting-room. He dodges Phepson, by going upstairs while Phepson was hunting about on the ground floor, and leaves the house later at his leisure."

"If he'd gone upstairs, he'd have met Dr. Chilvers coming down," Jimmy objected.

But Hanslet, thoroughly warmed up to his subject, swept this aside. "What if he did?" he demanded. "That house must be a regular rabbit-warren, with all sorts of perfect strangers burrowing about all over it. If Dr. Chilvers had met someone he didn't know on the stairs, he would have supposed he was a patient calling rather late on one of the other doctors, and wouldn't have taken any notice of him."

"You're full of ideas this evening," Jimmy remarked. "But it strikes me that you are just a little bit weak on motive. I haven't come across a convincing reason for anyone to want to murder Mawsley."

Hanslet snorted. "There's a lot you haven't come across yet, it strikes me. You tell me that Mawsley had put away a lot of money, and you don't even know who gets it. And let me tell you this. When a rich man dies a violent death, it usually turns out that his heirs know something about it."

Jimmy had no time to spare next day for the Mawsley affair. But Hanslet's suggestions had made sufficient impression for him to send for one of his subordinates, Detective-Sergeant King, and charge him with certain inquiries. "Go steady," was his final injunction. "We don't want it to get about that we're interested."

On Friday morning King made his report, telling his story with frequent references to his notebook. "I started off at the Tabby Cat, sir," he began. "I was pretty sure I should pick up the thread there, and so I did. The landlord, Mr. Buttermere, turned out to be a very decent chap, and quite ready to talk. I began by noticing a pair of horns hung up on the wall, and asked if this was where the Buffaloes met. I said I was very interested in them, because, although I was not a member myself, my brother-in-law in Manchester was very keen on them. That started Mr. Buttermere talking about them, and when I asked him who was the big noise in his branch, he said it was a Mr. Phepson, who was butler to a doctor in Harley Street, who had just died."

Jimmy laughed. "Good enough. It was easy enough after that, I daresay."

"I asked if the doctor's name wasn't Mawsley, sir," King replied. "I said I'd read about the inquest in the papers, and that it seemed very queer to me that a doctor should make a mistake like that. After that, all I had to do was keep quiet and listen. Mr. Buttermere said he knew more about it than most people, for Ted Rusper, Mr. Phepson's nephew, had been round to the Tabby Cat the evening after the inquest. But I picked up these points. Phepson came to the Tabby Cat every Tuesday evening, for half an hour or so, whether it happened to be the night of the Buffaloes' meeting or not. He came in about ten, after he'd been to see his sister, Mrs. Rusper. She was a widow, and her son Ted lived with her. Mr. Buttermere told me the address. He knew the

Ruspers well, for Ted often came in, except on Tuesday evenings, and Mrs. Buttermere was friendly with Mrs. Rusper.

"After I'd finished at the Tabby Cat, I went along to the address Mr. Buttermere had given me, and saw Mrs. Rusper. I'd got a cock-and-bull yarn all ready for her, about an old chap who'd been knocked down by a car in Harley Street and badly injured. We were looking for anyone who might have seen the accident, which took place about seven on the evening of Tuesday, January 8th. I said that we'd heard that her son went to an address in Harley Street about that time on Tuesdays, and perhaps he could tell us something."

"Very good," said Jimmy approvingly. "You've more low cunning about you than I knew. Go ahead."

"Mrs. Rusper told me that was quite right, sir," King replied. "Her Ted always used to go to a doctor's rooms in Harley Street on Tuesday evenings, to take charge there while his uncle who was the butler there was out. But he didn't go there any longer now, for the doctor had died not long after he got there one evening, and I had to listen to the story all over again.

"I got her back to the point after a while, and she told me that her Ted had been going to Dr. Mawsley's for a long time every Tuesday evening. For a matter of years, she said. Her brother Thomas Phepson was butler there, and Tuesday was his evening off. Tom would come round to see her, about half past seven as a rule, unless he had a Buffaloes' meeting. Sometimes they'd go out together, and sometimes they'd stay at home. He left her before ten, to look in at the Tabby Cat before he went back to Harley Street. She didn't think that her Ted had seen anything of the accident, or he'd have been sure to tell her about it when he got home that night.

"I said I thought I had better ask him, just the same, and she gave me the name of the shop he worked in. I went to see him there, found him a decent, quiet young chap. I started off with the accident but as it hadn't happened, he naturally couldn't tell me anything about it. I got him talking, and he told me he always went to Dr. Mawsley's on Tuesday evenings. All he had to do there was to keep his ear open for the telephone while his uncle was out. If it rang, as it sometimes did, he answered that Dr. Mawsley was out, but that he could take a message. He wrote this down, and gave it to his uncle when he came in. His uncle never left the suite until after the doctor had gone out, and always got back before he came in again."

"Young Rusper didn't give you the impression that he was hiding anything?" Jimmy asked.

King shook his head. "Not a bit, sir. He and his mother struck me as being plain honest folk, both of them. I'd be ready to swear that if there was any dirty work they know nothing about it."

"Neither of them talked about Dr. Mawsley, I suppose?" Jimmy suggested.

"Only about what happened to him that evening, sir," King replied. "Mrs. Rusper said that she had never been to his rooms and as far as she knew she had never set eyes on the doctor. But she did drop a remark about something her brother had said to her a little time back. He'd told her that it seemed to him the doctor was getting on pretty well with his lady secretary, and that he, her brother, didn't care for the girl overmuch."

"I've already gathered something about that," said

Jimmy. "It may only be that Phepson as an old servant didn't like the idea of anyone else about the place gaining too much influence with his master. You went to the house in Harley Street to have a look round, as I asked you?"

"Yes, sir," King replied. "I went there yesterday afternoon, and saw the porter. I asked him first what time he left the place, and he said seven o'clock on weekdays. So then I trotted out the yarn about the accident, which I said had happened about that time. That was only to get him talking, of course. I led him on to tell me when he came and went, and so on. Five days a week he comes at eight in the morning and leaves at seven. On Saturdays he leaves at one, and on Sundays he doesn't come at all, except in the winter when he looks in to stoke up the central heating."

Jimmy nodded. "That's very much what Phepson told me. Anything else?"

"I asked him how people got in after he'd gone, sir," King replied. "He told me that all the doctors who've got rooms in the house, and he said there were eight of them, not counting Dr. Mawsley, had keys. But he didn't think they ever had occasion to use them. They didn't come to work before nine or ten, and were mostly gone by six or a little later. On Tuesday last week, for instance, he'd seen them all go out before he left, except Dr. Chilvers and, of course, Dr. Mawsley. He remembered Rusper coming just before he left, and had a word with him before he went up. He told me he knew Rusper well, as he always came on Tuesdays about that time."

"Were there many people about while you were talking to the porter?" Jimmy asked.

"Any number, sir. There were people coming in

to ask for one or other of the doctors, or going out again, all the time I was there. The porter told me it was always like that, morning and afternoon."

This was all King had to say. When he had gone, Jimmy considered his report in the light of Hanslet's suspicions. It seemed more than ever unlikely that Phepson and his nephew were telling anything but the truth, so far as they knew it. But the possibility of intrusion remained. It was not to be supposed, with such a constant stream of visitors, that the porter checked the exits of all those he admitted. A visitor admitted during the course of the afternoon might have remained there indefinitely.

There was another point. According to the porter, the non-resident doctors, that is, all but Mawsley, had usually left by six or a little later. If it had not happened that on this particular evening Dr. Chilvers had formed an exception to the rule, Mawsley would have remained unattended for several minutes longer than had actually been the case.

10

That afternoon, with the Assistant Commissioner's approval, Jimmy took a train to Dorsetshire. Having secured a room at the Antelope, he went on to the police station, where he introduced himself to Superintendent Burford.

At Jimmy's first question, the local Superintendent raised his eyebrows. "Larch Hall!" he exclaimed. "Where Mrs. Mawsley lives? Is the Yard looking into that queer affair of the doctor's death, then?"

"Not officially," Jimmy replied. "We're feeling a mild curiosity, that's all. I propose to call on Mrs. Mawsley tomorrow morning, and I thought I'd like to have a little chat with you first."

"I'll tell you anything I can, of course," said Burford. "Larch Hall is a couple of miles or more from here, in a little village called Coverley. You can take a bus there, or I can run you out, if you like."

"The bus will be good enough for me," Jimmy replied. "I don't want to take up your time. What does the family consist of?"

"Mrs. Mawsley, her son and daughter," said Burford. "They've lived there a good many years now. It was Mrs. Mawsley who bought the place, I've always understood. The doctor only used to come down at the week-end."

"He came home regularly every week, I've been told," Jimmy suggested.

"Well, no, that's not quite right," Burford replied. "I remember that at one time he used to come down every week-end. But in the last year or two it hasn't been so often as that. More like once a fortnight or three weeks. The fact is, I fancy, that he was beginning to find life at Larch Hall not quite so comfortable as he'd have liked."

Jimmy remembered his visit to Briston Road, and what Dr. Hilworth had told him there. "Family quarrels?" he asked.

"I've never heard of there being any actual row," Burford replied. "You know what it is in country places, I daresay. The chauffeur lets his tongue wag in the pub, and the cook cackles to the farmer's wife, and one way and another a lot of gossip flies round. I don't know anything at first hand, only what my chap stationed at Coverley has told me. And that doesn't amount to a lot."

"Gossip usually shows which way the wind blows," Jimmy remarked. "What was the trouble?"

Burford shrugged his shoulders. "It doesn't do for a man to be away from home too much, especially when his children are growing up. Mrs. Mawsley is very much the mistress in her own house, and I daresay resents any interference, even from the doctor. Especially where the children are concerned. She looks on them as very much her own property."

"How many did you say there are?" Jimmy asked.

"Two, a girl and a boy," Burford replied. "The girl's the elder, a year older than her brother. Miss

Josephine Mawsley's a good-looking girl, but inclined to give herself airs. Quite the County, if you get me. You'll find Larch Hall fairly stinks of money. Mrs. Mawsley's father was a very rich man, and a big pot, I've been told."

"He was, I believe, a Bradworth manufacturer," said Jimmy. "What about the boy?"

"Young Jesse?" Burford replied. "Well, I hardly know what to make of him. He's been properly spoilt, I think that's his chief trouble. His mother wouldn't let him go to a public school. Said he was too delicate, and kept him at home. He used to go to a day-school in the town here, then later he had a tutor. There was a spot of trouble about him in the end, the tutor, I mean. He and the doctor didn't hit it off. Then Jesse went up to Oxford, but he didn't stay there very long. It was put about that his health wouldn't stand it. I don't know. Now he's back with mother."

"I'm a whale for gossip," said Jimmy. "What was the spot of bother about the tutor?"

"I'll tell you," Burford replied. "Let me see now, what was the fellow's name? Glossop, that was it. He lived at the lodge at Larch Hall, with his sister. Middle-aged chap, tall, dark, and good-looking, but with rather a shifty look in his eye, or so I always thought. The sister was one of those insignificant-looking people that nobody takes much notice of. They were at the lodge two or three years, till Jesse went up to Oxford. You might have thought that he wouldn't want a tutor any longer, but the Glossops stayed put.

"Then, for once, the doctor put his foot down. Mind you, this was only what was said at the time, and I can't vouch for the truth of it. As I've said, he never managed to hit it off with Glossop. And

118

he said that now Jesse didn't need him any longer, he'd have to go. In fact, the story went that the doctor told Mrs. Mawsley he wasn't coming to Larch Hall again while the Glossops were there. Whatever truth there may be in that, they went. That was about eighteen months ago, and, as far as I'm aware, they haven't been back since."

"Do you know where they went to?" Jimmy asked.

Burford shook his head. "Back where they came from, I suppose, and that was London. At all events, Glossop used to give out that he had held an important position there. It wouldn't altogether surprise me if he turned up again, now that the doctor's dead and Jesse is living at home again."

"Very likely," said Jimmy. "Apart from the doctor's dislike of him, how did Glossop get on with the family?"

"Very well, to all appearances," Burford replied. "And, as I see it, that was just it. The family and the Glossops were always together, while the doctor was only a week-end visitor. I daresay he felt out of it at Larch Hall, even to the extent of being rather in the way. But it was his own fault. He ought to have kept his family where they could all live together."

"Having money of her own, Mrs. Mawsley felt she could go her own way, I expect," said Jimmy. "I've been told that she didn't display any very profound grief at her husband's death, and I'm beginning to understand why."

"She saw so little of him that she'll hardly miss him much," Burford replied. "She's probably one of those women who spend so much affection on their children that they've none to spare for their husbands. Now then, in return for all the gossip I've given you, tell me the details of the doctor's death. I know no more than what I read of the inquest in the papers, and that wasn't very much."

Jimmy gave him a condensed account of what he had learnt of the affair. "There you are," he concluded. "You can make what sense of it you can. You knew him, and I didn't."

"I knew him, but I was not in any way intimate with him," said Burford. "We'd stop and exchange a word if we met in the street, that's all. I saw him last on the Monday before he died. He'd been to Larch Hall for the week-end, and I was outside the station when he drove up in the car that morning to catch the train back to London. We spoke to one another, about the weather, I think. You don't suspect foul play?"

"Personally, I don't," Jimmy replied. "All the evidence is against it. Either he committed suicide, or he made the very last sort of mistake you'd think a doctor capable of. Which was it?"

"Not suicide," said Burford emphatically. "Not unless he suddenly went clean off his head. He wasn't that sort. Besides, what had he got to commit suicide about? No, the coroner was right, and it was a mistake. He can't have been thinking about what he was doing when he took out that strychnine bottle."

Next morning Jimmy took the bus to Coverley. He alighted, and walked a quarter of a mile from the centre of the village to a lodge entrance. The lodge, he noticed, was empty, and he took it to be where the Glossops had lived. A short walk along a drive from the gates brought him to Larch Hall. As he approached the front door he saw, some little distance away across the park, a youth trudging along with a gun on his shoulder.

Jimmy was admitted by an elderly and rather

sour-faced parlour-maid, to whom he gave his card, with a request to see Mrs. Mawsley. She showed him into the morning-room, elaborately and ostentatiously furnished. The windows of this room looked towards the entrance by which he had come, and while he waited Jimmy stood looking out. He saw the youth again, this time walking rapidly towards the lodge, apparently to meet a man who had just come in through the gateway. Jimmy couldn't be certain at that distance, but he fancied that he recognized the man as a fellow passenger on the bus, who had got off just short of Coverley.

Before the pair met, the door opened and Jimmy turned to face Mrs. Mawsley. She was a tall, handsome woman in the early fifties, with a capable expression. The sort of woman, Jimmy thought, who would go her way guided by her own inclinations and without much regard for the opinion of others. She regarded him critically for a moment. "Well, Superintendent, what have you come to see me about?" she asked, pleasantly enough.

Jimmy felt instinctively that the direct approach would be the best line to take with Mrs. Mawsley. "I have come to see you in connection with the death of your husband," he replied. "And I can only beg you to forgive my intrusion."

"Sit down," Mrs. Mawsley said briskly. "Perhaps you can tell me how Dick made that ghastly mistake?"

"I wish I could," Jimmy replied. "I can only suppose that it was due to momentary aberration. When Dr. Mawsley was here during the week-end, did he seem preoccupied, in any way?"

"Dick was always more or less preoccupied when he was here," said Mrs. Mawsley. "He hardly ever seemed to take any interest in what we were doing.

121

He couldn't relax, and put his own work and affairs out of his head. I didn't notice, that week-end, that his behaviour was any different from what it usually was."

In spite of the readiness of Mrs. Mawsley's reply, it seemed to Jimmy that she was choosing her words with care. She gave the impression that, while not labouring under any profound sorrow, she was not prepared to discuss her husband with any frankness. Perhaps she had nothing to hide regarding his death, but there might be certain aspects of his life that she did not care to disclose. This was the thought that passed through Jimmy's mind as he asked his next question. "Dr. Mawsley had then no knowledge of Mrs. Somerthwaite's legacy?"

"Why, no, I'm sure he hadn't," Mrs. Mawsley replied. "Otherwise, he would have told me about it. As it was, the first I heard about it was when Mr. Forcett mentioned it at the inquest."

"Did you know Mrs. Somerthwaite?" Jimmy asked. "Or rather, Mrs. Gunton as she was when Dr. Mawsley attended her?"

"Mrs. Mawsley shook her head. "No, I never met her. She must have been Dick's patient before I married him. He gave up his practice in Bradworth immediately after that, and we went to London."

"I hope you won't think me very impertinent, Mrs. Mawsley," said Jimmy. "But the question I am going to ask you may throw some light on Dr. Mawsley's state of mind. Can you tell me anything of his financial circumstances?"

"You can set your mind at rest about that," she replied. "Dick never had any money troubles, at all events after he married me. He wasn't very well off before then certainly. I've sometimes wondered how he ever scraped together enough to buy his Brad-

have expected a will to be deposited was a lar[ge] desk with several drawers. But these were all h[alf] open, and a glance into them showed Jimmy th[at] they were as empty as the safe. Mrs. Mawsley h[ad] evidently made a clean sweep of all her husban[d's] belongings.

She returned, and handed Jimmy a small go[ld] snuff-box. He opened it to find that it containe[d] half a dozen white tablets. "Do you mind if I ta[ke] this with me?" he asked. "I'll return it within a d[ay] or two."

"Take it by all means," Mrs. Mawsley replied. "[Is] that all you want to know?" She walked with hi[m] across the hall to the front door where she sai[d] good-bye to him pleasantly enough. With an air [of] relief at being rid of a troublesome visitor, Jimm[y] thought, as he walked down the drive. What was [it] that she had been so anxious to hide, he wondere[d.] And why had she made such a thorough clearanc[e] of the contents of the safe?

As he approached the lodge, he became awar[e] of voices, and when he reached the gate he saw tw[o] men engaged in earnest conversation. They wer[e] sheltering behind the lodge, the walls of which hi[d] them from the windows of Larch Hall. One of the[m] was the youth he had seen on his arrival, still car rying the gun. Seen thus at close quarters, his strik ing likeness to Mrs. Mawsley told Jimmy that thi[s] must be her son Jesse. The other was undoubtedl[y] Jimmy's fellow-passenger in the bus. And lookin[g] at him with greater interest, Jimmy was reminde[d] of Burford's description of Glossop. Middle-aged[,] tall, dark and good-looking. This chap was all tha[t] and one might even concede him the shifty eye[,] Jimmy thought. The two interrupted their conver

worth practice. But since then things have been very different. My father left me very well off, and besides, once Dick got going as a specialist, he did very well indeed. There was no reason why he should not have retired long ago, but he was too fond of his profession."

Jimmy detected a patronizing note in her voice. It was clear that Mrs. Mawsley had not cared to consider herself as the wife of a doctor, even though he might be one of the leading specialists of the day. The Bradworth manufacturer's daughter had risen to the heights of a great lady, in her own estimation at least. But Jimmy had reached the stage towards which he had been steering. "One more impertinent question, Mrs. Mawsley," he said. "Did Dr. Mawsley leave any legacies in his will, to his butler, Phepson, for example?"

Mrs. Mawsley looked at him intently, as though striving to fathom the depths of his mind. "I know nothing of Dick's will, or whether he ever made one," she replied. "It isn't here. If it turns out that he never made a will, I shall, of course, see that Phepson is properly provided for."

"You say that Dr. Mawsley's will is not here?" Jimmy asked. "Are you perfectly satisfied of that?"

"Perfectly," she replied. "When I was in London last week, the Inspector gave me the things that were found in Dick's pockets when he had been taken to the mortuary. Among them was his bunch of keys. Mr. Forcett asked me to look for a docu-ment which Dick had told him was in the safe here. Come and see."

She got up and they left the room. Crossing the hall, they entered another room furnished as a study, and looking somehow as though it were rarely used, with a big safe standing against a wall. "This was Dick's own room," she explained. "And that is the safe where he kept all his papers. I looked through them and found the one Mr. Forcett wanted. I sent it to him, and he wrote back asking who Dick's executors were. I had to tell him that I had no idea. He had never told me, and I had never seen his will."

"You looked at all the papers there were in the safe?" Jimmy asked.

Mrs. Mawsley caught hold of the handle of the safe and swung open the door, to reveal an absolutely empty interior. "I looked through them all, and turned them out," she replied. "There was nothing there of any value. Only the document and a lot of old medical records, which I burnt, as they were of no use."

"You don't think the will can be anywhere else in the house?" Jimmy asked.

"I'm sure it isn't," Mrs. Mawsley replied shortly. "I've looked everywhere. I'm not sure what I ought to do about it, so I've asked my lawyer to come down from Bradworth and advise me. He'll be here this afternoon."

"Perhaps Dr. Mawsley employed a lawyer of his own?" Jimmy suggested.

She shook her head. "I don't think so. He never mentioned doing so to me. So far as I know, he always looked after his affairs himself. I don't even know how much money he had of his own. And it's quite likely he never made a will."

"If he didn't, his money will go to his family, as no doubt it would have done in any case," Jimmy remarked.

Mrs. Mawsley glanced at him sharply. "Of course!" she exclaimed. "Who else could Dick have left his money to? Not that it will make very much differ-

124

ence to us. My children and I have plenty alr[e]

Too much, perhaps, Jimmy thought. But [i]t seemed little object in pursuing that subject further. "Dr. Mawsley was in the habit of spend[ing] every week-end here, I believe?" he asked inn[o]cently.

Again that sharp, questioning glance. "Not ever[y] week-end," she replied. "Dick couldn't spare the time to do that. He was very busy, you know, so busy that he often had to refuse to see patients. And some of his patients lived in the country, and couldn't get up to London to see him. So he used to go and see them during the week-end, which was the only time he could spare from his consulting-room in Harley Street."

"I see," said Jimmy. "Now, just one more question, Mrs. Mawsley, and then I won't trouble you any further. I have been told that Dr. Mawsley used to take tablets regularly. Was that actually the case?"

For the first time the tension of Mrs. Mawsley's manner relaxed, and she smiled faintly. "Yes, that's quite true. Dick always used to drop a tablet in his glass when he took anything to drink. He carried a box of them in his pocket wherever he went. I don't know what they were made of, but he used to say they prevented him from having indigestion. He was always rather faddy about his food, which he liked quite plain."

"Can you tell me what became of that box [of] tablets?" Jimmy asked.

"It was handed over to me with the keys a[nd] other things," she replied. "I'll get it and sho[w] to you."

She went out, affording Jimmy the opport[unity] for a swift inspection of the room. The only [piece] of furniture except the safe in which one

125

sation to glance at him inquisitively, but did not speak to him as he passed.

When a return bus had taken him to Dorsetshire, Jimmy called again on Burford. "You were right, I fancy," he said. "Unless I'm mistaken, I saw your friend Glossop in earnest conversation with his pupil at the Larch Hall lodge, barely half an hour ago. It looked to me like a rendezvous."

"You're not likely to be mistaken," Burford replied. "It won't surprise me in the least if we see the Glossops established in their old quarters before very long. Well, how did you get on with Mrs. Mawsley?"

Jimmy frowned. "She puzzles me rather. She's not at all like what you'd expect a recent widow to be. She talks about her husband as though he was a perfect stranger. She even can't, or won't, tell me anything about his will. But she knows something about which she has no intention of letting on to anyone, I'm sure of that."

"Something about his death?" Burford asked. "Does she suspect he committed suicide, do you suppose?"

"No, I don't think it's that," Jimmy replied. "As I say, I'm puzzled. But I'd be glad if you'd keep your ears open for any further gossip from Larch Hall. I may come down to see you again, one of these days."

11

Jimmy went back to London, and that evening attended the weekly dinner party at Westbourne Terrace. Mawsley's name was not mentioned during the meal, but as soon as his guests were settled in the study afterwards, Dr. Priestley introduced the subject. "Have you found any opportunity of making inquiries into the matter which Oldland expounded to us last week, Superintendent?" he asked Jimmy.

"I have, sir," Jimmy replied, producing a sheaf of notes, and laying them on the table beside him. "My colleague, Sergeant King, and I have between us interviewed a number of people. If it won't try your patience, I will repeat their statements."

Dr. Priestley nodded, and Jimmy gave a detailed account of his investigation, to which his audience listened without interruption. "Well, there you are, sir," he concluded. "That's how the matter stands at present."

Although his attitude had been one of apparent somnolence, the Professor had not missed a word. "You have ascertained some very interesting facts," he said. "What deductions have you drawn from these statements?"

"First of all, sir, that the evidence given at the

128

inquest was absolutely reliable, as far as it went,"
Jimmy replied. "By which I mean that the statements of Phepson and Rusper can be accepted
without reserve. Hanslet was a little doubtful about
that, but I hope he's satisfied now."

"Yes, I'll allow you that," said Hanslet. "But, all
the same, I'm still not ready to wipe all possibility
of murder from the slate. You haven't proved that
someone else was not in the suite, without their
knowledge."

"That's quite true," Jimmy replied. "I'll stretch a
point, and grant you opportunity. But what about
motive?"

Hanslet shrugged his shoulders. "I stick to what
I said the other evening. What becomes of Mawsley's money?"

"His family gets it, apparently," Jimmy replied.
"And that brings us to Mrs. Mawsley. I can't make
up my mind as to how much she told me was the
truth, and how much prevarication. She denies all
knowledge of her husband's financial affairs, beyond that he had done very well since he got going
as a specialist. That may be true enough. She has
so much money of her own that her husband's earn-
ings hardly concerned her. Weedon told me that
the two establishments were run entirely separately,
Mawsley paying the expenses of the suite, and his
wife those of Larch Hall which, incidentally, must
be considerable. I gather that Mawsley didn't contribute to the family budget. All that is probably
true enough. But then we come to the matter of
the will.

"Did Mawsley ever make one, or didn't he? Weedon has no knowledge of one, and rather suggested
that Mawsley was the sort of person who wouldn't
have cared to devote his mind to such a document,

with its implications. Mrs. Mawsley says that her husband never told her that he had made a will, and that she had hunted everywhere without being able to find one. But still, I'm not altogether satisfied."

"Why are you not altogether satisfied, Superintendent?" Dr. Priestley asked quietly.

"Because I'm doubtful of Mrs. Mawsley's frankness, sir," Jimmy replied. "Let me deal with a minor point first. Phepson says that Mawsley spent every week-end at Larch Hall. Burford told me that of recent years he didn't spend every week-end there, but only came down once in a fortnight or three weeks. Mrs. Mawsley's explanation is that he came to Larch Hall whenever he could, but that he very often had to go to see one or other of his patients."

Hanslet laughed. "I don't think it's very difficult to untie that knot, Jimmy," he said. "I don't suppose Mawsley told his butler where he was going, every time he went away. Phepson may merely have assumed that he was going to Larch Hall. He may have gone to visit patients, or that may have been only the yarn he told his wife. From other things you've told us, it doesn't seem to me at all unlikely that he spent some of his week-ends enjoying himself."

"Quite," Jimmy replied. "But how much did Mrs. Mawsley find out about her husband's private affairs? That seems to me rather an important point. To get back to the will. If the safe originally contained Mawsley's papers, they aren't there now. Mrs. Mawsley says she burnt them, as they were of no value to her. Did they include a will, which she burnt with the rest, because she didn't approve of its provisions?"

"This is getting interesting," Oldland remarked. "Let's hear just what's in your mind, Jimmy."

"This," Jimmy replied. "Mrs. Mawsley says that her husband's money, more or less, would make no difference to herself or her children. It's quite possible that she flung some remark to that effect at Mawsley's head. Taking her at her word, he left his money elsewhere. He may have had relatives of his own, that we haven't heard of.

"But I have an idea that Mrs. Mawsley is by no means so contemptuous financially as she professes to be. Immediately after the inquest she approached Forcett and asked him what would happen to Mrs. Somerthwaite's legacy, now that her husband was dead. And she lost no time in sending him the document he wanted as proof of Mawsley's identity.

"My idea is this. She may or may not have known that her husband had made a will. If she did, she was not aware of its provisions. In the safe she found a will, and, on reading it, disapproved most strongly. She, therefore, destroyed it, knowing that if no will were found, Mawsley would be assumed to have died intestate, and his money would go to his family."

"I think you're on the right track, Jimmy," Oldland said. "But I don't see why you need drag in unknown relatives. It comes back to the suggestion I made to you the other evening. Mawsley made a will, leaving, I daresay, the bulk of his money to his family. But there were certain legacies attached, among them one to the Hilworth girl. Mrs. Mawsley saw no reason why she should part with good money to a girl of whom she may have thought she had cause to be jealous. Finding Miss Hilworth's name down for a thumping legacy may have opened her eyes a bit. She may have suspected how Mawsley spent the week-ends when he didn't come to Larch Hall. But, very naturally, she didn't want to advertise her husband's infidelities. Hence, her explanation to you that he had to visit his patients."

"Go on, Doctor," Hanslet said encouragingly. "You're coming round to my idea, I do believe, that murder isn't so entirely out of the question as Jimmy persists in thinking."

"I've already offered him a theory," Oldland replied. "Since then I've had time to elaborate it a bit. Mawsley made certain overtures to the girl, considerably earlier, one must imagine, than the day before his death. She agreed to comply with them, under certain conditions, one of which was that he should make a will in her favour. He did so, and having shown it to her, deposited it in the safe at Larch Hall. It's quite likely that he had it in mind to hoodwink her by destroying it at some later date.

"But she didn't give him the chance to do that. Her first step was to hot up the strychnine solution, which as originally made up, was so weak as to be harmless. But there, I'm bound to confess, I see a snag in my theory. According to her, Mawsley's pet pick-me-up was not strychnine, but the stuff he called M and C. Why didn't she add a good strong dash of strychnine to that? Mawsley dispensed the mixture himself, and he alone knew the composition of it. When subsequent analysis of the contents of the phial revealed the presence of strychnine, it would be assumed that drug was a normal constituent of the mixture.

"Never mind. Her next step was to go to her father with her pitiful tale, and get him to write his stinker to Mawsley. She guessed that, having read this effusion, Mawsley would feel the need of a stimulant. How she knew that he would choose strychnine is more than I can pretend to tell you. She counted on the letter being found, and the deduction being drawn that Mawsley had committed suicide to avoid exposure. She didn't, of course, reckon with Mrs. Mawsley destroying the will and so cheating her of her object."

But Jimmy shook his head. "Sorry, Doctor, but it's all a shade too fanciful. There are far too many slips between the cup and the lip, or the syringe and the forearm, if you like, for a dodge like that to have had a sporting chance of coming off. I can't help feeling that if Miss Hilworth had wanted to poison Mawsley, she'd have chosen some more direct method. No, if you and Hanslet insist on a murderer, I've got a more hopeful candidate than Miss Hilworth."

Hanslet laughed. "I'm not insisting, only rubbing in the possibility. Who's your candidate for the gallows?"

"The man I caught a glimpse of this morning," Jimmy replied. "What do we know of this chap Glossop? He was employed for some time as tutor to young Jesse Mawsley, during which period he and his sister lived in the lodge. They continued to live there for a time after Jesse had gone up to Oxford. Mawsley, we are told, didn't like Glossop and objected to this arrangement, and they left. A week after Mawsley's funeral Glossop reappears. He doesn't go straight up to Larch Hall, but meets Jesse for a confabulation at the entrance gate.

"Now, of course, there may be nothing in all that. On the other hand, Burford remarked to me, yesterday evening, that he wouldn't be surprised if

Glossop turned up again now that Mawsley was out of the way. I don't see why I shouldn't build up a theory of my own, no more fanciful than the doctor's."

Oldland glanced at Dr. Priestley, who was apparently paying not the slightest attention to the conversation. "We shall get rapped over the knuckles in a moment for indulging in blind guesswork. Never mind. Let's hear it."

"Although Mawsley may have disliked Glossop, we are told that he got on very well with his wife and children," Jimmy replied. "I don't think it's wildly impossible that Glossop did his best to ingratiate himself with Mrs. Mawsley. She's undoubtedly a rich woman, and that may have been his principal inducement. He's rather a striking looking chap, and I'm ready to believe that he has a way with him. It may be that Mawsley saw he was gaining an influence over his wife, and that was his reason for objecting to his presence at Larch Hall.

"I'm not suggesting that Glossop resorted to murder as a means of revenge for being turned out. His motive may have been considerably deeper than that. He may have believed that his influence with a widowed Mrs. Mawsley would prove sufficiently powerful to induce her to marry him. His appointment with Jesse this morning, and I'm pretty sure that it was an appointment and that Jesse was expecting him, was to sound him on his mother's probable reaction to his reappearance.

"So much for his motive. His opportunity he must have taken some pains to contrive. It is believed that when the Glossops left Coverley some eighteen months ago, they came to London. If so, he had plenty of time to spy out the land. Hanslet has already supplied a theory of how he got into the suite, and what he did while he was there."

"That's quite a creditable flight of imagination," Oldland remarked. "What do you say, Priestley?"

Dr. Priestley opened his eyes. "I say this," he replied. "After hearing what I have this evening, I am still by no means fully satisfied either that Mawsley committed suicide, or that he gave himself a fatal injection inadvertently. On the other hand, in spite of the ingenious theories which have been advanced, it would be difficult to persuade me that he was murdered."

"Oh, come now, Professor, that won't do!" Hanslet protested. "It's perfectly obvious that in this case at least there are only three alternatives, suicide, accident, or murder. Mawsley's death must have been due to one of them."

"In space it is perfectly obvious that there are only three dimensions," Dr. Priestley replied. "Length, breadth, and height. Yet a mathematician can prove, to his own satisfaction, at least, that a fourth exists. However, we need not labour that point. To my mind, the value of the Superintendent's investigations lies in the light they throw, not upon Mawsley's death, but upon his life and character.

"This appears to me to be of the first importance. Even if we take the narrowest view, the alternative which presented itself at the inquest, whether he committed suicide or made a fatal mistake, we must determine his disposition. Was his nature such that he was likely to take his own life, on what must have been a sudden impulse? Or, on the other hand, was he subject to fits of aberration, which led him to acts of almost incredible carelessness?

"We can reconstruct the outlines of his career from the various remarks which have been made. We first hear of him as a general practitioner in Bradworth. At that time his resources appear to have been meagre. Mrs. Mawsley remarked that she did not know how he scraped together enough to buy his practice. He seems to have been competent enough, if we may judge by his treatment of Mrs. Somerthwaite. He was undoubtedly ambitious, for his success in that case determined him to seek a wider reputation as a specialist.

"But Oldland will bear me out when I say that to carry out such a resolve, considerable financial resources were necessary. A lengthy period must elapse before an unknown man from the provinces can build up a remunerative practice in Harley Street, and during that period his expenses must necessarily be great. Dr. Knapp solved that problem by marrying a rich woman. We are entitled to speculate how far his choice of a wife was influenced by genuine affection, for that may have some bearing upon his subsequent conduct.

"The fact that he adopted his wife's name is, I think, indicative. It may be that his father-in-law wished him to do so, in order that the name might be perpetuated. We have been told, I think, that Mrs. Mawsley was her father's only child. But even so, the change was in accordance with his own inclinations. According to Mrs. Mawsley, he came to London immediately after his marriage, and he may well have wished to make a clean cut between the past and the future. All memory of the obscure and impoverished general practitioner, Dr. Knapp, was to be forgotten, and in his place was to rise the brilliant and prosperous specialist, Dr. Mawsley.

"We get a hint of that in the statement made by

Forcett to the Superintendent. He said, if I remember correctly, that the subject of Dr. Knapp of Bradworth did not seem to appeal to Mawsley, probably an understatement. It was not until the bait of his late patient and her legacy was held out that he became communicative. Even then, he appears to have touched upon the past as lightly as possible. His principal topic of conversation dealt with more recent years, and his successful career in Harley Street. That he should have talked in such a way, and so volubly, suggests a strong desire on his part to steer the conversation away from any reminiscences of the obliterated Dr. Knapp.

"Whatever his motives for marrying Mrs. Mawsley, and incidentally, hers for marrying him, she was prepared to finance his ambitions. We have it from Weedon that she did in fact do so. I find it hard to believe that there can have been any lasting affection on either side. It seems to have been a marriage of ambition, on Mawsley's part, for a prosperous career; on his wife's, to achieve a position in a more elevated society than that of Bradworth.

"These ambitions achieved, they tended to drift apart. Since their paths were divergent, this was only what might have been expected. No doubt the birth of the two children had considerable influence in this direction. I see no reason to dissent from Burford's opinion that Mrs. Mawsley was a woman who devoted herself to her children to the neglect of her husband. She was quite prepared to enjoy their company at Larch Hall, leaving Mawsley to his professional activities in London. It must not be forgotten that of recent years his financial dependence upon his wife had come to an end. He could go his own way, as she could go hers.

"I doubt that there was any expressed difference

of opinion between them. I see no reason why there should have been, for both were leading the lives they preferred. Differences no doubt cropped up from time to time on minor issues, as in the case of the tutor, Glossop. But on the whole I expect they went their respective ways, on a basis of mutual non-interference. This could hardly fail to lead to an estrangement which may at times have caused Mawsley some irritation. He may have been made to feel, probably quite inadvertently, that he was rather in his family's way at Larch Hall. His alleged remark to Miss Hilworth, to the effect he was tired of being treated by his wife and children as an unwanted stranger, seems to me to ring true.

"Now, what was Mawsley's character? He must have been not only persevering, but exceptionally able, to attain so distinguished a position in his profession. I might remark that a man who rises from obscurity to a level above that of his colleagues inevitably makes enemies in the process. Especially if his methods are so lacking in benevolence as to approach the ruthless. Oldland has told us that Mawsley avoided any but well-to-do patients, and his observation is confirmed by the incident Hilworth described to the Superintendent.

"I can almost see Hanslet's ears pricking at my remark. But I hasten to say that by enemies I do not mean those who would extend their hostilities to murder. What I wished to convey was the probability that Mawsley had incurred a considerable volume of dislike, to which he seems to have been completely indifferent. We may gather from Weedon's conversation that he was not a man to make friends. And so far we have met nobody who has displayed any real affection for him. The words of Mrs. Somerthwaite's codicil suggest that her legacy to him was impelled by gratitude rather than personal liking. Miss Hilworth conceived at first a profound admiration for him, for the doctor rather than the man, perhaps, but this admiration waned as she grew to know him better.

"Nor is there evidence of Mawsley's affection for any person. I exclude, of course, any casual intercourse he may have had with women, of which there is some suggestion. His interest in his wife and children appears to have declined almost to the vanishing point. We do not hear of his having any friend, male or female, to whom he was attached. The only person who was welcome at the suite, apart from lucrative patients, was his bank manager. It seemed that he liked Weedon, because he was useful to him as a source of advice upon his investments.

"And that brings us to the most striking feature of Mawsley's character, his devotion to money. Weedon's phrase, that he was a collector of it, expresses this most aptly. We are not to suppose that he was a miser, or that he did not spend money freely on occasions that seemed to him suitable. But his hobby, if I may employ the word, was to amass money for its own sake, and without having in mind any definite end to which it was ultimately to be applied. This frame of mind is not uncommon among those who in early life have been hard put to it financially. Their experience has taught them not only the value of money, but the misery, mental and physical, that can be caused an ambitious man by its scarcity.

"Of Mawsley's passion for acquiring money we have plenty of evidence. His delight at the news of his unexpected legacy, a delight at which Weedon expressed no surprise, is an apt illustration. The amount of the legacy, so far as he was concerned, could provide hardly more than an additional drop in the existing ocean of his investments. Yet, in addition to Forcett's account of his reception of the news, we have the illuminating evidence that, with an injunction that he was not to be disturbed, he proceeded then and there to work out the profit the legacy would bring him. Truly, the satisfaction of a collector in a newly acquired specimen.

"We must, then, ask ourselves this question. Would such a man, at the height of his career and his prosperity, have committed suicide? The answer to that question must surely be in the negative. People have recourse to suicide only in the last extremity, to escape from an intolerable position, real or imaginary. Can such a situation have arisen after Forcett's departure? It seems impossible. We are told that he spoke to nobody, either in person or on the telephone. Mawsley's only communication with the world outside his consulting-room was provided by the letters, until then presumably unopened. Hilworth's may have given him an unpleasant shock, but I find it impossible to believe that it drove him to immediate suicide.

"The second question, then, is this. What is the probability of such a man making so glaring a mistake? The fact that he kept such a variety of injections in readiness shows that he must have been perfectly familiar with their various uses and properties. We have been told that they were dispensed in accordance with his instructions. I am inclined to believe Miss Hilworth's statement that he ordered the strychnine injection to be made up of the proportion of eight grains of the drug to the liquid ounce. The Superintendent tells us that the phials were clearly labelled, in Mawsley's handwriting. We may assume that the primary purpose of the injections, with the exceptions of the M and C, was for use in experiments upon rats. Do you not agree, Oldland?"

Oldland nodded. "I do. The experiments being carried out to discover how any particular drug could be used to control a condition he had induced in one of the rats."

"Very well," said Dr. Priestley. "We may now endeavour to reconstruct events on the theory of accident. At eight minutes to seven his visitor left, and Mawsley remained alone in his consulting-room. Appearances suggest how he spent the next few minutes. While he made pencilled calculations regarding the legacy, he smoked his cigar and finished his cocktail. He then opened the letters which Phepson had brought him earlier in the evening.

"Although the letter alleged to have been written by Hilworth has not been found, I do not think we need doubt the statements made regarding it. Miss Hilworth is said to have posted it on Tuesday morning. A letter posted by Oldland at the same time was delivered at Mawsley's suite that afternoon. Phepson believes that he took four letters into the consulting-room, only three of which were subsequently found. We may assume, I think, that Hilworth's letter was among those opened by Mawsley between eight minutes to seven and ten minutes past.

"Having read his letters, Mawsley rose from his chair so abruptly as to overturn it. We may speculate upon the reason for his excitement. It may have been due to rapture at Oldland's offer of a patient so affluent as Sir Matthew Gussage. But I think it more probable that it was due to annoyance at the contents of Hilworth's letter. He jumped up from the table for the purpose of flinging the offending missive into the fire. This done, he went through the connecting doorway into the dispensary.

"He may have been in a state of some agitation or excitement. The fact that it did not occur to him to set the chair on its feet again suggests that he was. But can this state have been so violent as to obliterate all knowledge of what he was about? His actions were deliberate. Phepson says that a couple of minutes, maybe more, elapsed between his hearing the opening of the connecting door and the scream. Mawsley opened the poison cupboard, and selected from it not the phial containing M and C, but the one clearly marked as containing strychnine. He charged a syringe with an amount of this so large as to prove almost immediately fatal, pushed up his sleeve, and administered this injection. Does it seem credible?"

Oldland replied to this. "I started off, last week, by saying that it was incredible. But if you don't believe in suicide and won't entertain murder, it's what must have happened, all the same."

Dr. Priestley shook his head. "I can only repeat the analogy I have already drawn from the fourth dimension," he said.

12

Jimmy, considering the matter at his leisure next day, came to the conclusion that for once the Professor was looking for a mare's nest. It was all very well for him to refer obscurely to the fourth dimension, but this was a matter not of mathematics, but of hard common sense. The coroner, realizing this, had arrived at the only possible conclusion. Incredible though it might seem, Mawsley had somehow made a tragic mistake. Or, if he hadn't, if there was some flaw in the evidence, he had either committed suicide deliberately or been murdered. Whatever the Professor might say, there was no fourth alternative.

Suicide, in the light of Mawsley's character, seemed out of the question. The Professor had said, truly enough, that people only committed suicide to escape from an intolerable situation, real or imaginary. With what intolerable situation could Mawsley have been faced? His health had been sound enough, except for an occasional tendency to dyspepsia. He certainly hadn't killed himself because he felt a twinge of indigestion. He was annoyed by the way his family had come to treat him, but he could escape that annoyance by keeping away from Larch Hall. His finances were in a flourishing state, and his investments perfectly secure, in spite of the fluctuation in Peebles Corporation Stock. And he had several things to look forward to. The legacy, the whacking big fee he would no doubt have extracted from Sir Matthew Gussage, the appearance of his name in the Birthday Honours, to recall only three of his immediate prospects.

Remained Hilworth's letter. Following the Professor's reconstruction, with which Jimmy fully agreed, this had annoyed Mawsley to such an extent as to make him upset his chair. But had his annoyance been violent enough to drive him to suicide? Surely not. Even if Hilworth had threatened to expose him, and had carried out his threat, what then? Mawsley could have countered with a stark denial. At the very worst, it would have involved no more than the end of his career. Would that have mattered so much to him? The income from his investments would be ample for him to live upon. As Mrs. Mawsley had remarked, he might have retired at any time.

Murder, then, involving the presence of some unauthorized person in the dispensary? Hanslet's explanation of how that person had got in and out would serve. Jimmy knew very well that speculation as to motive was apt to be misleading. A might have a secret motive for murdering B unknown to anyone but himself and his victim. Putting motive entirely aside, then, what opportunity had presented itself to those associated with Mawsley?

Phepson and Rusper, first. They must be bracketed together, for one of them could not have committed the crime without the connivance of the other. Since they were already in the suite, their opportunity had been perfect. But Jimmy had a firm conviction that they were both telling the truth. Apart from that, it seemed to him that the technique was hardly one they would have employed.

Forcett next, since he had been the last person to speak to Mawsley. Phepson had let him out of the suite at eight minutes to seven. There was no evidence that he had left the house then. He might have slipped into the suite again, in the manner imagined by Hanslet. Against that was the fact that he was a complete stranger. His statement to that effect was confirmed by Phepson, who had never seen him before. It seemed highly improbable that a stranger should somehow have acquired a key with which to open the door of the suite. Or that he would have been able to find his way so readily into the dispensary.

Jack Thrisk, the rat-catcher. He also had seen and spoken to Mawsley that afternoon. He had been a fairly frequent visitor to the suite, and was perfectly familiar with the dispensary. He might have been aware that Mawsley had not locked the dispensary door after letting him out. He was familiar with the properties of strychnine, of which he always carried a supply. Given a key, he might have slipped back into the suite at any time. He might even have been in the dispensary during the interview between Mawsley and Forcett, next door.

Violet Hilworth, with or without the knowledge of her father, working daily in the suite, might well have obtained a key. She might have borrowed Mawsley's key on some pretext or other, and had a duplicate cut from it. She was, by her own admission, perfectly familiar with the dispensary and its contents. Had she been found there at an unusual hour, she could have invented some plausible pretext for her presence. But could a girl, single-handed, have overpowered Mawsley so effectively as to be able to drive the needle into him before he could call for help?

Wait a minute, though! What if Mawsley had offered no resistance? Jimmy's imagination set to work upon an entirely new theory. Suppose Mawsley had given her a key of the suite? She hadn't used it when she arrived in the mornings, because neither of them wanted Phepson to know she had one. Perhaps Mawsley, anticipating her return, had purposely left the dispensary door unlocked after Thrisk's departure. And, if he was indeed expecting her, his message by Forcett to Phepson, that on no account was he to be disturbed, would have been a very natural one.

Jimmy's imagination broke into a gallop. Violet Hilworth entered the consulting-room from the dispensary. Mawsley jumped up to greet her, overturning the chair in his delight. They would go out and have dinner together. But first of all Mawsley would have a stimulant to buck him up, as he'd had a hard day. They went into the dispensary together. Violet offered to give him the injection. It was so much easier for someone else to do it than to handle the syringe oneself. M and C, of course, as usual? Mawsley agreed. She opened the poison cupboard, took from it the strychnine bottle, charged the syringe, and gave the injection. What of Hilworth's letter? It might never have been written, or if it had been Violet might not have posted it. The fourth letter might have been of so little importance that Mawsley had thrown it into the fire.

The worst of it was, as Jimmy realized when he came down to earth, that this beautiful theory was quite impossible of proof. But, anyhow, Violet Hilworth's opportunity had been examined. Who came next on the list? Mrs. Mawsley, her son or her daughter might have got hold of a key. But, not very long after her husband's death, Phepson had spoken to Mrs. Mawsley at Larch Hall. It was to be presumed that the son and daughter had been at home at that time, or at all events not in London. What about Glossop, whose opportunity Jimmy had already outlined? His movements might be worth looking into. He could have learnt a good deal about the suite and Mawsley's habits. But could he have known where to lay his hands on the syringe and the strychnine?

As Jimmy cast about for any other likely candidate, he remembered a remark of Hanslet's. Someone who had legitimate business in the house, though not in the suite. What had kept Dr. Chilvers in his consulting-room beyond his usual hour that evening? Was it merely by chance that he was coming downstairs as Phepson ran up? Being one of the occupants of the premises, he could have secured a key to the suite by the simple process of trying a number in the lock until he found one to fit. He had a key of the house door, and so could get in at any time. During the early hours of the morning, for instance, when Mawsley and Phepson were in bed and asleep. By contriving to be summoned to Mawsley's aid, he could insure the success of his venture. If Mawsley had shown any signs of recovery, he could have given him a drop or two more, under colour of administering a counter-irritant.

With Dr. Chilvers the list seemed to be complete. Summing up, Jimmy was inclined to award the opportunity prizes to Phepson, Violet Hilworth, Chilvers, Glossop and Jack Thrisk in that order. Misleading as motive might be, it could be applied as a touchstone. It was difficult to imagine any reason for Thrisk wishing to kill the purchaser of rats at half a crown a head. Dr. Chilvers' motive was also obscure, unless it could be proved that he hoped to inherit Mawsley's practice. Of Phepson's innocence Jimmy was fully convinced. That left Violet Hilworth, expecting a legacy under a will which Mrs. Mawsley had possibly destroyed, and Glossop, anxious to return to the amenities of Larch Hall, and perhaps with designs on Mawsley's widow.

On Monday Jimmy sent for Sergeant King. "You're a wizard at worming things out of people," he said. "Make a note of this. Dr. Hilworth, 7 Briston Road, Hammersmith. He's got a daughter, Violet, who used to be Mawsley's secretary. Find out where she was between seven and half past in the evening of Tuesday the 15th. Don't let the girl or her father know that you're asking questions. You won't find it a particularly easy job, I'm afraid."

"I'll do my best, sir," King replied. "I was stationed in Hammersmith some years back, so I know the place well enough. I remember Dr. Hilworth's name, though I shouldn't recognize him if I was to see him."

Jimmy, careful not to neglect any clue, however unpromising, had sent for analysis the tablets from the gold snuff-box which Mrs. Mawsley had entrusted to him. He now took the box with him to the offices of Perring and Company in Broad Street. He was shown into Forcett's room, where he met with a cordial greeting. "Come in and sit down, Superintendent. I was just going to ring you up. I've had a letter from Mrs. Mawsley, in which she says that she has hunted all through Larch Hall, without being able to find any trace of her husband's will."

"What will happen if the will is not found?" Jimmy asked.

"A good deal of fuss and bother," Forcett replied. "It boils down to this in the end. Mrs. Mawsley will get half the estate for life, when it will go to her children. The other half will be divided equally between the children."

"In the course of your conversation with him, Dr. Mawsley did not mention having made a will?" Jimmy suggested.

Forcett shook his head. "The subject did not come up. It does occasionally happen that people put off making their wills until too late. But I shouldn't have expected a man in Dr. Mawsley's position to do that."

Forcett's tone indicated clearly that he had doubts about the matter. "It is, of course, no business of mine," he went on. "We can take no action until powers of administration of Dr. Mawsley's estate have been granted. But, had we been acting for him, we should not rest content till we had taken every possible step to find the will."

Jimmy smiled. "It's no business of ours, either," he replied. "The duties of the Yard don't include hunting for missing wills. Now, Mr. Forcett, I've brought something to show you. Have you ever seen it before?"

He took out the gold snuff-box and laid it on the desk. Forcett looked at it and nodded. "I have," he said. "In the hands of Dr. Mawsley, while we were talking in his suite in Harley Street."

"Can you swear to it?" Jimmy asked.

Forcett shook his head. "Lawyers learn to be very careful what they swear to," he replied. "But I have very little doubt that's the box I saw that evening. For one thing, gold snuff-boxes are not very common, these days. And for another, I noticed it particularly. When Dr. Mawsley took it out of his pocket, I thought for a moment that he was going to offer me a pinch of snuff. But instead of that he took a little white tablet out of it and dropped it in his cocktail. It fizzed as it dissolved, I remember."

"Did you see how many tablets there were in the box?" Jimmy asked.

"I can't say that I did," Forcett replied. "It wasn't full. I daresay there were half a dozen or so in it. Dr. Mawsley remarked that they were quite tasteless, and that he took them as a preventative of dyspepsia."

After some further conversation Jimmy left and returned to Scotland Yard. That afternoon the analyst to whom he had given the tablets came to see him. "Well, Jimmy, I've dealt with your samples," he reported. "I tackled each of them separately, as you asked me to, and found them exactly the same. One grain of papain, made up with a mixture of effervescing salts. Designed as a cure for indigestion, I imagine."

"I'm told that's what they were for," Jimmy replied. "Perfectly harmless, I suppose?"

"Perfectly," the analyst assured him. "You could swallow dozens of them without the slightest ill-effect. I don't know who or what you suspect, of course, but you can take it from me that those tablets wouldn't poison anybody."

But that, Jimmy reflected as the analyst left him, was not altogether conclusive. His mind had been toying with an idea which, as he realized, was very much on the fantastic side. But then the circumstances of Mawsley's death were in themselves fantastic. Any theory which could account for them deserved consideration, however extravagant it might seem.

This was the idea. There was no doubt about the cause of Mawsley's death. The post-mortem had revealed the presence of a lethal quantity of strychnine in his system. A phial of strychnine injection and a syringe had been found beside him in the dispensary. It had, therefore, been assumed that the strychnine found in the body had come from the phial. That Mawsley had administered himself a fatal injection.

The Professor had laid his finger on this point, and had mentioned the use of strychnine by rat-catchers. But there was another possibility. Everyone who had known Mawsley was aware of his trick of dropping a tablet into his beverage. Somewhere in the suite no doubt there was a supply of these tablets from which the snuff-box was from time to time replenished. It was unlikely, since the tablets were quite innocuous, that this supply had been kept under lock and key. At all events, during his examination of the contents of the cupboard in the dispensary, Jimmy had not noticed it.

Now, suppose that someone had inserted among this supply of tablets one and one only of exactly similar appearance, but of very different composition. With strychnine substituted for the harmless papain. Sooner, or later, Mawsley would have dropped it into something he was about to drink. And the beauty of the plan would have been that analysis of all the remaining tablets would show them to be perfectly innocuous. No proof that any one of them had been fatally poisonous would remain.

But there was one obvious and apparently insuperable difficulty. The poisoner could not possibly predict when the fatal tablet would be picked out. Even if he or she had been present when Mawsley dropped it in his glass, he wouldn't have recognized it, for the scheme involved it being indistinguishable from the rest. Had there been anything abnormal in its appearance, Mawsley would most likely have rejected it and chosen another. How then could the phial and syringe have been arranged in the dispensary, presumably as a blind, at the right moment?

Ignoring that difficulty for the moment, it seemed to Jimmy that the idea had its points. It was at all events a more probable technique of murder than lying in wait for Mawsley in the dispensary, overpowering him and forcibly administering an injection. It was certain, for Mawsley was bound to select the fatal tablet in time, and it was probably immaterial to the poisoner when he did so. Nobody else ran any risk of taking it, for it was not to be supposed that Mawsley shared his medicine with his friends.

The identity of the poisoner was bounded by very definite conditions. He, or again she, must have been aware of certain things, and have had certain facilities. That Mawsley was in the habit of dropping tablets in his drink, and where he kept his supply of them. Easy access to this supply, under circumstances which would not arouse suspicion. Ability to secure strychnine, and to make it up into a tablet of the requisite appearance.

It seemed that one person, and one person alone, conformed to these conditions. Violet Hilworth knew that Mawsley took the tablets, and even what they were made of, for she had mentioned papain of her own accord. In the course of her duties she would have learnt where Mawsley kept the tablets, and she could reach the spot without attracting attention. In the dispensary was a stock of strychnine, to which she had legitimate access. Being a qualified dispenser, she was no doubt capable of making up a sufficiently convincing tablet.

But the difficulty could not be shirked indefinitely. Could Violet Hilworth, having by some unexplained means insured that Mawsley should pick out the fatal tablet that evening, have arranged the phial and syringe in readiness? After Jack Thrisk's visit, obviously. And as Jimmy considered the point, a sudden thought struck him. Phepson had not actually seen her leave the suite that afternoon. He merely supposed that she had gone at her usual time, letting herself out. But suppose, with or without Mawsley's knowledge, she hadn't gone at her usual time, but had hidden herself in the bathroom, for example.

Meanwhile, King was carrying out the instructions Jimmy had given him. He made his way to Hammersmith, and walked slowly the length of Briston Road, in which the only spot of brightness was Dr. Hilworth's freshly polished brass plate. Looking about him, King saw on the other side of the road, almost opposite Number 7, an elderly woman sitting at a first-floor window. She was sewing busily, an occupation which did not prevent her keeping a sharp eye on the passers-by.

King looked at her intently, and when their eyes met he broke into a smile of spurious recognition. He knocked at the door, which after a short interval was opened by the woman. "Well, and what do you want?" she snapped.

"Why, you remember me, surely!" King replied heartily. "The copper that used to be on this beat, some years back."

"Well, I do seem to remember your face," she said. "So you've come back to these parts, then?"

King shook his head. "Only for the day, like. I'm on holiday, and thought I'd come along and see how my old friends were getting on. And when I saw you in the window there it all came back to me as if it might be yesterday. But my memory's so terrible bad I can't bring your name to mind."

"And I don't remember yours either," she replied. "My name's Miss Lynn, and I take in mending."

"Why, of course!" King exclaimed. "How did I come to forget that? My name's King, Harry King. Now you know."

"You'd best come in, now you're here, Mr. King," she said. "It's cold standing here." She led him up a flight of bare and creaking stairs to the room with the window overlooking the street. Having asked him to sit down, she picked up her sewing and began to talk, giving her visitor the life history of everyone in the neighbourhood.

"And Dr. Hilworth?" King asked, as soon as he found opportunity. "I see his plate's still up. He had three or four kiddies, I remember. But there, they'll be grown up and left home by now, I daresay."

"There's two of them gone away," Miss Lynn replied. "But the oldest, Miss Violet, is still with her father. Her mother's dead, poor lady. Miss Violet used to work for another doctor in the West End, but he died about a fortnight back and she's been at home since then. I expect she'll soon find another job, though, for she's a clever young lady."

"Why, you don't mean that she worked for Dr. Mawsley, that there was an inquest on?" King exclaimed. "He was a big pot in Harley Street, and it was brought in that he poisoned himself by accident."

Miss Lynn nodded. "Yes, that was the name. I read about it in the papers. It happened on a Tuesday, I remember, for that's the day I go across and see the doctor. I suffer from my ears something terrible, and he washes them out for me. And when I rang the bell that evening it was the younger girl, Miss Hester, who opened the door to me and not Miss Violet as usual."

"Miss Violet used to come home at nights, then, even when she was working?" King inquired.

"Oh, yes, she lived at home," Miss Lynn replied. "She's always looked after the doctor's house for him since her mother died. She'd go out at half past nine and be back at half past four, as regular as clockwork. And it was nearly always her who opened the door to people who called to see the doctor at six, which is his surgery time."

"And it was on this Tuesday, a fortnight ago, that her sister opened the door instead?" King asked.

Miss Lynn nodded. "That's right. But I did see Miss Violet, all the same. When I'd finished at the doctor's, I took along some mending that I'd done for old Mr. Swanton, and stayed chatting there for a while. And as I was coming back I met Miss Violet at the corner here. I said, 'You're late home this evening, Miss Violet,' and she told me she'd stayed up West to do a bit of shopping."

"You were surprised to see her come home so late?" King suggested.

"I don't know that I was surprised. The words just come into my mouth, like, for something to say. And it wasn't all that late, not more than half past seven, I suppose. And Miss Violet's always got a smile and a word when you meet her. Not like some folk, who go about with faces like a wet week-end and can hardly so much as pass the time of day. Why, I can tell you, Mr. King—"

And she wandered away into detailed descriptions of the failings of her neighbours. King listened sympathetically, putting in a word now and then, and eventually took his departure.

13

Jimmy received King's report on Tuesday morning. But by then other matters had arisen to claim his attention. For the next few days he found no time to devote to the Mawsley affair, though it was never entirely out of his mind. On Friday afternoon, finding himself in Kensington with an hour to spare before an appointment, he called on Oldland, with a view to seeking a piece of information.

"Hallo, Jimmy!" Oldland welcomed him. "How are you getting on? Solved the Mawsley mystery yet?"

Jimmy laughed. "Not yet, but I haven't given up hope. That's why I looked in to see you. What can you tell me about Dr. Chilvers, the chap that Phepson met on the stairs and called in?"

"Not a lot," Oldland replied. "I had the curiosity to look him up when I got back from the inquest. It seems that his line is disorders of the stomach. I don't think he's particularly well known, and I shouldn't imagine he's got a very extensive practice. And that's about all I can tell you."

"I see," said Jimmy. "Failing Mawsley, you wouldn't call him into consultation in the case of Sir Matthew Gussage?"

"Good heavens, no!" Oldland exclaimed. "That's not his line of country at all. I tell you, he deals with people's tummies, not their glands. If I had a patient with some form of gastric trouble, I might send him to Chilvers, but there are half a dozen other fellows whose names I should think of first. Chilvers isn't by any means a front rank man, as Mawsley was. And I'm sure I don't know who's going to take his place."

"Somebody will, no doubt," said Jimmy. "And how is Sir Matthew getting on?"

Oldland shook his head. "Not any too well, I'm sorry to say. In fact, he's been going down hill pretty rapidly these last few days. I got a man in to see him, the next best after Mawsley, but he hasn't got Mawsley's grasp of those particular troubles, I can see that. Meanwhile, old Matt's family are sitting round waiting for the end. And I'm afraid that their patience won't be put to any great strain."

"Do you suppose that Mawsley could have saved Sir Matthew's life?" Jimmy asked.

"If he couldn't, nobody else could, I'm sure of that," Oldland replied. "Put it this way, if you like. Mawsley's death has greatly diminished old Matt's chance of survival. While you're here, Jimmy, there's a question I want to ask you. You're an observant sort of chap. Did you notice anything unusual about Priestley when we were there on Saturday evening?"

"Why, no, I don't think so," said Jimmy. "Unless it was that he seemed rather more alert than he sometimes appears. Physically, I mean. There's no doubt that he's vastly interested in this Mawsley affair."

Oldland nodded. "Yes, I know. All the same, between ourselves, I'm rather worried about him. He had a queer attack yesterday, and I don't at all know what to make of it."

"A queer attack!" Jimmy exclaimed. "What sort of an attack? Nothing serious, I profoundly hope."

"Whatever it was, he seems to have got over it all right," Oldland replied. "He was as right as a trivet when I saw him this morning. I'll tell you about it. Between three and half past yesterday afternoon, Harold rang me up in a state of great agitation, asking me to come round at once, as Priestley had been taken ill, and seemed to be paralyzed. I went to Westbourne Terrace at once, and Harold met me in the hall. He told me that Priestley seemed to be getting over the attack, and took me into the study, where I found Priestley sitting in his usual chair, looking very limp. I asked him what was the matter, and he said he thought he'd had a fainting fit. He spoke very slowly, in a hoarse whisper. I told him to move his arms and legs, and found that he could do so, though stiffly, and with some difficulty.

"I sat there watching him for some time, and he got rapidly better under my eyes. Within half an hour his muscles were working normally, and he could talk perfectly well. I insisted that he should go to bed, and he got upstairs under his own steam. He said he would be all right, and wouldn't hear of having a nurse. He told me that he felt rather tired, and that a good sleep was all he wanted.

"Naturally, I wasn't satisfied, but I know Priestley too well to argue with him. It wouldn't have done any good, and might have made him worse. My own idea was, and still is, that he had a slight stroke, but I haven't told him so. As soon as I saw he was comfortable in bed, I went downstairs and got Harold to tell me the whole story.

"This is what he told me. Yesterday morning, Priestley seemed quite normal and in perfectly good spirits. He went out for a short walk after breakfast, and when he came in he went up to his laboratory, where he spent an hour or so. He then came down to the study, and set to work on a scientific paper he's writing, looking up references and dictating to Harold as he went along. Half an hour or so before lunch, he said that a glass of red wine would do them both good. He went down to the cellar himself, and came back with a bottle of burgundy, which he put down by the fire to warm. They went on with their work, and just before the lunch gong was sounded, Priestley took the bottle into the dining-room. You know how fussy he is about wine. Harold heard him draw the cork, and when he went into the dining-room he found the Professor had poured out a glass and was sipping it to test the temperature.

"Harold assures me that at lunch he shared everything that Priestley had. There can't be any question of the wine or anything he ate having disagreed with him. They had soup, roast pheasant and a savoury, and finished the bottle between them. After lunch they went back to the study. Harold says that he noticed Priestley seemed to drag his feet as he walked. They set to work again, and Harold soon saw that something was wrong. Priestley seemed to find difficulty in picking up his books and papers, and his voice got thicker and weaker. At last Harold ventured to ask if anything was the matter, and Priestley whispered it was nothing. The wine he had drunk at lunch had made him feel sleepy, that was all. But in a few minutes he had lost the power of movement altogether, and was unable to articulate. That was when Harold rang me up."

"It doesn't sound any too good," said Jimmy gravely. "Is there anything you can do about it?"

"Precious little, I'm afraid," Oldland replied. "Before I left the house I told Harold to ring me up at once if there was any change. He didn't, but I looked in again soon after seven and found Priestley sleeping as peacefully as a child. When I went round this morning, he was up and sitting in his study, and seemed perfectly normal. He insisted that it had been nothing but brain-fag, and that he didn't want any fuss made about it.

"Whether or not he guesses he had a stroke, I don't know. Anyhow, I talked to him like a Dutch uncle. I told him he had been working much too hard over that confounded paper of his, which not more than half a dozen people in the world would be able to understand when he'd finished it. I said the best thing he could do would be to go away for a change and forget it. Rather to my surprise, he seemed quite docile. He said that he might very possibly find time to go away next week for a few days. And he finished up by saying that he expected to see us there to dinner tomorrow. You'll be there?"

Jimmy shook his head. "I'm afraid not. I've got to go to Wales tomorrow morning for a conference, and I shan't get back till after the week-end. In any case, I haven't anything fresh to tell the Professor about Mawsley."

"You haven't discovered the fourth alternative that he was talking about, I gather?" Oldland suggested.

"I haven't," Jimmy replied. "I haven't begun to understand what he meant. Look here, Doctor. This stroke, or whatever it was, I can't say that I like the sound of it much. You don't think—?"

He broke off, at a loss for words into which to translate his thought. But Oldland interpreted his meaning. "That Priestley's brain is softening? Most certainly I don't. He's got all his wits about him, you may rest assured of that. And if he sets you the problem of a fourth alternative, I'll be bound he knows there must be a solution to it."

On his way to Wales next morning, Jimmy had leisure to consider what Oldland had told him. Had that curious attack from which the Professor had suffered really been a stroke? Could it not have been due to something he had eaten or drunk at lunch? Oldland had dismissed that possibility rather easily, on the ground that Harold had shared everything with the Professor, without exhibiting similar symptoms.

Jimmy was well aware that a detective's training and experience made him apt to suspect crime where possibly none had been committed. Hanslet, for instance, had from the first insisted that murder was the most probable explanation of Mawsley's death. But after making every allowance for this tendency, a faint possibility remained that an attempt, fortunately unsuccessful, had been made to kill the Professor.

How, Jimmy could form no very clear idea. It seemed quite on the cards that a drug existed which would, in small doses, produce the effects observed, and in larger ones cause death. Jimmy knew something about cumulative poisons, arsenic, for example. They could be administered in small doses from time to time, accumulating in the system with an eventual fatal result. Was it possible that the Professor was being subjected to something of the kind? That these mysterious attacks would recur till they ended in his death?

But, if that were so, who could be the poisoner? Not, Jimmy felt quite certain, Harold or any member of the household. Apart from a complete lack of motive, any such an idea was unthinkable. On the other hand, the Professor's reasoning had at various times brought several criminals to justice. A motive of revenge was understandable. Or even a desire to put an end to his reasoning before it could bear fresh fruits.

This last, however, seemed impossible. Nobody but the Assistant Commissioner and the Professor's immediate circle of friends knew that he had taken any interest in Mawsley's death. In any case, how could a stranger have introduced a drug, in such a way that nobody but the Professor would take it? He was not, for instance, in the habit of taking tablets, which might have been tampered with.

Still, Jimmy could not banish from his mind the sinister possibility that an attempt had been made on the Professor's life, and that it might be repeated. What was to be done about it? The Professor, though not a doctor of medicine, had an extensive knowledge of drugs and their effects. His remark to Oldland, that his symptoms had been due to brain-fag, showed that he had no suspicion that an attempt had been made to poison him. He apparently regarded the incident as the merest trifle.

Had he had a stroke, he would himself have realized the fact. And, knowing the danger of a recurrence, he would not have regarded that as a trifle. Was it possible that he had some idea of what had been attempted, but was unwilling to voice his suspicions until he was sure of his facts? That would be just like him, and might explain the unwonted docility with which he had accepted Oldland's suggestion that he should go away for a change. It would be quite natural for him to take himself out of harm's way until he was able to adduce convincing proof of the identity of the poisoner.

If a poisoner existed, and if his act had been intentional, Jimmy felt himself involved in the meshes of an intangible mystery. He began to see a parallel between the cases of Mawsley and of the Professor. It was perfectly certain that the Professor had not attempted suicide, if only for the reason that he would certainly not have bungled the job. It was inconceivable that, although he had been working in the laboratory that morning, he should have poisoned himself by accident. As in Mawsley's case, it was very difficult to form any really convincing theory as to how anyone else could have poisoned him.

Jimmy felt that he was once more faced with that elusive fourth alternative. But what could it be? Some occult power which dogged the footsteps of men eminent in their own line? That, of course, was nonsense. Neither Mawsley nor the Professor were men likely to be influenced by magic arts. And, anyhow, in a case of violent death there could be no fourth alternative. So, during his journey, Jimmy's thoughts revolved in a vicious circle.

The matter which had taken him to Wales demanded all his attention, and it was not until his return to London on Monday afternoon that he was able to return to the subject. His first move was to ring up Oldland, who was able to reassure him. The Professor had had no relapse, appeared perfectly well and hearty, and talked of going away for a change almost immediately. He proposed to be away for a few days, and to take Harold with him.

So far, so good, Jimmy thought. He next sought an interview with a friend of his, Sir Oswald Horsham, the senior official analyst attached to the Home Office. To him he repeated the symptoms which Oldland had described. Feeling that Dr. Priestley would prefer to keep his own secrets until such time as he chose to reveal them, he did not mention his name, giving Sir Oswald to understand that his inquiry was in connection with a case he had in hand. "Now, this is what I want to know," he said. "Is there any poison which would produce those effects?"

"Why, yes," Sir Oswald replied. "There are several vegetable alkaloids which might cause those symptoms. Hemlock, for instance, with which Socrates was bumped off, as you no doubt remember. It produces gradual paralysis, which eventually invades the muscles of respiration, causing loss of speech and finally death. Your man didn't take a fatal dose, I gather, and the symptoms passed off gradually, as they came on."

"Yes, fortunately," said Jimmy. "Would the stuff be easy to come by?"

"The poisonous principle in hemlock is coniine," Sir Oswald replied. "It would be extremely difficult for the ordinary person to get hold of the pure alkaloid. But spotted hemlock is common enough, and cases have been known of its leaves being mistaken for parsley. Anyone could brew for himself a decoction from the leaves, or better still, the unripened seeds of the plant, which would do the trick. I imagine that is very much how the Athenian executioners prepared the draught they presented to Socrates."

That evening Jimmy went to see Hanslet. "Sorry

I couldn't get to Westbourne Terrace on Saturday evening," he said. "You went, of course? How did you find the Professor?"

"Quite well and spry," Hanslet replied. "Although it seems he had a queer sort of attack one day last week. He wouldn't talk about it. He said it was due to overwork, but that it was all over and done with, and wasn't likely to happen again. He's going away for a bit this week, and seems quite excited at the idea. That is, if you can imagine the Professor getting excited about anything."

"He's keen enough when he gets his nose down to the scent of a problem," said Jimmy. "Look here, I saw Oldland on Friday, and he told me that in his opinion the Professor had had a slight stroke. Well, he may be right. But I have an idea that it wasn't a stroke at all, but an attempt at poisoning."

Hanslet looked at him sharply. "Eh!" he exclaimed. "And what makes you think that?"

"My naturally suspicious mind, I suppose," Jimmy replied. "I've no evidence, of course. But one can imagine the existence of a possible murderer. Someone who would sleep more securely in his bed if he knew the Professor was safely out of the way, perhaps. I asked Horsham, and he told me that hemlock would produce the symptoms we've heard about."

Hanslet puffed thoughtfully at his pipe. "Well, it didn't come off, thank goodness," he said. "And as he's going away, your poisoner won't get another chance for a bit. Do you really mean it, Jimmy?"

"I do," Jimmy replied gravely. "And I can't get it out of my head that it's got something to do with the Mawsley affair, and the Professor's interest in it. Where's he going?"

"He didn't say. He merely told us that he was

going to a place where he and Harold could enjoy a few days of leisure and relaxation. And, as I tell you, he seemed particularly pleased with himself. He's got something up his sleeve, I'm pretty sure of that. You're not thinking of having him shadowed, are you?"

Jimmy shook his head. "He wouldn't thank me for that. My idea is that he has a very shrewd notion of what happened to him, and prefers to unearth the details for himself. I can imagine that a personal problem like that would appeal to him enormously. And he'll be on his guard, anyhow."

"And you think that all this has something to do with the Mawsley business," said Hanslet. "Anything fresh there?"

"I'll tell you," Jimmy replied, and he proceeded to recount the results of his investigations during the past week. "So there you are," he went on. "I came to the conclusion that if Mawsley was murdered, the murderer must be Dr. Chilvers, Violet Hilworth, or that chap Glossop. From what Oldland tells us about Chilvers, he seems to be out of the picture, for he couldn't possibly benefit in any way by Mawsley's death. Of Glossop I know little or nothing. But I'd like to know where Violet Hilworth was between four and seven that evening."

"Well, I don't know," said Hanslet doubtfully. "You've got an idea that she may have killed Mawsley, after persuading him to make a will in her favour. After Mawsley's death his wife found this will, and destroyed it, because she didn't want the money to pass out of the family. What about having another chat with her?"

Jimmy shook his head. "She wouldn't tell me anything. I'm pretty sure that she found something among those papers in the safe which caused her considerable annoyance. It may have been the will, but if it was, she can't admit knowing what was in it without at the same time admitting she destroyed it.

"Besides, there's another very powerful inducement for her to hold her tongue. It's true that she likes to consider the medical profession as slightly below her dignity, but, all the same, her husband was a leading light in that profession. The coroner said some very nice things in expressing his sympathy, and the obituary notices have been most complimentary. I haven't a doubt she feels duly gratified.

"Now, even if she suspects her husband may have been murdered, I don't for a moment suppose she's burning with a passion to avenge him. I'm pretty sure that she would look on it as just one of those accidents which will happen, and that one must make the best of. Neither she nor her family will miss Mawsley in the least. I think one might go so far as to say that his death comes as a definite relief to them.

"That being so, her inclination would be to let sleeping dogs lie. She'd be very careful to drop no hint which might implicate Violet Hilworth. Just think of the scandal if the girl were to be arrested for Mawsley's murder! The whole story would come out, revealing the late Dr. Mawsley as not quite the pillar of respectability the world had been led to believe him to have been. His widow won't risk that, I'm quite sure."

"Perhaps you're right," said Hanslet. "Do you yourself believe that this girl killed him?"

"I haven't made up my mind," Jimmy replied. "She had every opportunity, and the necessary knowledge of drugs to enable her to set about it.

If Mawsley was murdered, she heads the list of suspects, in my opinion."

"*If* Mawsley was murdered," said Hanslet. "Now, Jimmy, I'll tell you something. I don't see how it's going to help you much, but you may as well hear it, for what it's worth.

"Last Saturday evening, at the Professor's, we didn't talk much about the Mawsley affair. I got the idea he was keeping off the subject, because he had rather lost interest in it. But Oldland happened to mention that he had seen you the day before, and that you'd been asking questions about Dr. Chilvers. He was very much amused at the idea you seemed to have got into your head, that Chilvers might have killed Mawsley so that Mawsley's patients would knock upon his own door in future."

"I'm bound to consider every possibility, however ridiculous it may seem to Oldland," Jimmy replied.

"Of course," said Hanslet soothingly. "I'm sure the Professor understands that. But he made a rather curious remark. He told us that he was practically satisfied Mawsley had not been murdered. And he went on to say that his death might well have been the indirect result of some incident in his past life."

"And what the dickens do you suppose he meant by that?" Jimmy demanded.

Hanslet shrugged his shoulders. "I haven't the remotest idea. He didn't explain, and changed the subject. Anyhow, I've told you. It's up to you to make what you can of it."

14

Since Jimmy's instructions were that he was to occupy himself with the Mawsley affair only in the intervals between more urgent matters, his investigation was bound to be scrappy. He had to content himself with collecting such items of information as came his way, and piecing them together.

For as yet nothing had transpired to justify official action on the part of the Yard. Jimmy might envisage the possibility that the evidence given at the inquest was incomplete, and that Mawsley's death had, in fact, resulted not from accident, but from homicide. But until he had obtained some evidence in support of that possibility, his hands were tied. His theories regarding a possible murderer were at present merely conjectural, with nothing tangible to support them.

And now, to complicate matters, came the Professor's cryptic remarks. First, that violent death could not always be classified under one of the three headings—accident, suicide, or murder, the latter of course including manslaughter, but that a fourth alternative might exist. Second, that Mawsley's death might have been the indirect result of some incident in his past life. What was a painstaking investigator to make of suggestions like that? Anyhow, the Professor had expressed his opinion that Mawsley had not been murdered. If he hadn't been, his case was no concern of the Yard.

Jimmy was very much inclined to leave it at that. In the light of the coroner's verdict, the Yard would never have taken up the matter, but for the Professor's suggestion. His own investigations had not disclosed a single fact which was in any way at variance with the verdict. According to Hanslet the Professor, having arrived at the conclusion that Mawsley had not been murdered, had lost interest in his death. The only question that remained was the original one, how had Mawsley contrived to make such a fatal mistake? And that was obviously unanswerable.

Such was Jimmy's frame of mind when a message was brought him, "From Supt. Burford, Dorsetshire, to Supt. Waghorn, C.I.D. Met. Police. Begins. Mr. and Miss Glossop now staying Larch Hall. Ends." Jimmy considered this. Interesting, but, after all, only what had been expected. Was it worthwhile making the acquaintance of this fellow Glossop? After this strenuous week-end in Wales, Jimmy was entitled to a day off. This was Tuesday, February 5th. He might take a busman's holiday next day, and go to Dorsetshire. He decided that he would.

He took an early train on Wednesday, and reached his destination about noon. Burford, whom he had notified of his intended visit, greeted him as an old friend. "I thought you might be interested to hear my news," he said. "I can embroider my message a bit. Glossop and his sister arrived at the station here on Monday afternoon. They were met by Mrs. Mawsley's car and chauffeur, and had a lot of luggage with them, as though they meant to pay a long visit. They are now staying at Larch Hall, in the house itself, not at the lodge."

Jimmy nodded. "I think we ought to have a quiet talk with Glossop, but not at Larch Hall. What do you suggest?"

"Easy enough," Burford replied. "I'll ring up my chap at Coverley. Tell him to see Glossop, and ask him to make it convenient to come here this afternoon. If he refuses to, we can take other steps. Will that do?"

"Very well," said Jimmy. "If he jibs, it'll be a sign that he's shy of meeting the police. Go ahead."

Burford rang up the local constable and gave him his instructions. Half an hour later the man telephoned to make his report. Mr. Glossop had seemed very much surprised at the request, and asked what the Superintendent had wanted to see him about. As the constable didn't know, he couldn't tell him. In the end, Mr. Glossop had said that he would be at the police station about three o'clock.

"Excellent," said Jimmy. "We'll interview him together, and hear what he's got to say for himself. I'm particularly anxious to know where he's been these last few weeks. Meanwhile, I hope you'll let me stand you lunch at the Antelope."

A few minutes after three, as Jimmy and Burford were sitting in the latter's room at the police station, a large and expensive-looking car pulled up outside. "That's Mrs. Mawsley's car and chauffeur," Burford remarked. "Yes, and that's Glossop getting out of it. Now we shall see."

"That's rather interesting," Jimmy replied. "He must have told Mrs. Mawsley what he wanted to go to Dorsetshire for. If he hadn't wanted her to know you had sent for him, he'd have come by bus."

Glossop was shown in. He nodded rather superciliously at Burford, then glanced in Jimmy's direction. As he did so he frowned, as though he had a dim recollection of having seen his face before, but could not remember when or where. He seemed to Jimmy more prosperous in appearance than when he had met him previously in the bus. And his manner was one of complete self-assurance. "Well, Superintendent," he said, addressing Burford with dignity. "May I ask what it is you want to see me about?"

"Sit down, Mr. Glossop," Burford replied heartily. "Merely a formality. This is my friend Superintendent Waghorn, from Scotland Yard, who will, I know, be pleased to make your acquaintance."

A light of comprehension flickered in Glossop's eyes. Clearly Mrs. Mawsley had told him of her interview with Jimmy, and now he recognized him as the man he had seen leaving Larch Hall. "How do you do, Mr. Waghorn," he said coldly. "This is not your first visit to this part of the world, I believe?"

The fellow was evidently on his guard, but that couldn't be helped. "We detectives get about quite a lot," Jimmy replied easily. "I should like to ask you a question or two, Mr. Glossop. First, would you mind telling me your full name?"

"Cecil Ernest Glossop," was the reply, given without hesitation. "Single, aged forty-nine."

"Thank you," said Jimmy, as he made a note. "And your address?"

"Why, you know that already!" Glossop replied. "Larch Hall, Coverley, in the county of Dorset."

"I know that you are staying at Larch Hall now," said Jimmy. "But that is not your permanent address?"

The crafty look of which Burford had spoken crept into Glossop's eyes. "I hope it is," he replied smugly.

"We seem to be at cross-purposes," said Jimmy. "What I want is your address before you came to Larch Hall on Monday."

"Then why didn't you say so?" Glossop replied, with more than a trace of insolence. "My sister and I had a flat in London, at Glaven Mansions, Paddington. But we've given it up."

"I see," said Jimmy. "Now, Mr. Glossop, would you be good enough to tell me your occupation?"

"I am a man of independent means," Glossop replied importantly. "Now and then I've taken up teaching, more as a hobby than anything else, being fully qualified to do so. Recently I accepted for a short while a post on the staff of the City Correspondence College, in the department of chemistry and physics."

"Prior to that, you accepted the post of tutor to Mrs. Mawsley's son, Jesse, I believe?" Jimmy suggested.

Glossop, after a glance in Burford's direction, nodded. "That is quite true. I saw Mrs. Mawsley's advertisement, and as I am very fond of the country, answered it. I was at leisure at the time, and after a visit to Larch Hall decided that the post would suit me. I have never regretted the decision, for I found my pupil to be a charming boy, though unfortunately rather delicate. In a very short time I became not only Jesse's tutor, but, if I may say so, a confidential friend of the family."

"A confidential friend of the family," Jimmy repeated slowly. "Including, of course, the late Dr. Mawsley?"

At the mention of Mawsley's name, Glossop's face

clouded over. "Dr. Mawsley and I failed to see eye to eye upon several matters," he replied stiffly. "I was not, of course, prepared to brook any interference on his part. I had been engaged by Mrs. Mawsley, and my salary was paid by her. Besides, Dr. Mawsley showed no concern whatever for the welfare of his family. His visits to Larch Hall were confined to the week-ends."

"You could hardly expect a busy Harley Street specialist to spend more time than that at home," Jimmy remarked. "It was because you had become a friend of the family that you stayed on after your pupil had gone up to Oxford?"

"That, of course, influenced my decision when Mrs. Mawsley asked me to do so," Glossop replied. "But the principal reason for my remaining was that neither Mrs. Mawsley nor I believed that Jesse's physical stamina would enable him to sustain the strenuous life of a University. We thought that if his health compelled him to come down, I could again be of assistance to him in his studies."

"I see," said Jimmy. "But by the time Jesse came down, you were no longer at Larch Hall. On whose initiative did you leave?"

"On my own, of course," Glossop replied loftily. "I am not one to outstay my welcome, or to hold any post on sufferance. I detected signs of friction on my account between Dr. Mawsley and his family. Naturally, I immediately resolved to remove the cause of that friction by taking my departure."

"Most tactful of you," said Jimmy. "You are, of course, aware of the circumstances of Dr. Mawsley's death?"

Glossop nodded. "I am perfectly well aware of them, for I attended the inquest, and heard all the evidence."

"You attended the inquest!" Jimmy exclaimed. "How did you come to do that?"

"At Mrs. Mawsley's request," Glossop replied. "I saw her at the Langham Hotel on the day following her husband's death, and she asked me to do so then."

"You went to see Mrs. Mawsley of your own accord?" Jimmy asked. "How did you know she was staying at the Langham?"

"I called on Mrs. Mawsley at her own invitation," Glossop replied with dignity. "On the Wednesday afternoon she called at Glaven Mansions. I was not at home, being occupied with my duties at the College, but Mrs. Mawsley saw my sister Edith. She told her of Dr. Mawsley's death, of which neither of us had at that time heard. Mrs. Mawsley told Edith that she was most anxious to consult me, and asked her to beg me to call on her at the Langham as soon as I came home. Naturally, being desirous of assisting her if possible, I did so."

"Of course," said Jimmy. "You heard the evidence at the inquest, and the verdict to which it led. Now, Mr. Glossop, you were acquainted with Dr. Mawsley. Can you suggest how he came to make such an extraordinary mistake?"

Glossop's crafty expression became more marked. "I'm not so sure, now, that he did make a mistake," he replied.

"Not a mistake!" Jimmy exclaimed. "Why, you don't think the coroner interpreted the evidence wrongly, do you?"

"Certainly not," Glossop replied. "His verdict was inevitable. But there may well have been secrets in Dr. Mawsley's past life, unrevealed until after his death, of such a nature to impel him to take his own life."

It seemed to Jimmy more than extraordinary that two such different men as Dr. Priestley and Glossop should independently arrive at the same conclusion. "What do you mean, Mr. Glossop?" he asked. "What secrets?"

But Glossop shook his head. "I do not feel at liberty to betray Mrs. Mawsley's confidence," he replied virtuously. "I may say this, however. After my arrival at Larch Hall on Monday, Mrs. Mawsley and I had a long conversation. In the course of this she disclosed to me that while going through her husband's papers, she discovered facts about his life that were hitherto unknown to her. In order to prevent these facts ever becoming known to her children, she destroyed all evidence of them."

This was very much what Jimmy had already guessed. But what had been the nature of this destroyed evidence? "I see, Mr. Glossop," he said. "By the way, did Mrs. Mawsley say anything to you about finding her husband's will while she was going through his papers?"

But this shot missed its mark, for Glossop did not wince. "Mrs. Mawsley told me that she had found no document of the kind," he replied. "And she also told me that you had already asked her that question, Mr. Waghorn."

Jimmy passed this off with a nod. "By the way, you were at Larch Hall the day I saw Mrs. Mawsley, weren't you?"

"I was not at Larch Hall itself," Glossop corrected him. "I did not think it fitting to intrude upon Mrs. Mawsley so soon after her husband's tragic death. I asked Jesse to meet me and to convey my sympathy to his mother. A day or two later I received a letter from Mrs. Mawsley, inviting my sister and me to resume our residence at Larch Hall. Under the circumstances, we felt that we could not do otherwise than comply with her wishes."

Jimmy glanced at Burford. "I do not think that we need detain Mr. Glossop any longer," he suggested.

Burford agreed that it would be quite unnecessary, and politely escorted Glossop to the waiting car, in which he drove off. As he reentered the room, Burford chuckled. "Well, what do you make of that chap?" he asked.

"He's an arrant hypocrite, as anyone can see," Jimmy replied. "He's wangled himself back into his comfortable quarters, and there, quite obviously, he means to stay. I wonder just how much he and Mrs. Mawsley are in one another's confidence?"

Burford shrugged his shoulders. "I shouldn't care to guess. Do you propose to see her again?"

"I don't see the use," said Jimmy. "The pair of them are obviously hand in glove. If I were to ask her now what secrets of her husband's past life she had discovered, she would be quite justified in telling me to mind my own business. It seems to me that the proper way to go about it is to check up on Glossop's movements first. He seems to have been in London at the time of Mawsley's death."

"I think you're right there," Burford agreed. "Glossop had every reason for wanting Dr. Mawsley out of the way. And if he's telling the truth, and Mrs. Mawsley went to his flat, they must have kept in touch after he left Larch Hall."

"The same idea has passed through my mind," Jimmy replied. "Was it a put-up job between them? Or did Glossop work it on his own, knowing that Mrs. Mawsley wouldn't inquire too closely into her husband's death?"

"Mrs. Mawsley is a strong-minded woman," said

Burford. "I don't know that she would have connived at murder in advance, but she might have
condoned it afterwards. And what's this story about
her finding secrets among her husband's papers?
Is that a very cunningly cured red herring?"

"I don't know," Jimmy replied. "When I was talking to her the other day, I felt sure she had found
something. It may be that the secrets she found
were revealed in a will, which she promptly destroyed. Glossop, you noticed, turned the matter
to his own purposes. He led us to believe that Mawsley's secrets were so devastating that they must have
driven him to suicide. I don't believe that, for a
moment."

"Neither do I," said Burford. "Dr. Mawsley wasn't
that sort of man. And there's this point. If his secrets were as lurid as all that, surely he would have
taken care that they died with him. He wouldn't
have killed himself before he had destroyed all in-
criminating papers which would otherwise be found
after his death."

Jimmy nodded. "That's a very good point. He
was at Larch Hall the previous week-end, and so
had every opportunity of doing so. We can take it
that when he left there on the Monday, he had no
intention of committing suicide the next day. In
fact, I don't believe the idea of suicide ever entered
his head. Only an hour or two before his death he
told Forcett that he would go down to Larch Hall
the following week-end and fetch the document he
wanted."

"Yes, you told me about that," Burford replied.
"I say, I wonder! That legacy was from a woman,
wasn't it? To a doctor who had attended her and
saved her life. What if that was said only for appearances' sake, and was not the true reason for

her generosity? Perhaps she was one of the secrets of Dr. Mawsley's past life."

"Well, that's a possibility," Jimmy agreed. "But where does it lead us? He may, long ago, have had an affair with this Mrs. Somerthwaite, of which she retained happy memories, as the legacy shows. But they had completely lost sight of one another since then. She didn't even know that the fascinating Dr. Knapp of her acquaintance had changed his name. Are we to believe that Mawsley was so heartbroken on being told by Forcett of her death that he killed himself out of hand? Forcett didn't mention that he showed any signs of grief whatever. Very much the reverse, in fact. Mawsley was as delighted with his news as a child with a new toy."

Burford laughed. "It does sound a bit far-fetched, when you put it that way. But there's this about it. If Mrs. Mawsley discovered this old affair between her husband and another woman, it might explain her attitude."

"It might," Jimmy replied doubtfully. "But, unless I'm very much mistaken, Mawsley had other and much more recent affairs. It seems to me more likely that she discovered some of them."

"What she discovered after her husband's death doesn't seem of any great importance," said Burford. "How do we know that something didn't come to her ears before he died? You've mentioned that girl who worked for him, for instance. Suppose that Dr. Mawsley and his wife had words that last weekend he was at Larch Hall? That she threatened to take proceedings for a divorce, perhaps. If she had, that would have queered his pitch professionally. On thinking it over, he may have made up his mind to take a quick way out."

Jimmy shook his head. "You knew Mawsley, and I didn't. All the same, you'll never persuade me that he killed himself deliberately. Everything I've heard about him contradicts the possibility. Well, it's time I went to catch that train. If I learn anything interesting about friend Glossop, I'll pass it on to you."

When he got back to London, he made his way to the address Glossop had given. Glaven Mansions turned out to be a down-at-heel block of small flats not far from the Harrow Road. After poking round for a while, Jimmy found a porter, whom he accosted. "Can you tell me the number of the Glossop flat?" he asked.

The porter looked at him surlily. "You're too late," he replied. "They've gone, both of them. Left here on Monday, and the van came to take away the furniture yesterday. And where they've gone to, I couldn't say."

"That's a nuisance," said Jimmy. "I want to see Mr. Glossop particularly. Do you know the address of the place where he works?"

"No, I don't," the porter replied. "All I can tell you is that while he was here he went out at nine regular and came back about six. I've heard that he's a school teacher of sorts, but whether that's right or not I can't say."

"Yes, that's what I've heard," Jimmy said. "He came back about six, you say. Did he go out much after that?"

The porter shook his head. "Not to my knowledge, he didn't. It's true he might have gone when I wasn't about. But, you can take it from me that the pair haven't much money to chuck about, and it's cheapest to stay home of an evening."

Further conversation with the porter was not very enlightening. The only item of interest Jimmy learnt was that the Glossops rarely had visitors. The only one the porter could remember recently was a lady in a posh fur coat who came in a big car one afternoon when Mr. Glossop was out. She must have seen Miss Glossop, for she stayed some little time. That must have been three weeks ago, or thereabouts.

Back at Scotland Yard, Jimmy summed up the Glossop situation. He had evidently contrived from the first to ingratiate himself into Mrs. Mawsley's good graces. Although Mawsley had spent so little time at Larch Hall, he had taken a dislike to this resident tutor. Very probably he saw that he was gaining too much influence over his wife and family. Mawsley had objected to Glossop staying on after Jesse had gone up to Oxford, and had carried his point.

So far all was plain sailing. But after that? Glossop's departure from Larch Hall had clearly not resulted in the breaking off of relations between him and the Mawsley family. Mrs. Mawsley had sought him out on the day following her husband's death. It would be very interesting to know exactly what passed between them at their interview. One thing was certain. Glossop and his sister had found their way back to Larch Hall, for good and all, this time. He had said he hoped it would remain his permanent address. In what capacity he meant to live there hardly mattered.

Looking at the matter from Glossop's point of view, Mawsley had been confoundedly in the way. While he lived, Glossop and his sister could never again hope to enjoy the fleshpots of Larch Hall, for which a flat in Glaven Mansions was a very poor substitute. Glossop's ambitions might have soared even higher. His appearance was presentable enough, and the evidence seemed to show that Mrs. Mawsley had already come to rely upon him to a considerable extent.

His motive, then, was fully apparent. But could he have found the opportunity? Could he have been present in the Harley Street suite on the fatal evening? He had been in London at the time. And he had let slip a possibly damaging admission. He had been employed at the Correspondence College in the department of chemistry and physics. If that were true, and he were qualified for the job, he might be presumed to know something about poisons and their effects.

15

Dr. Priestley's choice of a holiday resort was curious. Certainly the Queen's Hotel at Bradworth, where he and Harold installed themselves, was comfortable, not to say luxurious. But one would hardly have thought that the heart of a busy manufacturing town was exactly the place in which to seek that leisure and relaxation for which he had expressed a desire.

It was on Tuesday, February 5th, that he and Harold reached Bradworth. He had told Harold nothing of his intentions, though it was pretty obvious that his choice of Bradworth had been influenced by the Mawsley affair. After his many years' association with the Professor, Harold knew him pretty well. He was in no way misled, as Hanslet had been, by his apparent loss of interest in the circumstances of Mawsley's death. He was well aware, from past experience, that his employer never relaxed his grasp of a problem until he had arrived at a satisfactory conclusion. And he could tell now, by his behaviour and the shrewd, alert look in his eyes, that the Professor was following a track after his own heart.

One thing which puzzled him was the Professor's attitude towards the mysterious attack which had caused so much concern to his friends. He never alluded to it, or complained in any way of its effects. When they had settled in at the Queen's Hotel, Harold ventured to ask him whether he felt perfectly fit after the journey. The Professor's reply had been enigmatic. "You need have no apprehensions as to my health, my dear boy. The symptoms I exhibited the other day may have seemed alarming, but they have happily left no after effects, and are, I assure you, most unlikely to recur. Their cause may possibly be revealed, before very long."

With that, Harold had to be content. But he began to wonder whether Oldland's diagnosis had been correct. If the Professor had had a stroke, the only thing that could happen before very long to reveal the fact would be a second one. It was perfectly clear that he anticipated nothing of the kind. He was, for some secret reason of his own, thoroughly pleased with himself.

After dinner, on the evening of their arrival at the Queen's, Dr. Priestley sent Harold to find a copy of the Bradworth Directory. He spent some little time turning over the pages of this, and making notes of names and addresses on a slip of paper. This he finally tore into two halves, one which he handed to Harold. "You will find there the addresses of five persons of the name of Knapp," he said. "It is possible that one or more of them may be related to the Dr. Knapp who was in practice here, years ago. I want you to call on them all in the course of tomorrow."

"Very good," Harold replied. "What excuse would you like me to give them for calling?"

"It hardly matters," Dr. Priestley replied. "I can safely leave that to your own ingenuity. You will not, of course, allow any of these people to think that any doubt exists of the correctness of the verdict on Mawsley's death."

Next morning Dr. Priestley and Harold set out, taking different ways. The former took a taxi to an address he had found in the directory the previous evening, Hawthorn Mill. On reaching the building, he found inscribed upon it the designation of the firm to which it belonged, David Mawsley and Son, Ltd. He entered the inquiry office, handed in his card, and asked if he might see the manager, on a matter of historical interest.

After a short interval he was told that Mr. Warburton would see him, and he was shown into the manager's room. Mr. Warburton was a burly Yorkshireman, grey-haired and elderly. He looked from his visitor to the card which had been passed on to him with a slightly puzzled air. Evidently distinguished scientists with strings of letters after their names were rare birds at Hawthorn Mill. But when he spoke it was genially enough. "Let me offer you a chair, sir. I'm very much honoured by this visit, I'm sure. Will you tell me what I can do for you?"

"That is very soon explained," Dr. Priestley replied. "One of my hobbies is to dabble in genealogy. A friend of mine, who is aware of this, has asked me to trace particulars of the Mawsley family, to a branch of which, I believe, this mill belongs."

"Belonged, you should say, sir," said Mr. Warburton. "It's many years now since there was a Mawsley in the firm. But you've come to the right man, all the same, for I've been here ever since I left school as a nipper. I can just remember seeing old Mr. David, who started the business. Wonderful old boy! Lived till he was ninety-five."

"I am indeed fortunate," Dr. Priestley replied.

"No doubt, if you will be kind enough, you can give me the particulars I am seeking."

Mr. Warburton swung his chair round, and laid his hands upon his knees. "It'll be a pleasure," he said. "As I tell you, Mr. David started the business. That was long before my time, somewhere back in the middle of the last century. Quite in a small way, you understand. He was a mill hand himself, and had saved a bit of money and got some of his friends to help him. At least that's what I've heard.

"When I came along, fifty years ago now, the place was just Mawsley and Son, with no Limited stuck on the end. Mr. David was the Mawsley, and Mr. Jesse the Son. It was always the joke among us lads that though we'd always been taught that David was the son of Jesse, it turned out that it was the other way about. Mr. Jesse had a sister, who died before she got married. Mr. David had no other children.

"It was Mr. Jesse I knew best, for Mr. David had retired by the time I came here. And Mr. Jesse was the one to make things hum. He built up the business until it became one of the biggest in Bradworth. He made his pile, as anyone in the town will tell you. But it was a great sorrow to him that he had no son, only a daughter. He'd have liked to have seen a son of his to carry on the business after he'd gone. As it was, when he felt he was getting on, he sold out to a limited company. They kept the name, naturally, but there's no Mawsley left in it now. And I've always said that giving up the mill killed Mr. Jesse, for he died barely a year later."

"He had a daughter, you say," Dr. Priestley remarked. "What became of her?"

"Yes, he had a daughter," Mr. Warburton replied,

with a slow smile. "Miss Wilhelmina. She was called after the Queen of Holland, who visited Bradworth just before she was born. And I've wondered if that put ideas into her head from the start. Anyhow, as she grew up, the mill wasn't good enough for her, no, not by a long way."

Mr. Warburton's smile broadened, and his manner became confidential. "There's no harm in my telling you about it now. Why, even at the time there must have been plenty who guessed what was in the wind, though nothing was said that came to my ears. You see, it was this way. I'd worked myself up till I was assistant manager to Mr. Jesse, and famously we got on together. He'd take me along to the big house he'd built, and treat me just as though I was his own son. And, God bless him, that's what he wanted to make me.

"You see how it was, I daresay. It was Mr. Jesse's idea that if I was to marry Miss Wilhelmina, he'd leave everything to us, and the mill would stop in the family. But that didn't suit Miss Wilhelmina, and I don't know that she's to be blamed. I might have risen to be next below her father, but all the same I was nowt but a mill hand really, as my father and grandfather had been before me. And Miss Wilhelmina was a young lady who'd been to the most expensive schools Mr. Jesse could find for her. High tea wasn't what she wanted any longer, if you understand me."

"Perfectly," Dr. Priestley replied. "I very much appreciate your confidence, Mr. Warburton. I do not think that I need offer you my sympathy."

Mr. Warburton broke into a chuckle. "Sympathy!" he exclaimed. "No, there's no need of that. What should I have done with all that brass? And as for Miss Wilhelmina, I soon got over the loss of her. I married a good, steady, hard-working lass, and I've never had reason to regret it. It was better so, I know that well enough."

"No doubt it was," said Dr. Priestley. "And Miss Wilhelmina. What became of her?"

"She married a doctor," Mr. Warburton replied. "His pockets were none too well lined, I was told, but that didn't matter. He looked and spoke like a gentleman, and that was good enough. Although I went to the wedding, his name's gone clean out of my head. But that's of no consequence, for he changed it to hers when they were married. That was Mr. Jesse's idea, I don't doubt. He wanted to keep his name alive, although he had no son of his own."

"Did Mr. Jesse approve of the marriage?" Dr. Priestley asked.

"It wasn't what he'd intended," Mr. Warburton replied. "But Mr. Jesse was wrapped up in his only child. He wouldn't have stood in the way of her marrying the man she had set her heart on. He was terribly lonely after she'd gone away from Bradworth. All alone in that big house, with nobody but the servants to talk to. You see, very soon after the wedding the doctor sold his practice here and went to London to live. It broke Mr. Jesse up, I do believe. It wasn't so long afterwards that he packed up and sold out. And, as I've said, within the year he was dead."

"What did he die of?" Dr. Priestley asked.

Mr. Warburton shrugged his shoulders. "It's my belief he died because he didn't see the good of going on living. He caught a chill, and didn't seem to have an ounce of fight left in him. Double pneumonia, they called it."

"His son-in-law came here to attend him in his

189

last illness, no doubt?" Dr. Priestley suggested.

"His daughter was sent for, and she was with him at the end," Mr. Warburton replied. "But her husband didn't come down. I daresay he thought that Mr. Jesse had enough doctors looking after him already. There was old Dr. Porter, who's dead now, Mr. Jesse's regular doctor, and two or three others called in, but they didn't seem able to do anything much. Mr. Jesse's son-in-law came down for the funeral, that was all."

"And what about Mr. Jesse's will?" Dr. Priestley asked. "He left everything to his daughter, I suppose?"

"Everything but a few legacies," Mr. Warburton replied. "He remembered me to the tune of ten thousand pounds. For the help I'd given him at the mill here he wrote it down as. But I wondered then and I still wonder sometimes whether it wasn't really because he felt I'd been disappointed, and wanted to make it up to me the best way he could. Mr. Jesse died worth a lot of money. Best part of a quarter of a million, the will was proved at. And that was after he'd settled a whacking big sum on his daughter when she got married."

"She must be a very rich woman," Dr. Priestley remarked. "You have had no communication with her since her father's death?"

Mr. Warburton shook his head. "Not a word, by mouth or letter. I can't even tell you where she's living now. In London somewhere, I don't doubt. I heard in a roundabout sort of way a year or two ago that her husband had become a big pot there. Well, if that's so, she's got what she wanted, I daresay."

Evidently Mr. Warburton had not heard of Mawsley's death, and Dr. Priestley saw no need to enlighten him. In the course of further conversation, he mentioned the name of Mrs. Gunton, but Mr. Warburton did not remember ever hearing it. "If you want the London address, I can give you a tip," he said, as his visitor rose to go. "Whitwell and Reepham, the lawyers, are sure to know it, for they acted for Mr. Jesse, and did all the business when he died. You'll find their office in Duke Street here. No, don't thank me, sir. The pleasure's been mine."

Dr. Priestley left Hawthorn Mill, his fingers numb from Mr. Warburton's hearty grip. But he did not follow up his hint. Although he was inquisitive on the subject of Dr. Knapp, whose very name Warburton had forgotten, it was most unlikely that Whitwell and Reepham could, or at all events would, give him exactly the information he sought. They would certainly ask inconvenient questions as to why a complete stranger should display interest in the affairs of a client of theirs. He returned to the Queen's Hotel, not at all dissatisfied with the results of his expedition.

Although Mr. Warburton had been unable to enlighten him upon the antecedents of Dr. Knapp, he had disposed of one of the tentative theories which Dr. Priestley had formed. He felt tolerably certain that the key to the mystery of Mawsley's death was to be found in the past, and had considered the fact that his father-in-law had died not very long after his marriage. That death might not have been due entirely to natural causes.

Put in its simplest terms his reasoning had been this. It might be assumed with practical certainty that Dr. Knapp had married Wilhelmina Mawsley for her wealth, actual or potential. If he were to establish himself as a specialist in Harley Street he would need considerable financial assistance. It

191

might have been that his wife had been unable to furnish this assistance in full measure until she had inherited her father's fortune. In order to enable her to do this, Mawsley had employed his medical knowledge to his father-in-law's detriment. This action on his part had somehow come to light, and had led to his own death.

But, if Warburton could be believed, and Warburton was at least transparently honest, this theory could be discarded. During his last illness Jesse Mawsley had been attended by a formidable array of physicians, among whom his son-in-law had not been included. Even if he had operated from a distance, incredibly through the agency of his wife, the medical talent assembled would surely have defeated his machinations. Besides, there had been no need for such a drastic step. In Warburton's words, Jesse Mawsley had settled a whacking big sum on his daughter when she got married. This would surely have provided sufficient funds to finance the Harley Street venture.

Meanwhile, Harold had been carrying out his allotted task. The first Knapp on the list Dr. Priestley had given him was the owner of a small tailor's shop, and a youngish man. He made no difficulty about answering Harold's questions, but could give him no help. He was not a Bradworth man, but came from another part of the county. He had taken over his present business five years earlier, and before that had had no connection with the town. None of his relatives had ever been a doctor, and this was the first he had heard of a Dr. Knapp having at one time practised in Bradworth.

The second Knapp was an elderly woman, the widow of a mill foreman. Once satisfied that Harold's call was not in the attempt to sell her something, she became loquacious. She had been born and bred in Bradworth, and the furthest she had ever been from the town was to Blackpool at the wakes. Yes, she did remember that many years ago there had been a Dr. Knapp, but she didn't know that she had ever seen him, and couldn't say what had become of him. He was no relation of her husband's. The only relations he had were farmers in the North Riding.

Harold located the third Knapp in a semi-detached villa on the outskirts of the town. He had some difficulty in gaining access to him, for the door was opened by a pleasant enough but very deaf woman, who seemed unable to grasp what he wanted. However, he was finally shown into the parlour, where an elderly man with a pinched face and wearing glasses was reading a newspaper in front of a gas fire. "This gentleman wants to see you, Mr. Knapp," the woman shouted, as deaf people so often do. "But what about I can't rightly make out."

Mr. Knapp nodded and laid aside his newspaper. "All right, Mrs. Prout," he said. Then, as she left the room, "I'm afraid my housekeeper is rather deaf. Perhaps you will sit down, and tell me what I can do for you?"

"Thank you, Mr. Knapp," Harold replied. "My name is Merefield. I have been asked to make inquires concerning a Dr. Knapp, who at one time practised in Bradworth, and, as you bear the same name, I wondered if you could help me."

"You mean Richard Knapp, I expect," said Mr. Knapp. "What do you want to know about him?"

Harold had prepared himself for this. "Yes, Richard was the Christian name," he replied. "This Dr. Knapp took the name of Mawsley on his marriage.

193

He died in London three weeks ago, and no will of his has yet been found. I am trying to trace any relatives of his who may know something of it."

Mr. Knapp raised his eyebrows. "Richard's dead, is he!" he exclaimed. "I hadn't heard of that. But then it isn't likely that I should, for I haven't had anything to do with him since we were nippers. I'm a relative of his, right enough, for I'm his first cousin. But I can't tell you anything about his will. It's not likely that he left me anything."

"His first cousin," said Harold. "You must have seen a good deal of him when he was in practice here?"

"No, you're wrong there," Mr. Knapp replied. "Richard and I weren't on friendly terms in any way. For one thing, he was a doctor in a black coat, with a brass plate of his own, while I was only a grocer's assistant. And, for another thing, his father and mine had quarrelled over money, many years ago."

"You can tell me something of your cousin's early life, perhaps?" Harold asked politely.

"Why, yes, I can tell you that," Mr. Knapp replied. "Our family had always been in the grocery line. When Richard and I were kiddies, my father had a little shop in the town here, and his father had another in the village of Woolhough, some miles out. It was when my grandfather died that the pair of them got to loggerheads, and after that I didn't see much of my uncle and aunt, or Richard either, for that matter. But I heard about him from time to time, naturally enough. He was the only child, and was always a bright lad, a lot brighter than I ever was, as I'm the first to say. And he made up his mind early that he wanted to be a doctor.

"Well, my uncle and aunt they scraped and saved

194

to have him educated properly. How they managed is more than I can tell you, for the takings of the village shop can't have come to much. Richard got a scholarship, as I heard, and that must have helped a bit. Anyhow, when he'd grown up and passed his examinations he got into the hospital here, as a student at first. And it was while he was there that my uncle and aunt both died. What they had to leave him I don't know, but it must have been precious little.

"And one fine day, why, it must be thirty years ago now, I heard that cousin Richard had bought the practice in the town here of a doctor who had died. I couldn't believe my ears at first, and one evening I slipped round to look at the plate. There it was, right enough. Mr. R. E. Knapp, with a lot of letters after it. Where he got the money from is more than I was ever able to fathom. I didn't ask him, naturally."

"Was he in practice here for very long?" Harold asked.

"Not more than a couple of years or so," Mr. Knapp replied. "Cousin Richard was always a sharp one, with his eye on the main chance. I did hear that he was very well thought of here, as a clever young doctor. People who weren't satisfied with their own doctors were getting in the way of sending for him. But that wasn't good enough for Richard. He wanted to get rich a lot quicker than that. So what must he do but get spliced to the wealthiest girl in the town, Jesse Mawsley's only daughter. We didn't see much of him in Bradworth after that. He'd hardly left the church when he was off up to London, and his missus with him. Well, well, so he's dead now, you tell me. How did that happen?"

"He died very suddenly, as the result of an accident," Harold replied. "By that time he had become one of the leading London specialists. What became of his practice here? He sold it, I suppose?"

"He must have sold it, for it was taken over by Dr. Ramsbury," Mr. Knapp replied. "He had it for some years, then moved on to a larger house. He's not an ordinary doctor now, the sort you send for yourself when you're ill, I mean. He's what they call a consultant, and a pretty big pot in his way, by all accounts. He's one of the heads at the hospital, and he's got a fine house out on the Craven Road."

After some further conversation, in the course of which Mr. Knapp insisted that he should join him in a glass of sherry, Harold went back to the Queen's Hotel. He found Dr. Priestley there, and they went in to lunch together.

16

While they were eating their meal, Harold reported the result of his morning's work. "I'm afraid it hasn't got us much further," he said apologetically. "Although the retired grocer was Mawsley's cousin, he didn't seem to know much about him. They were not on speaking terms while he was here, and after he left they completely lost touch with one another."

"You have done very well," Dr. Priestley replied approvingly. "In an investigation of the type upon which we are engaged one can only expect to proceed step by step. I am particularly struck by what you have learnt of Mawsley's successor in the practice here. Mr. Knapp's description of him suggests that he must be Dr. Lionel Ramsbury, who is well known in the world of physics as well as medicine. I have corresponded with him from time to time, and I seem to remember that his address was Bradworth."

Dr. Priestley paused, and after a thoughtful interval continued. "I shall be glad to take the opportunity of our being here to become personally acquainted with Ramsbury. Apart from our mutual interests, it is possible he may be able to throw further light upon Mawsley's antecedents. He will no doubt be as familiar with my name as I am with his. Will you make it your business this afternoon to ascertain whether he is indeed Dr. Lionel Ramsbury, F.R.S.? A reference to *Who's Who* at the public library should suffice for this. If you find that he is, proceed to get in touch with him. Tell him that I am staying in the town, and should much appreciate an appointment to pay my respects to him."

Harold carried out these instructions and announced the result to Dr. Priestley later in the day. "He is Dr. Lionel Ramsbury. As soon as I had made sure of that, I rang him up. He knew your name at once, and seemed delighted at the chance of meeting you. He told me that the evening was the only time he could be sure of being undisturbed. He suggested that you should dine at his house at eight this evening, and you could have a long talk afterwards."

So it came about that Dr. Priestley made Ramsbury's acquaintance. He was a man in the late fifties, with a friendly and energetic manner. "I'm delighted to meet you in the flesh, Dr. Priestley," was his greeting. "As you may well imagine, I read everything you write, and though I don't always agree with your conclusions, that only adds zest to my interest. Come along, we've just time for a glass of sherry before dinner."

After dinner Ramsbury took his guest to the library, a handsome room lined with books. A bright fire was burning in the grate before which were drawn up two deep and luxurious arm-chairs. As they entered the room Ramsbury switched off all the lights, with the exception of a single shaded reading lamp which radiated a soft, diffused glow. "Men love darkness rather than light," he remarked. "Not necessarily because their deeds are evil, but because they find it more restful to the eyes. Make yourself comfortable, and let's talk."

As it turned out, Ramsbury did most of the talking at first, and Dr. Priestley found himself in the role of an appreciative listener. It was not for some time that he found a suitable opportunity for introducing the subject he had at heart. Then at last, taking advantage of a pause in one of his host's scientific expositions, he put the question. "By the way, you knew Dr. Mawsley of Harley Street, did you not?"

Ramsbury sat bolt upright in his chair. "Mawsley!" he exclaimed. "Why, it's most extraordinary you should mention his name. A young lawyer chap came to see me some weeks ago, asking about him. And the next thing was I saw an account of his death and an obituary notice in the *Lancet.* Poor old Richard! What an extraordinary death for a man like him. You knew him, too?"

"I never met him," Dr. Priestley replied. "But the circumstances of his death were indeed so extraordinary that on hearing them my curiosity was thoroughly aroused. I find it very difficult to explain how a man of his knowledge and experience could have made a mistake of that nature."

"I quite agree with you," said Ramsbury. "Richard, at least when I knew him, was one of those inhuman machines that just can't make mistakes. I can only imagine some sudden and inexplicable failure of the mind."

"The name of the lawyer who came to see you was Forcett, was it not?" Dr. Priestley asked. "He was inquiring about Dr. Knapp?"

"Yes, that was the name I remember," Ramsbury replied. "Decent, smart young fellow, I thought. I'll tell you the whole story. He rang up from somewhere in the town, asking for an appointment, and I gave him one. When he had produced his credentials, he told me that he had heard I had at one time taken over the practice of a certain Dr. Knapp. His firm was trying to trace a doctor of that name. Could I tell him the present whereabouts of my predecessor?

"It struck me that if anything unpleasant was involved, Richard wouldn't thank me for putting the hounds on his scent. So I asked this young chap Forcett why he wanted to trace him. He told me that at one time Knapp had had a patient, Mrs. Something or Other, who at the time had been Mrs. Gunton. This lady had recently died, leaving a legacy in very vague terms to a Dr. Knapp, who had attended her while she was staying in Bradworth.

"I knew then that Richard was the man he was after. Long ago, I knew Mrs. Gunton's parents. They're both dead now. Her father was a mill-owner. And I knew she had been living with them while her husband was abroad in the last war. She had some glandular trouble or other, but nobody seemed able to do much for her till she called in Richard, who was brilliantly successful. He was a clever chap, there's no getting away from that."

By this time Dr. Priestley had learnt that only an occasional comment on his part was necessary to stimulate Ramsbury's conversation. "You knew Richard Knapp, as he was then, before you succeeded to his practice?" he asked.

"Knew him!" Ramsbury exclaimed. "Rather! We were students at the hospital here together, and got quite chummy. As far as one could get chummy with a chap like Richard, that is. Didn't I say he was an infallible machine? Even as a student, he had an uncanny trick of being always right. That was the trouble with him. All head and no heart.

"I haven't the slightest idea who his people were, for he never spoke of them. But I always imagined that he sprang from a pretty humble source, and it was fairly obvious that he had a terrific struggle to make both ends meet. Not that he ever spoke about it, or tried to borrow money from his friends. He was extraordinarily reserved, and didn't make many friends, for that matter. Men were repelled by his aloofness, and were also, I daresay, jealous of his abilities. The brilliantly successful student is rarely popular with his fellows. Men were repelled, I said. But there was something about him that women seemed to find irresistible."

A lump of coal became dislodged in the glowing fire, and a sudden flame leapt up. The light from it shone upon Ramsbury's face, hitherto hidden in the shadows of his chair. Dr. Priestley observed with some surprise that his expression had become one of profound sorrow.

The flame died down, and after a longish pause Ramsbury went on. "There was a girl, a charming and entirely lovable girl. Even after all these years— but there, you didn't come here to listen to romantic bleatings. We're both of us old enough to have got over the follies of our youth. If we haven't, we've nobody to blame but ourselves. I'll tell you the story as objectively as I can.

"You must know that I was a year senior to Richard, and qualified that much before he did. We didn't lose sight of one another, for I got a job on the staff of the hospital. And there I met a young nurse, Doris Leyton. I won't attempt to describe her to you. The scientific mind is in search of facts rather than fancies. I'll only say that she was an orphan of good family, with the sweetest nature I have ever known, and was believed to have a little money of her own. Yes, and she was beautiful, at all events in my eyes.

"You've guessed already that I fell head over ears in love with her. And I flattered myself she liked me. But, like a fool perhaps, I said nothing. The fact was I was tongue-tied, and didn't know how to set about it. Doris wasn't the sort of girl you could make love to at first sight. Besides, a budding house physician hasn't got much to offer in the way of worldly prospects. Usually he's got some years of hard struggle before him. Then there was that rumour, and so far as I was concerned, it was only a rumour, that she had money. I didn't want her to think I was after that. I thought I could safely wait until I had built up some sort of position for myself.

"That was the position when Richard qualified, and in turn got a position on the staff. After that it wasn't very long before I realized I'd lost my chance. Psychology is not my specialty, and a long experience, professional and social, has only served to make the psychology of women more obscure to me. I've been happily married now for many years. But I don't feel that I understand my wife's thought processes any better than I did at the beginning.

"But that's by the way. I told you that Richard was irresistible to women. I'd seen that already when we were walking the wards together. The majority of female patients don't like young students messing them about, but the way they all took to Richard was pathetic. Anyhow, to cut a long story short, Doris fell for him, utterly and immediately. I don't suppose that everybody spotted that as quickly as I did. But I loved her, and I could tell, every time she spoke to him or looked at him, that in the literal sense of the word she worshipped him."

The fire had died down, and in the soft glow of the shaded lamp only the outline of Ramsbury's figure was visible. But by the restless clutching and unclutching of the hand laid on the arm of his chair, Dr. Priestley could tell that the wound of those days would never be fully healed. For a few minutes a deep silence prevailed, before Ramsbury resumed abruptly. "It hurt. It hurt most damnably. But what was I to do? I had no claim on her. I was no more to her than just an ordinary member of the staff whom she happened to like. If she chose Richard to fall in love with, that was no affair of mine whatever. But I wondered, even then, what the end of it all would be. Didn't I say he was all head and no heart? A woman who loved as she so obviously did wouldn't be content with a merely intellectual companionship. I didn't believe she could ever find true happiness with him. And, to put the matter bluntly, it was quite clear that Richard couldn't afford to take a wife. He would surely never marry Doris and live on whatever her pittance might be.

"One supposed that he realized he could hardly do that. You could never tell what Richard's intentions were, he was far too remote and inscrutable for that. But it was quite evident that Doris had made up her mind. We all imagined that they had come to some mutual understanding, and were only waiting to get married until Richard had got on in the world a bit. None of us doubted that he would get on, and that very rapidly."

Ramsbury laughed mirthlessly. "His first step was even more rapid than we had expected. An old G.P. in the town here died, and it became known that his practice could be acquired for two or three thousand or thereabouts. My people were rather keen to buy it for me, but I wouldn't let them. I felt that I wanted the experience of another year or so at the hospital before I launched out on my own. And then one day, Richard said he had a piece of news for me. He was leaving the hospital. I was very much astonished, and asked him where he was going to. He replied that he wasn't going very far, for he'd just bought old Dr. Wilson's practice.

"I didn't ask him where he got the money from. One doesn't venture to put that sort of intimate question to a man like Richard. He may have had friends and relations in the background somewhere that he could call upon. I don't know. Anyhow, he put up his plate, and it wasn't so very long before it began to get about that he was going ahead. There was never the slightest doubt about his ability, and he was lucky enough to bring off one or two rather spectacular successes, the case of Mrs. Gunton among them. He was spoken of as a rising young man. Doris stayed on at the hospital. I expected every moment to hear that she and Richard were going to get married."

Ramsbury leant forward to put some more coal on the fire. "What I did hear was something very different," he continued deliberately. "And I had no difficulty in hearing it, for the news was published with a great flourish of trumpets. An engagement was announced, and the marriage would shortly take place, between Dr. Richard Knapp and Wilhelmina, the only daughter of Jesse Mawsley Esquire. I was never so amazed in my life. Where and how he had met the girl I don't know, but he must have played his cards magnificently. Everybody knew that Jesse Mawsley was the richest man in the town, and that he had nobody to leave his money to but his daughter.

"I'm afraid my reaction was entirely selfish. It seemed to me that the chance I had lost had been miraculously offered to me again. Doris was away when the news broke. How much she knew about it, whether she and Richard had at any time contemplated marriage, I shall never know. Of one thing I am certain, that she was utterly devoted to him. How he could have failed to reciprocate that devotion is more than I can understand. I can only suppose that his ice-cold ambition was proof against any sentiment of affection.

"He asked me to go and see him, and I went. I found him affable enough, but just as distant as ever. He told me that immediately after his marriage, which was to take place within a few weeks, he proposed to leave Bradworth and try his fortunes in London, and wanted, therefore, to dispose of his practice. He knew of the suggestion that had been made at the time of Wilson's death that I should buy it, for I had told him myself, and he thought I might like the first offer now. He also told me that, in accordance with his prospective father-in-law's wishes, he was about to take the name of Mawsley, to which he hoped to add fresh lustre.

"That was the way he talked, and he meant every word of what he said. I never met a man with such a serene confidence in his own destiny. He was certain, even then, that, backed by his wife's money, he had the ability to become one of the world's leading specialists. And not only ability, but ruthlessness. Perhaps it was hardly surprising that during the whole course of our interview, a pretty long one, Doris' name was not mentioned.

"Well, after consultation with my people, I made

him an offer, which he accepted, for the practice. But that, to my eager mind, was only a trifle. I wanted to see Doris and speak to her. What I was going to say I didn't in the least know. Something that would make her understand how ready I was to take Richard's place. I knew within a little when she was due back from her holiday, but the days went by and she didn't turn up. At last I plucked up my courage, and asked the matron as flippantly as I could when we were going to see Nurse Leyton back again. She told me that we wouldn't see her back again. Nurse Leyton had written to her from London, resigning her post on the grounds that she was about to be married. Didn't I think that the hospital staff might like to subscribe to a wedding present for her?"

"Dear me, all this is most extraordinary!" Dr. Priestley murmured. "Who did Miss Leyton marry?"

"I don't know!" Ramsbury replied violently. "I never saw Doris again, after the announcement of Richard's engagement, and only heard of her once more. All I could think of was that my chance had gone again, and for good, this time. It hit me pretty hard, I may tell you. My first impulse was to clear out and seek my bread among strangers. It seemed to me that everyone in Bradworth must be smiling at my discomfiture, though, of course, they weren't really. But I couldn't do that, for the arrangements for my taking over Richard's practice were already made."

"Did I understand you to say that you heard of Miss Leyton once more?" Dr. Priestley asked.

"Yes, once, and that was all," Ramsbury replied. "It was about a year after Richard's wedding. Did I tell you that I acted as best man? By time this I was established in his old practice, and doing fairly well. I don't think the patients found me as brilliant as he had been, but at all events there were no open complaints. I kept up my connection with the hospital, and one day when I was there the matron stopped for a word with me.

"She was a real good sort, that woman, and I fancy had a pretty shrewd idea of what I'd been through. She told me she had had a very nice letter from Nurse Leyton that was. The letter said that her husband had been posted abroad, and that she wouldn't be able to join him for a considerable time. She wanted some occupation till then, so she was going to take a post in a nursing home, somewhere near London. Would the matron be kind enough to send her a reference, and remember her to her friends at the hospital. That was all."

"Do you recollect Miss Leyton's married name, or the address of the nursing home?" Dr. Priestley asked.

"I don't," Ramsbury replied. "All this was thirty years ago, you must realize, and I made no attempt to memorize them at the time. You see, I'd told myself pretty firmly that all that was over and done with, and the sooner forgotten the better. I've heard no more of Doris since that day. But forgetting doesn't come so easily."

A silence followed Ramsbury's words, broken after an interval by Dr. Priestley. "May I ask how much of what you have told me you imparted to Forcett, when he came to see you?"

"As soon as I knew what he wanted Richard for, I told him that the Dr. Knapp he was after was now known as Dr. Mawsley, and was a big noise in Harley Street," Ramsbury replied. "He was very grateful for that information, and asked me for any details of his career, so that he could make identification yet more certain.

"I took quite a fancy to that young fellow. He was so obviously keen and alert, yet very much more human than the average young lawyer. And I liked his manner, the quiet deference of a younger man towards his elder. I'll go so far as to say that I felt there was some queer sympathy between us, as though I had known him all his life, though, of course, as a matter of fact, I'd never set eyes on him before.

"That being so, I was ready enough to tell him what I could. Much what I've told you, but perhaps not in such wearisome detail. I gave him a sketch of Richard's life in Bradworth, as I knew it. I didn't clothe the bare bones with the flesh of my experience, of course. It wasn't necessary. All he wanted was a few facts which he could apply as a test to a legatee's identity. I told him, for instance, that Richard had been a student at Bradworth Hospital, and subsequently for a short time a house-physician there. Also that he had married Jesse Mawsley's daughter, rather to the astonishment of his friends, who had expected him to marry one of the nurses. But I refrained from telling him of my own interest in that particular nurse.

"He was a whale for facts, was that young man. I found myself subjected to a searching but extremely courteous cross-examination. He wanted names and addresses of everyone concerned, and the date of any incident I mentioned, all of which he made a note of. He was most apologetic about giving me so much trouble, but as he explained, he had to be morally certain that Dr. Mawsley was indeed the person referred to in the will before he approached him. And I'm bound to say he was extraordinarily grateful. But, I say, Dr. Priestley, I'm boring you with all this long-winded reminiscence."

"On the contrary," said Dr. Priestley. "You have entirely captured my interest. I believe that in order to understand the circumstances of Mawsley's death, it is necessary to have a clear picture of his life. Did you keep up your friendship with him after he left Bradworth?"

"We corresponded for a while," Ramsbury replied. "Almost entirely on professional matters. His patients that I had taken over, and so forth. But it soon petered out, and since then the only news I've had of him has been at second-hand. I know, of course, that he had climbed to the top rung of the ladder. I gather, Dr. Priestley, that you know the details of his extraordinary death. I should be very glad to hear them."

Dr. Priestley replied to this request with a succinct account of the matter. "Well, that's amazing!" Ramsbury exclaimed when this had come to an end. "The infallible machine must have slipped a cog at last, for Richard was the last man in the world to commit suicide. There could be no suspicion that he was murdered?"

"I hardly think so," Dr. Priestley replied. "The question has been raised, but any theory of murder involves, in my opinion, too many improbabilities. I am perfectly certain that Mawsley administered the fatal injection with his own hand."

17

It was long after midnight when Dr. Priestley got back to the Queen's Hotel. Next day he remained in bed for breakfast, and did not get up until just before lunch. After that meal he dictated to Harold some notes on the information he had derived from Ramsbury in the course of the previous evening.

"We have now a fairly complete outline of Mawsley's earlier life," he remarked as he came to an end. "I think we may accept Ramsbury's statements as correct, for his interest in Nurse Leyton has engraved events upon his memory. As we have no clue to Miss Leyton's present name or whereabouts, we cannot endeavour to trace her. But it would be interesting to know more about her friendship with young Dr. Knapp, and whether they remained in communication after their respective marriages."

"Mrs. Mawsley might be able to tell us something about that," Harold suggested.

"She might be able to tell us, but I think it most unlikely that she would consent to do so," Dr. Priestley replied. "We have heard Jimmy's account of his conversation with her. I am inclined to imagine that until her husband's death she remained unaware of the existence of Miss Leyton as, being ignorant of her married name, we must continue to call her. After all, her friendship with Dr. Knapp would not be common knowledge outside the circle of the hospital staff, with which, presumably, Wilhelmina Mawsley had no contact. And it may be that on going through her husband's papers, Mrs. Mawsley found evidence of his early affections."

"A will which, in her opinion, was rather too favourable to Miss Leyton?" Harold asked.

Dr. Priestley nodded. "Very possibly. Her manner as reported to us very strongly suggests that she made some discovery regarding her husband which she was not prepared to impart. Perhaps no more than a letter signed Doris, but none the less sufficiently revealing. But that is really beside the point. Her discovery was not made until after her husband's death, and cannot, therefore, have influenced the event itself.

"A more profitable field of speculation would appear to offer itself. Ramsbury could hardly be described as reticent, or in any way sparing of his confidences. To me, a personal stranger, he was ready to reveal a page of his past life of which the bitterness still remained. He took a fancy to Forcett, with whom he conceived an immediate bond of sympathy. How much did he tell him, and how much did Forcett's native shrewdness enable him to deduce from what Ramsbury did not say?"

"Forcett can't have been vastly interested in a romance which must have come to an end before he was born," Harold ventured.

"Not in the romance as such," Dr. Priestley agreed. "But his duty was to learn all he could about a Dr. Knapp. He subjected Ramsbury to cross-examination, with a view to ascertaining all possible details. His intention was, no doubt, to use these details as the foundation of questions to be subsequently put to Mawsley. If he answered them correctly, his identity with Dr. Knapp would be established.

"I cannot ignore the possibility that herein lies the explanation of Mawsley's death so soon after Forcett's interview with him. Quite unexpectedly this complete stranger had recalled to his memory a passage from the past which he had done his best to forget. I do not say that he was driven to commit suicide by remorse. But I do contend that Forcett's conversation may have contributed directly to his death. Was it merely because he wished to concentrate on the terms of the legacy that he gave orders he was not to be disturbed?

"However, this at the moment is little more than pure conjecture. It would be profitable, I think, for you to make Forcett's acquaintance. I see no reason for employing any subterfuge, though I should not approach him directly on the subject of Mawsley. We have to bear in mind the professional reticence of a lawyer. I seem to remember that his firm, Perring and Company, have been concerned in more than one notable criminal case. You might tell Forcett quite frankly that you are interested in criminology and are seeking information. With this opening, it should not be difficult for you to introduce Mawsley's name. From that point, I can safely leave matters to your discretion. If you find it convenient to introduce my name, you may do so."

Dr. Priestley and Harold returned to London on the following day, Friday, and Harold immediately set to work to find some plausible pretext for getting in touch with Forcett. Among the contents of the bookcases in the study were many volumes of law reports, going back several years. Harold ran through these, picking out the names of the various

212

firms of solicitors mentioned in them. At last he found a reference to Perring and Company. They had acted for the plaintiff in an action for damages brought against a firm on whose premises the plaintiff had met with an accident through failure of an elevator. The proceedings as reported were in no way exciting, and had taken place three years previous. But the pretext would serve.

On Saturday morning Harold rang up Perring and Company, and asked to be allowed to speak to Mr. Forcett. "I hope you will forgive this approach by a complete stranger, Mr. Forcett," said Harold. "My name is Merefield. I am in search of information on a matter of personal interest, and I believe you could give it to me."

"I shall be glad to help you if I can, Mr. Merefield," Forcett replied. "What is it about?"

"Well, it's rather too long a story to tell over the phone," said Harold. "And I don't want to intrude on your time, as I know you must be very busy. Could we meet after office hours, one day next week?"

"Why, yes," Forcett replied. "I am nearly always at home in the evenings, from nine o'clock onwards. If you care to call on me then, I shall be very pleased to see you. My address is 21 Paston Street, off the Fulham Road."

Having ascertained that it would be convenient for him to call soon after nine on Monday, Harold rang off. He read up the meagre details of the elevator case, and made himself familiar with the names of those concerned.

That evening, Dr. Priestley's usual guests assembled for dinner. Naturally their first inquiries concerned his holiday, whether he had enjoyed himself, where he had been, and if he felt perfectly fit again.

But the Professor was evasive. He and Harold had spent a very pleasant time. They had found a place where they had been thoroughly comfortable, and had made several interesting acquaintances. As to his health, it had never been better. The incident of the previous week had been a trifle, best forgotten.

Mawsley's name was not mentioned until they were sitting in the study after dinner, when it was introduced by Oldland. "Have you given any more thought to that queer business of Mawsley?" he asked.

"I have not entirely dismissed it from my mind," Dr. Priestley replied. "Perhaps the Superintendent has some further information which he may care to impart to us?"

Jimmy replied to this invitation with an account of his interview with Glossop. "He's got what he's after so far," he went on. "He made no secret of the fact that he expects Larch Hall to be his permanent address in future. Whether he means to rest content with establishing himself there as the friend and protector of the family, is more than I'm prepared to say. He certainly seems to be very much in Mrs. Mawsley's confidence."

"Did he bump off the doctor so as to be able to marry her?" Hanslet asked. "It doesn't seem likely that Mrs. Mawsley, who you tell us is in her own estimation a very fine lady, would marry a chap who, after all, is no more than her son's tutor. If she thought of marrying again, she'd fly higher than that, surely."

"Wait a minute," Jimmy replied. "A couple of days ago I went to the City Correspondence College, and had a chat with the Principal, as he calls himself. He wasn't a bad sort of a chap in his way, and told me that he had known Glossop for a good many years. It was he who saw Mrs. Mawsley's advertisement for a tutor, and put Glossop on to it. He also told me that though Glossop was driven to live by his wits, he came of very good family, and that his grandfather was an Earl."

Oldland chuckled. "That answers your objection, Hanslet," he said. "Mrs. Mawsley, the manufacturer's daughter, raises herself in the social scale by marrying a doctor, who, assisted by her wealth, becomes a well-known specialist. But that doesn't satisfy her for, after all, a doctor, however eminent, is still only a professional man. So she connives at the murder of her husband in order to be free to marry the grandson of an Earl. Why, it's good old-fashioned melodrama! What do you say, Priestley?"

"I can hardly claim to be an authority upon melodrama," Dr. Priestley replied. "But I hardly think it likely that Mrs. Mawsley connived at her husband's death, or, for that matter, that this man Glossop murdered him. What I find most interesting in his conversation with the Superintendent is his reference to Mrs. Mawsley's discoveries after her husband's death. Facts about his life that were hitherto unknown to her. That was Glossop's expression, was it not?"

"Those were the words he used," Jimmy replied. "I daresay he was speaking the truth, for when I saw Mrs. Mawsley I got the impression she had found something. But I'm pretty sure she'd never reveal what it was. Glossop said that she had destroyed all evidence of the secret."

"And yet it may be that the secret led indirectly to Mawsley's death," said Dr. Priestley dreamily. "Though I do not for a moment suppose that Mrs. Mawsley realizes that. I feel quite sure that she was guiltless of any attempt to conceal essential facts. Facts, I mean, which in her view might have led to her husband's death."

"Well, I don't know," Hanslet objected. "If she destroyed his will that is surely concealing an essential fact."

"You do not quite follow my train of thought," Dr. Priestley replied. "If the provisions of that will were such that they provided some person with a motive for contriving Mawsley's death, the document might have pointed to that person's identity. In which case I should agree with you that its destruction by Mrs. Mawsley amounted practically to collusion on her part. But here we are on very speculative ground. We do not know that any will existed. Indeed, from what we have been told, and particularly from the remarks of Mr. Weedon, it would seem quite possible that Mawsley never made one. My personal opinion is that between his death and any hypothetical will he may have made, there is no connection whatever."

"You choose to be obscure, Priestley," said Oldland. "Can't you give us your considered opinion in plain words?"

Dr. Priestley smiled faintly. "I cannot do that," he replied. "I will not deny that I have arrived at a considered opinion. In asking me to express this in plain words, you no doubt expect me to describe in detail the influences which led Mawsley to administer to himself a fatal injection of strychnine. That I cannot yet do. I can comply with your request in this form. My opinion is in agreement with the coroner's verdict. Mawsley's death was due to an error on his part. But I would add a rider to the effect that he was led to commit this error by circumstances beyond his immediate control."

Oldland shrugged his shoulders. "You seem to take a perverse delight in deepening the obscurity of the fog," he said. "I can only suppose you to mean that somebody had been monkeying with the injection."

"That is far from my meaning," Dr. Priestley replied quietly. "I feel sure that we may dismiss from our minds any such suspicion. And, at the same time, the hypothesis that any unauthorized person entered the suite. Mawsley's death was due directly to his own mistaken act."

Dr. Priestley paused, then turned to Jimmy. "I owe you my apologies, Superintendent. When I first considered the matter, I came to the conclusion that the circumstances of Mawsley's death might have been such as to justify the intervention of the police. That, in fact, he might have been deliberately murdered, or at least have intentionally committed suicide. I no longer believe in the likelihood of either of these alternatives. The police, therefore, may rest content with the coroner's verdict, as they would have done but for my ill-judged intervention. I can only repeat my apologies, which I trust you will convey to the Assistant Commissioner."

"Well, that's that," said Hanslet. "The case is closed, then?"

"So far as any criminal investigation is concerned, the case is closed," Dr. Priestley replied. "We need discuss it no further."

On Monday evening Harold set out to call on Forcett. He found 21 Paston Street to be a draper's shop, at that hour closed and shuttered. By the shop was a side door, with a bell-push beneath which was a small brass plate with the name G. L. Forcett.

Harold rang the bell, and very shortly heard footsteps descending a stairway within. The door opened, to reveal Forcett. "Mr. Merefield?" he asked. "I'm glad you've come along. Come up to my rooms, and I'll see what I can do for you."

He led the way up the stairs to the second floor, which was equipped as a residential flat, and showed Harold into a comfortably furnished room in which a fire was burning. "This is my hermit's cell," he said. "I'm not married, and don't keep a resident housekeeper, so I'm all alone. Sit down, and we'll talk."

"It's very kind of you, Mr. Forcett," Harold replied. "I'll explain myself. I am employed as secretary by Dr. Priestley, of whom you may perhaps have heard. My employer takes a keen interest in any unusual incident of which he reads reports. It is one of those I want to ask you about."

"I've heard of Dr. Priestley as a distinguished scientist," said Forcett. "Science is one of the things I dabble in, besides the law. I shall be very flattered if I can help him in any way. What is the incident?"

"The Professor has been devoting some attention to the case of a Mr. Hellifield, who was injured in an elevator accident some time ago," Harold replied glibly. "On looking up, at his request, the report of the action for damages brought by Mr. Hellifield, I found that your firm had acted for him."

Forcett nodded. "We did. But may I ask why you applied to me rather than to one of the partners?"

"Because I didn't know their names," Harold replied. "But I knew yours, for you see I'd heard about the inquest on Dr. Mawsley, who died a little while ago, and I saw that Mr. Forcett, of Perring and Company, had given evidence. So when I rang up, I asked for Mr. Forcett. You don't mind, do you?"

"Not in the least," said Forcett. "It has led to our meeting. So Dr. Priestley is interested in Mr. Hellifield's action for damages? I wasn't actively concerned in the case, but so far as I remember, it was quite a hum-drum affair."

"The Professor is always on the look-out for possibilities that haven't occurred to other people," Harold replied. "He's been wondering whether the accident was as simple as it looked. Whether the machinery of the elevator might not have been tampered with, for instance."

Forcett smiled. "Dr. Priestley appears to have an inquiring mind," he said. "After the accident the elevator was examined by engineers, who reported some gadget or other had broken as the result of a hidden flaw in the metal. It's all coming back to me, now you mention it. I'll tell you the story, as I remember it."

He proceeded to do so, while Harold listened with every appearance of interest. From this the conversation drifted to other cases in which Perring and Company had been engaged. "The firm's activities cover a very wide field," Forcett went on. "I'm only an articled clerk at present, though I'm promised a partnership when I've passed my final exams this year. Then, of course, I shall devote myself to one particular branch. Meanwhile, I'm expected to deal with anything that may crop up. If you look at my library, you'll get some idea what that means."

Harold got up and glanced at the books which filled several wide shelves. "My word!" he exclaimed. "I'd no idea a lawyer had to read all that. You've got quite a collection of books on forensic medicine, I see. I recognize most of them, for that's a subject in which the Professor has always been interested."

"Yes, that's how I come to know his name," said Forcett. "I try to keep abreast of current scientific literature. Forensic medicine is the line I shall concentrate upon, when I get the chance."

Harold sat down again. "I mentioned the inquest on Dr. Mawsley just now," he remarked conversationally. "The Professor and I heard all about it, for a friend of ours attended. It seems amazing that a man like that should make such a mistake."

"It was," said Forcett dryly. "I feel I have a peculiar interest in the matter, as I was the last person to hold any conversation with him. And that was only by the merest chance. The senior partner gave me the job of tracing the Dr. Knapp mentioned in Mrs. Somerthwaite's codicil, and that's how I came to meet him."

"It must have been a pretty difficult job," said Harold artlessly. "How did you set about it?"

"By going to Bradworth and asking questions," Forcett replied. "I learnt that a Dr. Knapp had at one time practised there, that some thirty years ago his practice had been taken over by Dr. Lionel Ramsbury, who still lived in the town as a consultant. I was granted an interview with Dr. Ramsbury, and found him most illuminating, far more so than I had any reason to expect. He told me sufficient details about Dr. Knapp's past life to make my subsequent course perfectly plain sailing. And as soon as he told me that Dr. Knapp had taken the name of Mawsley and was now established in Harley Street, any difficulty in locating him was removed."

"You had, of course, to make quite certain that Dr. Mawsley was your man," Harold suggested.

"And for that purpose I suppose you asked Ramsbury about his early days in Bradworth. I wonder,
now!"

"I certainly asked him a few questions with a view
to confirming his identity," Forcett replied. "What
do you wonder?"

"Whether, in the course of those questions, you
inadvertently touched upon a sensitive point," said
Harold. "And that he was so upset in consequence
that he made that extraordinary mistake, not knowing what he was doing."

"That almost amounts to the suggestion that I
drove him to suicide," Forcett replied lightly. "It's
quite true that he didn't seem anxious to dwell on
his early days, when he was an unknown man. He
liked to forget all that. But I can assure you that
when I left him he displayed no intention whatever
of committing suicide."

Shortly after this Harold left Forcett's rooms and
returned to Westbourne Terrace, where he found
Dr. Priestley waiting up for him. "He doesn't seem
to think much of the idea that he may have said
something to disturb Mawsley's peace of mind," he
said, when he had reported his conversation with
Forcett.

"Perhaps not," Dr. Priestley replied. "I certainly
agree with him it is highly unlikely that anything
he said would have driven Mawsley to suicide.
Everything we have heard tends to suggest that
Mawsley had every motive for prolonging his life
rather than terminating it. The fourth alternative
of which I spoke the other day is now, I believe,
discernible. You have done very well, almost too
well, perhaps."

After a long interval of silence, which Harold did
not venture to break, the Professor went on, rather

more briskly. "I am beginning to share Ramsbury's interest in this young man, and should like to meet him. As you tell me he is a student of forensic medicine, we already have a common bond of interest. Will you write him a note, Harold? Suggest to him that as he is acquainted with my name, he might care to meet me in person. With that end in view, ask him to name any evening this week, with the exception of Saturday, that it would be convenient for him to dine here."

18

Harold carried out these instructions, and in due course received a politely worded reply from Forcett. He would be honoured to accept Dr. Priestley's kind invitation for Thursday.

The Professor, on being told of this, expressed his satisfaction. "Excellent!" he said. "We should have a very pleasant evening. No doubt the subject of Mawsley's death will crop up in the course of it. Oldland, I think, should be present. It was he who first aroused our interest in the matter, and he is our authority for what took place at the inquest. Will you ring him up and invite him?"

"Very good," Harold replied. "And what about Hanslet and Jimmy?"

"Certainly not!" Dr. Priestley exclaimed sharply. "They will no doubt be here on Saturday, as usual."

On Thursday evening the Professor's guests arrived at the appointed time. Harold introduced Forcett, and after an interval for a glass of sherry, the party went in to dinner. During the meal Dr. Priestley led the conversation on to various scientific matters. Forcett's remarks revealed considerable technical knowledge on his part, but his manner was courteously deferential, and he did not thrust his own ideas upon his host or Oldland.

After dinner the four adjourned to Dr. Priestley's study, where Forcett refused Harold's offer of a cigarette. "Thanks very much, but I very rarely smoke," he said. "I seem to be one of the very few people of my generation who haven't acquired a craving for tobacco. I'm very often considered a crank in consequence."

"A very wise crank," Oldland remarked, as he took a cigarette from the box Harold handed to him. "I smoke like a chimney myself, and it doesn't do me any good. Neither nicotine nor alcohol are really necessary to the human system, but the effects of both are very pleasant. I should hate to have to go without them."

He poured himself out a whisky and soda, and the company arranged themselves, Dr. Priestley in the chair behind his desk, with Harold beside him, Oldland and Forcett in arm-chairs before the fire. "I hope you will forgive a personal question, Mr. Forcett," said the Professor. "How did it happen that you, with your obvious scientific tendencies, took to the law as a profession? Was it a matter of heredity?"

"I'm only an amateur of science, sir," Forcett replied deprecatingly. "The law wasn't in my blood, for so far as I know there has never been a lawyer in my family. But even as a boy it struck me as offering a promising career, and for some reason it appealed to me. So when the opportunity cropped up, I jumped at it."

"Wise man," Oldland muttered from the depths of his chair. "The law's a lot more profitable than medicine, for instance, I'll wager."

"I'm not so sure," Forcett replied. "I've come across some very prosperous doctors lately, in the course of my duties. In my case the opportunity of becoming a lawyer came almost by chance. Among my mother's friends was the then senior partner in the firm of Perring and Company. Old Mr. Perring, we called him, to distinguish him from his son, who became the head of the firm when his father died some years ago. While I was still quite a lad, old Mr. Perring made my mother an offer to take me into the office as a junior clerk. To learn the trade, as he put it. As soon as she told me of this, I jumped at it, as I say, and I've been with the firm ever since."

"In which, I understand, you are shortly to become a partner," Dr. Priestley remarked. "Well, Mr. Forcett, I congratulate you. But I cannot help wondering how, in the course of your legal studies, you found time to devote to scientific pursuits?"

"That again was due to chance, which seems to have played a large part in my life," Forcett replied. "If my mother had never met old Mr. Perring, I might never have become a lawyer. And if, shortly after I joined the firm, it had not become concerned in an elaborate dispute concerning patent rights, I might never have acquired an interest in science. It's the way things happen, I suppose.

"You may wonder how an important case like that should affect a humble junior clerk. It was this way. In order to understand properly the points at issue, some elementary knowledge of chemical and other scientific processes was necessary. Since, as it happened, everyone in the firm, with the exception of myself, had enjoyed a classical education, they were unaware of even the rudiments of these matters. Old Mr. Perring said that as I was the latest from school, it wouldn't do me any harm to go back there. So I spent six months attending classes in the necessary subjects, in the course of which I acquired a keen interest in them."

"You, therefore, devoted yourself to the study of forensic medicine?" Dr. Priestley suggested. "Perceiving this to be one of the subjects in which science and the law converge?"

"Not immediately, sir," Forcett replied. "There was an intermediate step. When, a year or two later, one of the firm's clients, a manufacturing chemist, got at loggerheads with one of his competitors, old Mr. Perring decided that, as I had acquired some knowledge of chemistry and physics, I was the man to unravel the details. He had, I fancy, no very clear conception of scientific terminology, or of the differences between chemistry, physics and pharmacy. It appeared to him, no doubt, that since a chemist dispenses physics, his business must necessarily involve the practice of both physics and chemistry."

Oldland laughed. "It's a trap lots of people fall into. You didn't disabuse the senior partner?"

"I did not," Forcett replied. "He wasn't the sort of person you could argue with on a subject like that. Instead, I spent a month in our client's establishment, where I took an intensive course of pharmacy under his chief assistant. It was this experience which showed me how valuable a knowledge not only of forensic medicine as such, but of theoretical chemistry and physics as well, might be to a lawyer."

"That has been proved before now," Dr. Priestley remarked. "I need only mention Sir Edward Marshall Hall's brilliant defence in the Seddon case. You say a theoretical knowledge, but it usually happens that theory leads to practice. And laboratory work of any kind is most fascinating. Have you ever indulged in it?"

"Only on the most humble scale," Forcett replied. "I have collected from time to time enough apparatus for me to follow some of the simpler tests described in the textbooks. I have no ambition to become an expert myself. But in my opinion a lawyer should be able to understand what the experts are talking about, especially where medical evidence is involved."

"As, for instance, in Mawsley's case," Oldland remarked. "I've seen you before, Mr. Forcett, though you aren't likely to have picked me out of the crowd. I was at the inquest, and heard all the evidence, yours included. I suppose it was because of your contact with the world of medicine that your firm set you to trace this Dr. Knapp?"

Forcett smiled. "Partly that, I daresay. But mainly because nobody else in the office had the time to spare just then."

"And you discovered that Dr. Knapp had become famous as Dr. Mawsley," said Dr. Priestley. "He must have had exceptional ability to rise from the position of an unknown general practitioner to that of a specialist of world-wide reputation."

"No doubt, sir," Forcett agreed dryly. "But he would never have got on as he did but for other people's money."

"Mrs. Mawsley, I understand, is a rich woman," Dr. Priestley remarked. "But Mawsley must have had resources of his own. He was able to buy a practice in Bradworth before he met his future wife, was he not?"

This apparently simple question seemed to cause Forcett some difficulty, for he hesitated frowning quite a while before he replied. "So I have been given to understand, sir. Of course it may be that Dr. Knapp had more funds at his disposal than his friends believed. Or possibly our late client, Mrs.

Somerthwaite or her parents may have helped him. The wording of her codicil shows how high an opinion she had of him."

Something about this answer made it ring, to Dr. Priestley at least, not quite true. But he passed it over, and went on. "So you made an appointment with Dr. Mawsley, and called on him. You had never met him before?"

"Never!" Forcett exclaimed almost violently. "I may have heard his name, for I suppose most people had, but it didn't impress itself on my memory in any way. I certainly never set eyes on him until I was shown into his consulting-room that evening. We were complete strangers to one another."

"Yes, I am quite sure of that," said Dr. Priestley. "And what impression did this complete stranger make on you, may I ask?"

"Not at all a favourable one," Forcett replied deliberately. "I don't mean that I was offended at the coldness of his reception of me, for that was only natural. He could not have been expected to extend a particularly warm welcome to the representative of a firm of solicitors quite unknown to him. In fact, it was the reverse of the medal that revolted me. His sudden switch over to excessive geniality when he heard about the legacy. He was so excited, yes, I think that is the very word, that it never occurred to him to express the slightest sentiment of sorrow at the news of Mrs. Somerthwaite's death. In his eyes she was merely a patient, remembered only on account of the success he had achieved in the treatment of her case."

"While she, for her part, had always remembered him with gratitude," said Dr. Priestley. "You gained the impression that Mawsley was a man without heart, incapable of any genuine affection. And this, to use your own expression, revolted you. Yet Mawsley was married, and the father of a family."

Forcett seemed to feel the warmth from the fire, for he took out his handkerchief and mopped his face with it. He made no reply to this last observation, and Dr. Priestley continued. "The father of a family. Do you know, Mr. Forcett, I am inclined to believe that in that fact is to be sought the clue to the extraordinary circumstances of Mawsley's death. A full knowledge of his relations with women, before and after his marriage, might well be revealing. I am something of a student of human nature, as you may perceive."

Oldland was becoming conscious that he was the witness of a fencing match, the purpose of which he could not perceive. At all events, there was a growing tension in the atmosphere, which he thought it would be as well to relieve. "Who was it who said that the proper study of mankind is man?" he asked, with rather forced levity.

Forcett seemed to welcome this, as a hard-pressed fencer would a breathing space. "Pope, I believe," he replied. "I came across the quotation in a crossword puzzle the other day, and had to look it up. You speak of Mrs. Mawsley, sir," he said to Dr. Priestley. "I have met her only once, though I have corresponded with her. She approached me after the inquest wanting to know who would now be the recipient of the legacy. I told her that would depend upon the provisions of her husband's will, and suggested where she might find that document. She has since written me to say that though she has searched for it, she has been unable to find it. It seems very strange."

"That Mrs. Mawsley should have been unable to find her husband's will?" Dr. Priestley suggested.

"It may be that he never made one. Did he mention having done so, in the course of your interview with him?"

"Certainly not, sir," Forcett replied. "There was no reference whatever to the subject of his own will. I was able to suggest to Mrs. Mawsley where it might be deposited, for in the course of conversation Dr. Mawsley had spoken of a safe at Larch Hall, in which was a document affording proof of his identity. My suggestion was that the will might be there, too."

"A very natural assumption," said Dr. Priestley. "Now, although there is no evidence that this will ever existed, you find it very strange that Mrs. Mawsley failed to find it. This rather suggests you consider it possible that Mrs. Mawsley did in fact find a will, and having read it suppressed it, as not being to her liking."

Forcett shifted uneasily in his chair. "I shouldn't like to accuse her of having done anything of the kind," he replied.

"Perhaps not," said Dr. Priestley. "But what you have said reveals that you have considered the possibility. I will put the question to you quite frankly. Have you at any time, even before your interview with Mawsley, considered it likely that he had made a will? And that that will was in favour of some woman other than his wife, or of her children?"

Forcett seemed stunned by this question, and it was a second or two before he could find words in which to answer it. "No, no, sir, that's impossible!" And then, rapidly and incoherently, he went on. "He'd never have done it. That idea never entered my head. He'd abandoned all thought of her, long ago."

A curious change came into Dr. Priestley's tone
230

and manner. From being dry and incisive, his voice became quite gentle and full of sympathy. "I think I understand, Mr. Forcett. Your mother's maiden name was Doris Leyton?"

The silence which ensued was broken only by the slow ticking of the clock, and seemed to continue interminably. At last Forcett rose slowly from his chair. "It is time I bade you good night, sir," he said with dignity.

"It is not yet time for that, Mr. Forcett," Dr. Priestley replied quietly. "You have said too much, and yet too little. A link in the past existed between your mother and Mawsley. You knew this before you made the appointment to call upon him. I do not wish to threaten you, but merely to show you that your best policy will be one of complete candour. Superintendent Waghorn, whose acquaintance you have already made, is a friend of mine. A hint from me might enable him to discern the truth. You would prefer, I think, to retain your secret."

Forcett stood for a while swaying on his feet, then, with an air of defiance, resumed his seat. "I should have known from Mr. Merefield's hint the other evening," he said quietly. "He asked if I had touched on a sensitive point, and so drove Mawsley to his mistake. But I supposed he was merely guessing. What do you want me to do?"

"I want you to tell me about your mother," Dr. Priestley replied. "And before you speak, I want you to understand this. If I am satisfied that you have told the whole truth, I will give you my most solemn undertaking that no word of what you have said will travel beyond the four walls of this room."

"I am bound to accept that," said Forcett wearily, after an interval. "You know already who my mother was, though I did not know myself until quite recently. You want me to tell you about her? I will tell you this. She was the sweetest natured woman who ever lived. If utter love and self-sacrifice are the ultimate virtues, she is now among the saints in heaven, where to those who forgive, all is forgiven."

He paused, and then went on more briskly. "The first thing that I remember as a small child was my mother being out all day, and a woman coming to look after me and take me out. We lived in a cottage near Tunbridge Wells. I wasn't particularly interested in the woman, whose name I have forgotten, but my mother I adored. I always looked forward to her coming home in the evening, when we were alone together, we two.

"As soon as I was old enough, I went to school, a little private day-school it was. And there I made the surprising discovery that other children had fathers as well as mothers. Of course, I couldn't keep this to myself, and had to ask my mother why I hadn't got a father, too. She told me that he had gone away to a far country, and died there, soon after I was born. I wondered, even then, how he could have gone away and left her.

"And then, as time went on, I got to know other things. My mother was a nurse and spent her days in a nursing home in the town. I understood, as I grew older, that she did this to make more money. She had a very little of her own, but this was not enough for us to live comfortably and to send me to the sort of school I ought to go to. After the first preparatory school, I went to a grammar school, where I got on remarkably well. I didn't seem to find any difficulty in learning. And I had only one ambition, to qualify myself for some good job, and earn enough money for my mother to live with me instead of slaving at nursing.

"Things were at this stage when old Mr. Perring had a severe illness and became a patient at the nursing home. My mother looked after him, and he was profoundly grateful to her. I've wondered since whether if she had given him the slightest encouragement, he would have asked her to marry him. He'd been a widower for some time. I suppose she let him know that the only way he could show his gratitude was through me. At all events, one day after he had left the nursing home and gone back to work, she sent me up to Broad Street to see him.

"I was fifteen at the time, and had a youthful conceit of myself. But as soon as I was shown into the presence, all that deserted me, and I felt like hiding under the table. Old Mr. Perring was most imposing in appearance, with a head of snow-white hair, and a pair of eyes that seemed to bore into one's soul in a vain attempt to find anything worthwhile there. His room was like the inner sanctuary of some temple dedicated to the god of law, all incredibly heavy furniture and enormous tomes in leather bindings that smelt of the ages. However, he was very nice to me in a dry sort of way, and asked me several questions. I suppose my answers must have been satisfactory, for he dismissed me with the promise that as soon as I had matriculated, he would find a post for me in the office as a junior clerk. After that, my future would depend upon my application to my work and studies.

"Well, so it turned out. Within a couple of years I was in the office, living in a room in Bermondsey, and going down to my mother for the week-ends. We'd got it all fixed up. As soon as I was properly dug in at Perrings' she was to give up the cottage and the nursing home, and take a flat somewhere in London, where we could be together. I could see that she regretted the idea of giving up her nursing. She was one of those selfless women who are not happy unless they are devoting themselves to other people. But, as usual, she was prepared to sacrifice her own desires to mine."

Forcett paused, and his face darkened. "It didn't come off," he went on abruptly. "Before I had been with Perrings' for many months, she contracted some sort of septic poisoning, and within a week she was dead. But, before she died, she told me that she had a confession to make. She wanted me to know the truth about herself and me."

Again that tense silence fell upon the room, until Forcett continued in a voice so low as to be scarcely audible. "This is what she told me. It began long ago, when as a girl, Doris Leyton, she was on the nursing staff of a big hospital. There she met and fell in love with a medical student, whom through-out her story she referred to as Dick. She wouldn't tell me anything more about him than that, or even where the hospital was. But she made it perfectly clear that in spite of everything, her love for him had never faltered. She shared her devotion for him only with myself.

"She and Dick became engaged, but as they did not mean to get married for a while, they did not make this public. Their arrangement was that when Dick was qualified, he should buy himself a practice as soon as opportunity offered. He had no money of his own, but she had a few thousand left to her by an uncle, and she was only too glad to let him have this. As soon as he had found the practice and got settled in it, they were to be married.

"The opportunity arose. A practice became available, and she gave Dick the money to buy it. She told me that Dick was one of the cleverest people who ever lived, and that from the start he was a brilliant success as a doctor. There seemed no reason why they should wait any longer. There was indeed every reason why they shouldn't. My mother went away for her annual holiday, having arranged with Dick that they should be married shortly after her return.

"While she was away, Dick wrote to her. She didn't care to talk to me about that letter, which must have been about the most brutal ever penned. In it Dick said he would have to break off the arrangements they had made, for he had become engaged to a very rich woman. She would understand that his career must come first.

"That letter, I know, must have broken my mother's heart. But she never said a word to me about her feelings. She told me that, of course, she understood that Dick's happiness and his career were all that mattered, and that she wrote back to him to tell him so. But what she did not tell him was that she was faced with a personal problem. She was determined never to do or say anything that might put obstacles in his way. She had freely and gladly given herself to Dick, and by now she knew that she had become an expectant mother.

"She still had a little money left, though most of what she had had she had given to Dick. She came to London, whence she wrote to the hospital, resigning her post on the grounds that she was about to marry. In due course I (the baby) was born. She took the name of Forcett, and invented a fictitious husband who had been sent out to the Far East and had died immediately on his arrival there. As soon

235

as she could, she found a new job at the nursing home, and took the cottage near by. With her baby and her work, she told me, she was happy enough.

"When she was thoroughly settled in her new life, she wrote to my father. She said that she felt it was only fair to him to let him know that he had a son. There would never be any question of her asking for his help, for she was quite independent. She would have liked to have called the boy after him, but had been afraid this might possibly give a clue to his parentage. She had, therefore, called him Godfrey, after her own father, and Lionel, after a friend whom Dick knew, who had always been kind to her. This letter she signed merely with her Christian name, giving no address. So far as she knew, she told me, Dick had never made any attempt to trace her.

"That was all she would tell me. She wasn't going to incur any risk of my disturbing Dick's peace of mind. She said that she had heard about him now and then, through the nursing home, and that he was building up a wonderful name for himself. It had all been for the best, for if she had married him, she would not have been rich enough to start him on his career. It was obvious that she idolized him, and that she regarded her own happiness as a very humble sacrifice to lay on his altar. She died content in this thought."

Dr. Priestley broke the silence which followed Forcett's last softly spoken words. "Your mother was indeed a saint," he said gently.

"Say rather a martyr," Forcett replied, raising his voice to its normal level. "And martyrs may be avenged. I don't quite know what I made of all this at the time. I was rather too young to realize the full extent of my mother's tragedy. But as I grew older, it became my firm intention that if ever I found the man who had ruined her life and happiness, I would exact the final punishment.

"Whatever may be the outcome, my motive remains beyond question. There was nothing sordid about it, no thought of extorting money. You hinted just now, sir, that my father might have left a will in favour of my mother or of the child she had borne him. I can imagine nothing more unlikely, for that incident in his life was over and done with. Forgotten, perhaps, until it was recalled to him on the evening of his death. Even had he done so, and I had been able to reveal myself as the rightful legatee, I would not have touched a penny of his money. From the time of my mother's death onwards, I have always felt confident of my ability to carve out a career for myself by my own exertions."

"Your desire was to avenge your mother's wrongs upon the man responsible for them," Dr. Priestley suggested.

"Exactly, sir," Forcett replied. "That, and nothing else. But how was I to fulfil that desire? My mother, possibly guessing what my instinct would be, and wishing above all things to shield the man to whom she was still passionately devoted, had given me no clue to my father's identity. When, after her death, I looked through the few papers she had left, I found nothing to throw any light upon the past. All that I knew about my father was that he was, or had been, a doctor, and that his Christian name was Dick or Richard.

"It was only by chance that I learnt who he was. I've said already that chance has played an important part in my life. But surely it was the finger of Providence that directed me. When, some weeks ago, the firm was called upon to deal with Mrs.

Somerthwaite's will, I was entrusted with the task of tracing the Dr. Knapp there mentioned. I went to Bradworth, and there got in touch with Dr. Ramsbury.

"From what he told me, I had very little doubt that Dr. Mawsley of Harley Street was the legatee I sought, and that so far my task was accomplished. But early in our interview, I realized that some of the things he mentioned might have another and more personal significance. He spoke of Dr. Knapp as Richard, and said that having married the richest woman in Bradworth, he had left the town to set up in London. With what seemed to be rather elaborate casualness he mentioned that while he was a student at the hospital Dr. Knapp had been on very good terms with one of the nurses there, and that he had been generally expected to marry her. Finally, there was the rather curious coincidence that Dr. Ramsbury, who had known both Dr. Knapp and this nurse, had the Christian name of Lionel.

"I had to handle him very carefully because for some reason he seemed reluctant to talk about the nurse. But I did manage to get out of him that about the time Dr. Knapp's engagement was announced, she had left the hospital to marry someone else, whose name he did not know. Finally, as though as an afterthought, I asked him her name, and he told me it was Doris Leyton. I knew then that I had identified not only the legatee, but also my own father."

19

Forcett's voice ended upon an uncertain, shaky note, as though he were overcome by his emotions. Very quietly Oldland poured out a stiff whisky and handed it to him. "Drink that!" he commanded.

With a trembling hand Forcett took the proffered glass, and drank deeply from it. And as he set it down, Dr. Priestley spoke. "I will ask you to believe that you have my sympathy, Mr. Forcett. And I may repeat my assurance that our conversation this evening is entirely confidential. Some days after your return from Bradworth you sought an interview with Mawsley. It may make it easier for you if I describe what I believe to have taken place in the course of that interview. If any of my details are inaccurate, you may correct me."

Forcett made no reply, and after a pause Dr. Priestley continued. "The account you have given of your conversation with Mawsley is perfectly truthful, so far as it goes, but it is not complete. He was distant at first, as might have been expected, but thawed when the purpose of your visit was explained to him. He became so genial in fact that he invited you to have a cocktail with him. You could not have known in advance that he would do so?"

The whisky seemed to have restored Forcett's equanimity. "I didn't," he replied. "I went to the suite prepared to seize on any opportunity that might arise. If it had not, I meant to arrange matters so that subsequent meetings between us would have been necessary. I knew I could contrive that one of these meetings would involve a meal together. As it turned out, no difficulty would have presented itself in that respect. He told me that evening that he was going out to dinner soon after seven, and invited me to come with him. It was after the cocktails had been brought in, so I was spared the necessity of accepting."

"Just so," said Dr. Priestley. "The cocktails were brought in, and each of you mixed his own. To your astonishment, and perhaps dismay, Mawsley added a tablet to his. I use the word dismay, for you were ignorant of the composition of the tablet, and it might have the effect of acting as an antidote to the drug you proposed to employ. However, you decided to proceed. Mawsley turned aside to his desk in order to procure a pencil and a sheet of paper. While he was thus engaged, you dropped into his cocktail a small and non-lethal dose of coniine."

Forcett stared at him in surprise, but without resentment. "Are you a magician, sir?" he asked.

"Not a magician," Dr. Priestley replied. "Only an old man who has devoted his life to the interpretation of facts. The remains of Mawsley's tablet were still effervescing in his glass, thus concealing the fact that anything else was dissolving in it. And when Mawsley went on to sip the cocktail without suspicion, you knew that the first stage of your plan had succeeded. You had no compunction in proceeding to the second?"

"None whatever, sir," Forcett replied readily. "As you have deduced, the dose of coniine I had given him was far from lethal. He would have recovered from it in a couple of hours at the most. I had been afraid that at the last moment I might relent. But his conversation had filled me with such loathing that I could feel no belated softness towards him. He had talked of nothing but himself and his accomplishments. The position he had made for himself in the world, the money he had derived from his scores of wealthy patients, his big estate in the country, his successes with women, the fact that he had been promised a knighthood in the near future. No word of humility, or of regret for anything that had happened in the past."

From Oldland's chair came a voice hardly above a murmur. "Thou fool! This night thy soul shall be required of thee."

Dr. Priestley nodded in approval. "And you could hardly fail to contrast this bombast with the circumstances of your mother's life," he said. "Now, I am aware of the effects produced by a relatively small quantity of coniine. For some time Mawsley experienced no symptoms beyond a growing lassitude, which he probably attributed to the reaction after a busy day. He offered you a cigar, which, in spite of the fact that you were not in the habit of smoking, you accepted. He discussed with you the proceeds of the legacy, making notes as he did so. He finished the cigar he had been smoking on your arrival, and laid the stub in the ashtray.

"Meanwhile, the coniine was producing its effect, gradually at first, but with increasing rapidity. Before Mawsley could have realized that his lassitude was due to a toxic agent, he was past taking any

241

steps to help himself. His muscles had become paralyzed, until he could move his limbs only with difficulty, and finally, not at all. His organs of speech were similarly affected, so that he could not cry out above a whisper. But all the time his brain remained clear and capable of receiving impressions. Indeed, coniine has the curious effect of rendering the subject unusually receptive of suggestion. Under its influence, Mawsley would to some extent be in a hypnotic state. He would be inclined to follow directions which normally he would have rejected. On the other hand, his power of understanding what was said to him would not be decreased. Are not these the effects of coniine, Oldland?"

"I'm no toxicologist," Oldland replied. "But I'm beginning to wonder how you come to know so much about the stuff."

Dr. Priestley passed this by, and once more addressed Forcett. "You had been watching Mawsley very closely, and when you judged that the time had come, you revealed yourself. You charged him with the abominable way in which he had treated your mother and told him that your intention was to exact vengeance. In so doing, you were perfectly safe. Had Mawsley survived that evening, he would not have ventured to take action, for by so doing the scandal of his past life would be revealed to the world. You had, of course, no intention that he should survive. But how did you learn that there was a supply of strychnine in the dispensary, next door?"

"He practically told me so himself, sir," Forcett replied. "After I had come back from Bradworth I had made all inquiries I could about Dr. Mawsley and his activities. I heard not only that he was the leading authority on glandular diseases, but that he had written articles in the medical journals describing the effects of various drugs in controlling these diseases. From this I inferred he kept a supply of drugs on the premises.

"Earlier in our conversation, when he was boasting about the marvellous cures he had effected, I asked him as innocently as I could whether he dispensed his medicines for his patients himself. The idea seemed to amuse him, and he told me that specialists didn't do that sort of thing. The only dispensing that was done in the place was for the purpose of experimenting upon rats, and that he left to his secretary. There was a room devoted to this beyond the door, which he indicated. But I hadn't been counting on the chance of that, and had brought with me a hypodermic syringe and a bottle of strychnine injection, which if necessary I should have left ready to his hand."

"I see," said Dr. Priestley. "Your plan had been prepared to cover every eventuality. I can understand how you acquired a knowledge of poisons and their effects. Nearly all the standard textbooks in forensic medicine, of which you are a student, contain a section devoted to toxicology. But the poisons themselves are, perhaps fortunately, not easy to obtain. May I ask from what source you obtained them?"

"You know so much already, sir, that I see no harm in telling you," Forcett replied. "I have mentioned that in the course of my legal duties I took an unofficial course in pharmacy in the establishment of a manufacturing chemist. By that time my decision to punish the man who had betrayed my mother, should I ever succeed in identifying him, had been made. I did not then know what form the punishment would take. But when I had completed the course, I took away with me a collection of drugs in small quantities.

"The only drugs available to me were those commonly used in medicine—morphine, strychnine, and hyoscine, for example. Coniine was not among them. It was not until considerably later that, as you surmised, I read of the properties of coniine in one of the textbooks. I saw then how a non-lethal dose of this drug could, under suitable circumstances, be used to achieve my end. And I learnt that it could be prepared fairly simply from a native plant.

"My next holiday I devoted to a walking tour, exploring the country until I found a patch of spotted hemlock, growing wild. I picked a quantity of the unripe seeds, and on my return to London prepared from these a supply of the drug. I do not pretend that I obtained the coniine in any high degree of purity. But I drank a small quantity in solution, and experienced exactly the sensations you have described."

Dr. Priestley nodded. "Thank you, Mr. Forcett. You, of all people, will understand my love of accuracy in detail. Having reduced Mawsley to a state of helplessness, and having revealed your identity to him, you prepared the scene as you wished it to be discovered. Your purpose was to provide indications that Mawsley had been perfectly normal, physically and mentally, and in every way capable of action, after your departure. On his desk were four unopened letters. You opened these and glanced through them. Perhaps you did not notice that one of them was from Dr. Oldland here, but another of them attracted your attention.

"It was an unpleasant letter, and perhaps you hesitated about what to do with it. If you left it for others to find, it might suggest that its contents had driven Mawsley to suicide. But I think you reflected that nobody who knew him would believe that he would have taken so serious a view of the matter. It was your endeavour to create appearances which would suggest that, after your departure, Mawsley had behaved in his usual manner. You asked yourself what he would have done with such a letter, and came to the probably correct conclusion that he would have destroyed it. You, therefore, threw it and its envelope on the fire.

"Continuing your policy of producing favourable appearances, you carried out further details. Mawsley had not begun a second cigar. You placed the one which you had yourself smoked half through beside the stub in the ashtray. You rinsed out Mawsley's glass, then poured into it a drop or two of the gin and lime juice. You removed the tray from the central table to the one at the side of the room. You were then ready to take your departure. But I do not understand how you could feel confident that, on regaining the use of his limbs, Mawsley would administer to himself such a powerful injection of strychnine as to prove immediately fatal."

"I can explain that, sir," Forcett replied, and in his tone was almost the pride of achievement. "The dose of coniine I had introduced into his cocktail was not lethal. He would have recovered from its effects in due course, even if I had not taken steps to accelerate his recovery."

"Ah!" Dr. Priestley exclaimed. "Now I begin to understand. You told us that you had brought a supply of strychnine with you?"

"Exactly, sir," Forcett replied. "You are no doubt aware that strychnine is to some extent an antidote to coniine. In cases of poisoning by coniine, a small, and, of course, non-lethal injection of strychnine is recommended as part of the treatment. This, then, is what took place. As you have supposed, I explained myself and my motives to him very fully, and in terms which he could not fail to understand. By this time he was unable to move a muscle, or to utter any sound beyond the rasping of his breath. Then I took a further step. I charged my syringe with an injection representing a quarter of a grain of strychnine, and administered it to him. I chose the nape of the neck for the purpose. The hair would hide the prick from any casual inspection subsequently, and search for it in that particular place was not likely to be made.

"I was gambling partly on the probability that he was not very strong on toxicology. Few people, even doctors, unless it happened to be their speciality, were likely to keep in their heads a list of poisons and their antidotes, still less the dose of antidote required to counteract the poison. But I was gambling still more upon the receptiveness to suggestion induced by coniine. I knew that, helpless though he was, he could hear and understand everything I said to him. While under the influence of the coniine, he was, so to speak, capable of being hypnotized."

"That is true," Dr. Priestley remarked. "And, of course, you made use of this condition to further your own ends."

"I did, sir," Forcett agreed. "I told him that by now he must have realized that the state in which he found himself was due to the administration of some drug. This, I went on, was indeed the case. In order to keep him quiet while I told him what I had to say, I had introduced into his cocktail an amount of coniine, large enough to produce the effect I required, but not so much as to be fatal.

"I impressed upon him repeatedly that I had devoted myself to an extensive study of toxicology, in view of the very opportunity which had now arisen. I rubbed it into his consciousness that, after a comparatively short period, he would have recovered from the original dose of coniine. But I told him, and repeated my statement several times, that the injection I had just given him was a further quantity of coniine. His system, I declared, was now absorbing no less than eight grains of the drug, an amount from which he could not recover.

"I described to him what would happen. The paralysis which he now experienced would gradually spread until it invaded the respiratory muscles, when death would ensue through inability to breathe. That would probably not happen for a while, and he would have plenty of time to meditate upon the unpleasant position he was in. And, for that matter, to ponder the tantalizing fact that an antidote was at hand, if only he had the physical power to reach it. He had told me that in the room next door he kept an assortment of drugs. Among these, no doubt, was strychnine, which he probably knew was the antidote to coniine.

"He had one chance, I went on to tell him. It takes a little time for coniine to permeate the system, as he would know by his experience of the action of the first dose. He would soon be recovering from the effects of that dose, but I had now administered a second. It would be a race between recovery from the first dose, and the second dose taking effect. There might be a very short interval between the two, during which he would have some control of his muscles.

"I said that I did not think this would occur. I had judged the first dose as nearly as I could to make the occurrence possible, but most improbable. I wanted him to know the added torture of the hope due to gradual recovery being dashed by the return of the paralyzing symptoms induced by the second dose. Still, the remote chance remained, and Providence might be on his side. But if he did become able to move his limbs, he would have to be quick, very quick. If any respite were allowed him, it could be for no longer than a few seconds.

"At this point I opened the door he had pointed to, and found that it led into what I heard later was called the dispensary. Incidentally, there was a tap and a sink, and it was here that I thoroughly washed out the cocktail glass. There was also a cupboard, locked, but with the key in place. In this I found, among other injections, one labelled strychnine. I took this out and put it on the bench.

"Then I went back to the consulting-room and told him what I had done. The strychnine was there, I had laid it ready to his hand, but it was a million to one against his being able to reach it. If only he could, an injection would save his life. I would even tell him the quantity that would be required. To be effective, the quantity of antidote to counteract the poison should be in the proportion of one to four. I had given him eight grains in all of coniine, and an injection of two grains of strychnine would, therefore, be necessary. Two grains. It was worth his while to remember that. Two grains!"

Forcett's voice had risen with excitement as he described the scene. Now it fell again to his normal placid tone. "Of course, I stretched a point there. A quantitative estimate of the antidote that will be required in any given case is rarely possible. I was practising a form of hypnotism. I counted on impressing those two words on his mind so powerfully that, as soon as he was able, he would give himself an injection containing that quantity.

"I tried to foresee everything that might happen after I left. I had said nothing but the truth when I told him that strychnine was, if not actually an antidote, at least a factor in the treatment of coniine poisoning. Actually, I had given him a small non-fatal dose of coniine in his cocktail, and followed this up with an equally non-lethal injection of strychnine. In a very short time he would in any case recover from the effects of the coniine. The strychnine I had given him would make his recovery doubly sure, and would accelerate the process.

"My own experience led me to believe that he would regain the partial use of his limbs before he did his power of speech. As he became aware of this, he would believe that the rare chance I had told him about had occurred in his case. His mind would be concentrated, to the exclusion of everything else, upon reaching the strychnine before the paralysis returned. By the time he was able to move, he would still be unable to use his voice to call for help. But there was the bare possibility that he might ring the bell for the butler.

"I didn't think this very likely, for even if he had he couldn't have explained what he wanted, and he would have been wasting what he believed to be vital seconds. But I was taking no chances. The bell is rung by means of a push at the end of a length of flexible cord, leading to a fitting on the wainscot, the cord being long enough to allow the push to be laid on the desk or the table. It was lying on the table during our interview. As I left the room, I pressed the push, then dropped it on the floor beside the desk, in rather an awkward corner. I knew very well that he would not waste time groping for it there."

Dr. Priestley nodded. "You left the room, and stood for a moment in the doorway, where you spoke a few words intended for the butler's ears. You then shut the door, and addressed the butler, who, summoned by your ringing of the bell, was standing in the hall. You told him that Mawsley had given orders that he was not to be disturbed until he went out. He had told you of his intention of going out to dinner soon after seven, so you were on safe ground there. The butler then let you out of the suite. Did you leave the building immediately?"

"I did," Forcett replied. "And I did not return until ten o'clock next morning. I should like you to realize, sir, exactly how matters stood when I left. I did not cause his death, which was entirely due to his own action. If he had not given himself that injection, if in fact he had done nothing at all, he would have fully recovered from the effects of the coniine, and would have been alive and well at this moment."

Forcett paused, and then went on reflectively. "I could not, of course, be certain that my suggestion would be acted upon. But even if it had not, and he had lived, my end, which would have been his punishment, would have been achieved. For the rest of his life he would have been haunted by the knowledge of my existence, and of my ability to expose him. Such exposure would involve the loss of most of the things he had boasted about to me so confidently. The constant threat of being flung from his pedestal would have been intolerable. At the same time, I should have been in a position of perfect safety. He could not take proceedings against me, for to do so would merely be to precipitate the exposure."

"Let me assure you that I fully realize how matters stood when you left," Dr. Priestley said. "You did not know that your suggestion had taken effect until you reached the suite next day?"

"I had a pretty shrewd idea that it had, sir," Forcett replied. "I estimated that in twenty minutes or so after I left he would have recovered sufficiently to get as far as the dispensary. At the end of that period I rang up the suite from a public call-box. I knew that the butler would answer it. If he did, I was going to ask him to tell his master, when he was at liberty to do so, that I had found I should not be able to keep my appointment next morning until a few minutes after I had arranged, and hoped this would cause no inconvenience. When I got no reply to my call, I knew that something very much out of the ordinary must have happened."

"Quite so," said Dr. Priestley. "Very much out of the ordinary, indeed. I owe you my thanks, Mr. Forcett. I had solved the problem of Mawsley's death to my own satisfaction, but you have thrown light upon certain of the details which remained obscure. You have, in fact, afforded me a very entertaining evening."

At the note of finality in Dr. Priestley's tone, Forcett stood up. "I'm glad I've been able to capture your attention, sir," he said dryly. "But I'm bound to ask what steps you mean to take about it."

"Steps?" Dr. Priestley replied irritably. "It is not for me to take any step whatever. Once more I repeat that I regard everything you have said as being in the strictest confidence. Your actions are, in my opinion, best left before the bar of your own conscience. Before you go, Mr. Forcett, I should like to offer you a word of advice."

Forcett, already on his way towards the door, paused. "I should be grateful for it, sir," he said.

"I should not carry my experiments in toxicology any further," Dr. Priestley replied. "Good night."

20

"Well, I'm damned!" Oldland exclaimed, when Forcett, escorted by Harold, had left the room. "That's the most astounding dodge I've ever heard of. Are you too tired to tell me now what put you onto it?"

"I'm not at all tired," Dr. Priestley replied. "I feel pleasantly stimulated by the confirmation I have received of my solution of the problem. You will admit that I have maintained that Mawsley's death was not due to accident, suicide, or murder, and that a fourth alternative should be sought?"

"Yes, I'll admit that," said Oldland, as Harold returned quietly to the room and took his seat. "What I can't make out is how you guessed what that fourth alternative had been. It beats me."

"I think I may justly claim that it was not entirely guesswork," Dr. Priestley replied. "When you first told us about the case, in giving your account of the inquest, you made the difficulty sufficiently plain. All the evidence showed that Mawsley must himself have administered the fatal injection, no other person being present when he did so. If this were indeed the case, only one of two alternatives seemed possible, suicide or accident.

"Suicide appeared out of the question. No reason was suggested at the inquest, nor has any been discovered in subsequent investigation, for Mawsley taking his own life. There was the further objection, which I think you were the first to raise: having at his disposal a remarkably complete assortment of poisons, it was unlikely that he would have chosen from among these for purposes of suicide the one producing the most painful effects.

"Regarding accident, implying that Mawsley had in error given himself a lethal injection, believing it to be innocuous, the coroner used the word extraordinary, an expression which you fully endorsed. It was more than extraordinary in the case of a man of his knowledge and experience. As I considered the matter, the conviction grew upon me that it could not have been a mistake in that sense. The more I heard about Mawsley from those who had known him, that conviction grew.

"As you are aware, I suggested to Jimmy that the police might investigate it. There was always the remote possibility of some flaw, or some lacuna, in the evidence, and that the injection had been forcibly administered by some other person. From the first I never believed that this could have been the case, but it was necessary to eliminate the possibility. It was only natural that the training of Jimmy and his colleagues should lead them to seek for a criminal with more or less obvious motive and opportunity. But none of the individuals they suggested to fill this part seemed to me entirely satisfactory.

"This, then, was how the matter stood. It seemed to me that Mawsley's death could not be explained by any one of the stock alternatives of the police, accident, suicide or murder. I began to wonder whether a fourth alternative might not be conceivable, and perhaps unwisely put my thought into words. It must have seemed to the trained investigator so illogical as to suggest an advanced stage of senile decay of my reasoning powers."

"No fear of that," Oldland remarked. "But it sounded a bit incomprehensible, I'll admit."

"I daresay it did," said Dr. Priestley. "When I made the remark, the nature of this fourth alternative had not occurred to me. But I set to work on the idea, taking as my starting point the supposition that, for once, things were exactly as they seemed, that, deliberately and of his own volition, Mawsley had given himself the fatal injection. Not, I felt sure, by mistake or for the purpose of suicide. Why, then? It was some little time before the answer dawned upon me. Not for the purpose of taking his life, but of saving it.

"Under what circumstances, then, would Mawsley have had recourse to strychnine in such a quantity? Only, it seemed to me, if he had believed his life to be in danger as the result of poisoning by some drug to which strychnine was an antidote. But why, if that had been the case, had he not summoned aid? The only possible answer was that the effects of the drug upon him were such as to render him unable to do so. Was there a drug which would produce such effects, and to which strychnine was a recognized antidote? A study of various textbooks on toxicology showed me that there was such a drug—coniine.

"You are well aware that in my laboratory I have a variety of substances which from time to time I employ in the course of research. Among them was a sample of hemlock leaves, *conii folia*, in the language of pharmacy. From these I prepared an infusion, a small and, I hasten to add, carefully calculated quantity of which I swallowed in a glass of burgundy. The resulting effects both you and Harold witnessed."

"Confound you, Priestley!" Oldland exclaimed. "What the devil do you mean by leading us up the garden path like that? You gave us both the fright of our lives. If I'd known, I'd have given you such a drastic and unpleasant treatment that you'd have thought twice before playing such a trick as that again. But now I understand how you came to know so much about coniine and the effect it produces."

Dr. Priestley smiled. "It was precisely because I had no desire to undergo your treatment that I did not tell you the cause of my symptoms. I wished to experience not only the progress of the effects produced by the drug, but also the manner of their disappearance. Forcett described these quite accurately, and I have little to add to his description, except to emphasize the curious effect of the drug in making the patient responsive to suggestion. When I carried out the experiment, it was my firm intention not to allow Harold to send for you. Up to a point, I was able to resist his suggestions that he should do so. But when I was fully under the influence of the drug my resistance broke down. In other respects my brain was normal. I could understand perfectly what Harold said to me. I could follow the rather difficult train of thought of the work on which we were engaged. I realized quite clearly that in a short time the paralysis would pass off, leaving no ill-effects. But, as he persisted, I became temporarily convinced that he was right. Had I been able to speak, I should have concurred audibly in his wish to send for you."

"I fancy Harold would have sent for me, however

violently you disapproved," said Oldland. "I hope you'll have sufficient consideration for your friends not to do it again. I will say on Jimmy's behalf that he guessed what your trouble had been. Only he thought that someone had been trying to poison you."

"I am very sorry to have caused so much concern," Dr. Priestley replied contritely. "I didn't sufficiently realize the affection my friends had for me. But to proceed. I had to my own satisfaction established the possibility that Mawsley had had recourse to strychnine because he was suffering from coniine poisoning, which he believed would otherwise prove fatal. The next question was, how had this poisoning occurred?

"Again, accident or an attempt at suicide seemed to be ruled out. Mawsley would not have taken coniine by mistake, any more than he would have given himself a fatal injection of strychnine by mistake. If his intention had been suicide, he would not have struggled to the antidote which would have frustrated his aim. The probabilities seemed to point to the coniine having been administered intentionally by some other person.

"If that was the case, when had it been administered? My own experience of the effects of the drug, and of the rate at which they developed and passed off, determined that in Mawsley's case he must have been given it within very few hours before his death. The earliest opportunity that I could allow was when his tea had been brought to him, about half past four. It might be that coniine had been introduced into something he had eaten or drunk then. It might, for instance, have been dissolved in the teapot. But this could only implicate

Phepson and, apart from any other consideration, it seemed unlikely that Phepson had made a study of coniine and its properties.

"On these grounds, the tea seemed to be ruled out. The next person who had been in Mawsley's company was the rat-catcher. Originally, before the idea of coniine occurred to me, I envisaged the possibility that he might have been in some way responsible for Mawsley's death from strychnine poisoning. But he was as unlikely as Phepson to be familiar with coniine. His responsibility might also be ruled out.

"Then came the incident of the cocktails. It seemed to me that the nature of these made them an ideal vehicle for the administration of coniine. In the course of my experiments I had learnt that in the presence of an alkali, the drug emits an unpleasant mouselike smell, but that in the presence of acids this smell was not appreciable. The cocktails consisted of gin and lime-juice, the latter containing citric acid. If then coniine had been an additional ingredient of such a cocktail, its presence would probably have remained undetected.

"In considering how it might have been added, a very interesting point arose. We heard, from several independent sources, that Mawsley was in the habit of dropping a tablet into his drinks. These tablets were composed mainly of papain, and he habitually carried a box of them in his pocket. Forcett told Jimmy that Mawsley dropped one of these tablets into his cocktail. It was just conceivable that a substitution had been effected. That a tablet, or tablets, composed of coniine instead of papain, had been surreptitiously placed in the gold snuff-box.

"At that point I considered the matter from another point of view. My own experience, again, told me that if Mawsley had taken coniine, he must have done so before Forcett left him. Further, that at the time of his leaving, Mawsley must already have been exhibiting symptoms of paralysis and loss of speech. Yet Forcett had calmly walked out with a promise to call next morning, and a message to the butler that his master was not to be disturbed. Surely the most complete stranger would hardly have behaved so callously. He would at least have said to Phepson, 'I don't altogether like the look of Dr. Mawsley. He told me to give you orders not to disturb him, but all the same, I should go and see him, if I were you.' On the other hand, if Forcett had given him the drug himself, his behaviour was just what might have been expected.

"But that line of argument seemed to end in a blind alley. There was never the slightest doubt that Forcett was a complete stranger to Mawsley, or that his errand was perfectly genuine. Mawsley had not recognized his name, or his face when he was shown into the consulting-room. Neither Phepson, nor any of Mawsley's associates, had seen or heard of him before. The firm of Perring and Company would hardly connive at the forging of a codicil by any of their clerks. What possible motive could this complete stranger have had for giving Mawsley a dose of coniine within a few minutes of his first introduction to him? And, still more puzzling, how did he happen to have such an uncommon drug available at that moment?

"I could not imagine that Forcett had been an agent, acting on behalf of some other person. The only way out of the impasse was to suppose that he was not in fact a stranger, and that he had made preparations in advance to take advantage of his genuine errand to effect his purpose. But here again was a difficulty. Forcett, as I have said, was unknown to any of Mawsley's associates of recent years. If there had been any previous communication between them, it must have occurred many years ago. Probably before Mawsley's marriage, when he was practising in Bradworth. So I decided that Harold and I would spend a short holiday in that town."

"Oh, so that's where you went, was it!" Oldland exclaimed. "Well, I hope you both enjoyed yourselves."

"We did," Dr. Priestley replied equably. "And it was there that, through Harold's efforts, I was enabled to make the personal acquaintance of Dr. Lionel Ramsbury, whose name you heard Forcett mention just now. We already knew one another by correspondence, so I had little difficulty in gaining his confidence. He turned out to be one of those people who delight in reminiscence. As soon as I mentioned Mawsley's name, very little encouragement on my part was necessary to induce him to tell me the story of his early years. And from what he told me, I deduced the possibility that Forcett was the son of Dr. Knapp and Doris Leyton."

"Well, I congratulate you," said Oldland. "When I first told you the yarn, I made it pretty clear that to me such a mistake on Mawsley's part seemed incredible. My word, that young fellow has inherited all his father's ability, and, for that matter, all his ruthlessness. It's just about the neatest job I ever heard of, and it had the additional merit of being from his point of view absolutely fool-proof."

"Almost," Dr. Priestley agreed. "There was, however, the risk that traces of coniine might be discovered post-mortem in Mawsley's system."

Oldland shook his head. "That risk was negligible. At the time of the inquest there was no question of foul play. Consequently, none of the big bugs, like our friend Horsham, was called in. The post-mortem work was left to the district analyst. His job was the straightforward one of determining the cause of Mawsley's death. He started on the perfectly correct assumption that it had been due to strychnine poisoning, and the quantity of that drug he found in the body proved conclusively that had been the case. Having established this fact, he had no reason to waste his time looking any further. Even if he had detected the presence of coniine, it would have been in quantity insufficient to cause death, and might, therefore, be disregarded."

Dr. Priestley nodded. "You are probably right. Forcett, as a lawyer, was no doubt aware of the procedure that would be followed. He gave us to understand that he left no loophole for failure. The coroner's verdict was in one sense correct. Mawsley died as the result of a mistake on his part, a mistake due to misconception."

He paused, and after a while went on dreamily. "My own experience enables me to picture the scene following Forcett's departure from the consulting-room. It is true that in my case no antidote was employed, whereas Forcett administered a small injection of strychnine. The effect of this would be to accelerate Mawsley's recovery from the symptoms due to the coniine he had swallowed, and this no doubt was Forcett's intention. He wished to precipitate the end, for if Mawsley had remained incapable too long, his condition might have been discovered, in spite of the instruction that he was not to be disturbed.

"Comparatively soon, then, within a few minutes after Forcett had left him, Mawsley, whose mental perception remained unclouded throughout, became aware that the paralysis of his muscles was diminishing. Perhaps he first became aware that he could slowly flex his fingers. This must have filled him with a wild and unreasoning excitement. He was still under the influence of suggestion. His son's words were ringing in his head. The remote chance he had mentioned had been granted. The effects of the first dose were wearing off before those of the second had taken control. And two grains of strychnine would counteract the eight grains of coniine he had been given.

"If only he could reach the dispensary. His whole will was concentrated on that overmastering longing. Two grains of strychnine would save his life, two grains, if he could only reach them. One full syringe of the injection already prepared in the dispensary. But he was helpless, bound to his chair as securely as though by steel chains. And the only sound he could produce was a low hoarse rasping in his throat.

"But despair gradually gave place to hope. Infinitely slowly, as it must have seemed to him, but actually in a few minutes, the power returned to his muscles. Every second of this period he must have dreaded to feel a cessation of the improvement, and the subsequent rapid deterioration which could end only in death. But at last he found that with supreme difficulty he could move his arms, his legs. He probably made more than one attempt to rise from his chair before he finally succeeded in doing so.

"When at last he did succeed, his movements were so uncertain and clumsy that he overturned the chair. Phepson, listening impatiently in the hall, heard the sound of this. He also heard another sound, the significance of which escaped us at the time. He heard the rattling of the handle of the communicating door between the consulting-room and the dispensary. Why should Mawsley have fumbled with so familiar a handle, thus causing it to rattle? Because his muscles were not yet under full control. But he was able to achieve the one object upon which his whole will was set. He reached the dispensary bench, charged a syringe full of the injection, and administered this. The result, though contrary to his expectation, was of course inevitable."

"As Forcett, of course, very well knew," Oldland remarked. "He was fully prepared for what he would find at the suite next morning."

"His second visit formed an essential part of his plan," Dr. Priestley replied. "He was very naturally questioned as to Mawsley's condition when he left him. Of this he gave a misleading account, declaring that Mawsley had then been in a perfectly normal state, mentally and physically. He was able to produce corroborative evidence of that, by pointing out the sheet of paper with Mawsley's notes upon it, the half-smoked cigar, the removal of the tray to the side table, and so forth. All these appearances, according to him, had been produced after his departure. The only possible inference from this, since no one else had entered the room, was that Mawsley had produced them himself. There was no reason to doubt Forcett's veracity. Actually, as we know, Mawsley made the notes before he was overcome by the coniine, and Forcett produced the remaining appearances while Mawsley was helpless in his chair."

"Yes," said Oldland. "The whole affair was very

thoroughly thought out. But what now? Do you really mean to let that young parricide get away with it?"

"Parricide!" Dr. Priestley exclaimed. "Have you taken leave of your senses? Forcett committed no crime, certainly not that of parricide. He did not even cause Mawsley any serious bodily harm. He gave him a non-lethal quantity of coniine, followed by an injection of an antidote which, but for Mawsley's own action, would have restored him to normal in a very short space of time. Forcett certainly cannot be charged with murder."

"No, I suppose not," Oldland agreed. "And, if he were, there isn't a tittle of evidence against him. What he told us just now wouldn't cut any ice. He could very easily turn round and say that it was only a yarn he had spun to satisfy the curiosity of a pair of inquisitive old men. Then, if Mawsley wasn't murdered, in effect he committed suicide."

"Certainly not!" said Dr. Priestley. "Suicide involves the deliberate intention of taking one's own life. Mawsley's recourse to strychnine was in pursuance of a desire not to end his life, but to prolong it. Nor did he make any mistake about what he was doing. Mawsley's case demonstrates that there is a fourth alternative to the three generally accepted—accident, suicide or murder."

"It's a very pretty problem in ethics," Oldland replied. "Forcett contrived his father's death, without being guilty of it. And I think he was fully justified. We've heard a good deal about Mawsley from one source and another, but very little that we can put on the credit side of his moral account. It certainly seems to be the case that his death has plunged nobody into any lasting depths of grief."

"His patients may have cause to regret him," Dr. Priestley remarked.

"Oh, yes, his patients," Oldland agreed. "Old Matt Gussage's last chance has vanished, I'm afraid. But I was thinking of his friends and relations, and his family in particular. If Mrs. Mawsley, as seems to me quite likely, found that letter written by Doris Leyton, she will feel absolved from any necessity for mourning her late husband's memory. She will probably acquire a new social brilliance by marrying the grandson of the Earl.

"As for the other people whose names have cropped up in connection with the case, their lives won't be greatly affected. Mr. Weedon and the rat-catcher have both lost a useful customer. No doubt Mrs. Mawsley will have the decency to pension off Phepson. He's pretty sure to go and live with his sister and enliven his declining years by attending the meetings of the Buffaloes at the Tabby Cat. Violet Hilworth won't have any difficulty about finding another job. But I'm wondering what Forcett will do, now that he knows his secret is out."

"You heard what I told him," said Dr. Priestley. "His actions are best left before the bar of his own conscience. If capital sentence is passed at that bar, he has the means at his disposal for carrying it out. But I sincerely hope that he will take to heart the last piece of advice I gave him. I think he will. Indeed, I feel sure he will."

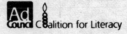